Mickey Spillane was born in Brooklyn, New York, on March 9, 1918. His novels have sold in the millions and his hard-as-nails character P.I. Mike Hammer was the first in the private eye thriller genre to make the New York Times bestseller list. Spillane has been honoured by the Mystery Writers of America with the Grand Master Award, and with the Private Eye Writers of America 'Eye' Lifetime Achievement Award; he is also a Shamus Award winner.

Spillane lives with his wife, Jane, in South Carolina.

THE BIG KILL

Mike Hammer slugs it out with a two-timing, still luscious ex-Hollywood starlet who's using everything she's got to block the trail of a vicious killer.

Books by Mickey Spillane
Published by The House of Ulverscroft:

SOMETHING'S DOWN THERE
ONE LONELY NIGHT

MICKEY SPILLANE

THE BIG KILL

Complete and Unabridged

ULVERSCROFT
Leicester

First published in Great Britain in 2003 by
Allison & Busby Limited, London

First Large Print Edition
published 2006
by arrangement with
Allison & Busby Limited, London

British Library CIP Data

Spillane, Mickey, *1918* –
    The big kill.—Large print ed.—
    Ulverscroft large print series: mystery
    1. Hammer, Mike (Fictitious character)—Fiction
    2. Private investigators—New York (State)—New
    York—Fiction 3. Detective and mystery stories
    4. Large type books
    I. Title
    813.5′4 [F]

    ISBN 1–84617–178–4

01 168 394 5

Published by
F. A. Thorpe (Publishing)
Anstey, Leicestershire

Set by Words & Graphics Ltd.
Anstey, Leicestershire
Printed and bound in Great Britain by
T. J. International Ltd., Padstow, Cornwall

This book is printed on acid-free paper

To Marty

1

It was one of those nights when the sky came down and wrapped itself around the world. The rain clawed at the windows of the bar like an angry cat and tried to sneak in every time some drunk lurched in the door. The place reeked of stale beer and soggy men with enough cheap perfume thrown in to make you sick.

Two drunks with a nickel between them were arguing over what to play on the juke box until a tomato in a dress that was too tight a year ago pushed the key that started off something noisy and hot. One of the drunks wanted to dance and she gave him a shove. So he danced with the other drunk.

She saw me sitting there with my stool tipped back against the cigarette machine and change of a fin on the bar, decided I could afford a wet evening for two and walked over with her hips waving hello.

'You're new around here, ain't ya?'

'Nah. I've been here since six o'clock.'

'Buy me a drink?' She crowded in next to me, seeing how much of herself she could plaster against my legs.

'No.' It caught her by surprise and she quit rubbing.

'Don't gentlemen usually buy ladies a drink?' she said. She tried to lower her eyelids seductively but one came down farther than the other and made her look stupid.

'I'm not a gentleman, kid.'

'I ain't a lady either so buy me a drink.'

So I bought her a drink. A jerk in a discarded army overcoat down at the end of the bar was getting the eye from the bartender because he was nursing the last drop in his glass, hating to go outside in the rain, so I bought him a drink too.

The bartender took my change with a frown. 'Them bums'll bleed you to death, feller.'

'I don't have any blood left,' I told him. The dame grinned and rubbed herself against my knees some more.

'I bet you got plenty of everything for me.'

'Yeah, but what I got you ain't getting because you probably got more than me.'

'What?'

'Forget it.'

She looked at my face a second, then edged away. 'You ain't very sociable, mister.'

'I know it. I don't want to be sociable. I haven't been sociable the last six months and I won't be for the next six if I can help it.'

2

'Say, what's eatin' you? You having dame trouble?'

'I never have dame trouble. I'm a misanthropist.'

'You *are*?' Her eyes widened as if I had something contagious. She finished her drink and was going to stick it out anyway, no matter what I said.

I said, 'Scram.'

This time she scowled a little bit. 'Say, what the hell's eatin' you? I never . . . '

'I don't like people. I don't like any kind of people. When you get them together in a big lump they all get nasty and dirty and full of trouble. So I don't like people including you. That's what a misanthropist is.'

'I could a sworn you was a nice feller,' she said.

'So coulda lot of people. I'm not. Blow, sister.'

She gave me a look she kept in reserve for special occasions and got the hell out of there so I could drink by myself. It was a stinking place to have to spend the night but that's all there was on the block. The East Side doesn't cater to the uptown trade. I sat there and watched the clock go around, waiting for the rain to stop, but it was as patient as I was. It was almost malicious the way it came down, a million fingers that drummed a constant,

3

maddening tattoo on the windows until its steady insistence rose above the bawdy talk and raucous screams of the juke box.

It got to everybody after a while, that and the smell of the damp. A fight started down at the other end and spread along the bar. It quit when the bartender rapped one guy over the head with an ice stick. One bum dropped his glass and got tossed out. The tomato who liked to rub herself had enough of it and picked up a guy who had enough left of his change to make the evening profitable and took him home in the rain. The guy didn't like it, but biology got the better of common sense again.

And I got a little bit drunk. Not much, just a little bit.

But enough so that in about five minutes I knew damn well I was going to get sick of the whole mess and start tossing them the hell out the door. Maybe the bartender too if he tried to use the stick on me. Then I could drink in peace and the hell with the rain.

Oh, I felt swell, just great.

I kept looking around to see where I'd start first, then the door opened and shut behind a guy who stood there in his shirt sleeves, wet and shivering. He had a bundle in his arms with his coat over it, and when he quit

4

looking around the place like a scared rabbit he shuffled over to one of the booths and dropped the bundle on the seat.

Nobody but me had paid any attention to him. He threw a buck on the bar, had a shot then brought the other shot over to his table. Still nobody paid any attention to him. Maybe they were used to seeing guys who could cry.

He set the drink down and took the coat off the bundle. It was quite a bundle, all right. It was a little kid about a year old who was sound asleep. I said something dirty to myself and felt my shoulders hunch up in disgust. The rain, the bar, a kid and a guy who cried. It made me sicker than I was.

I couldn't take my eyes off the guy. He was only a little squirt who looked as if he had never had enough to eat. His clothes were damp and ragged, clinging to him like skin. He couldn't have been any older than me, but his face was seamed around the mouth and eyes and his shoulders hung limply. Whatever had been his purpose in life, he had given up long ago.

But damn it, he kept crying. I could see the tears running down his cheeks as he patted the kid and talked too low to be heard. His chest heaved with a sob and his hands went up to cover his face. When they came away he bent his head and kissed the kid on top of his head.

All of a sudden my drink tasted lousy.

I turned around to put a quarter in the cigarette machine so I wouldn't have to look at him again when I heard his chair kick back and saw him run to the door. This time he had nothing in his arms.

For about ten seconds I stood there, my fingers curled around the deck of Luckies. Something crawled up my spine and made my teeth grind together, snapping off a sound that was a curse at the whole damn world. I knocked a drunk down getting around the corner of the bar and ripped the door open so the rain could lash at my face the way it had been wanting to. Behind me somebody yelled to shut the door.

I didn't have time to because I saw the guy halfway down the street, a vague silhouette under the overhead light, a dejected figure of a man too far gone to care any more. But he was worth caring about to somebody in the Buick sedan that pulled away from the curb. The car slithered out into the light with a roar and I heard the sharp cough of the gun over the slapping of my own feet on the sidewalk.

It only took two of them and the guy slammed forward on his face. The back door flew open and another shadow ran under the

6

light and from where I was I could see him bend over and frisk the guy with a blurred motion of his hands.

I should have waited, damn it. I shouldn't have tried a shot from where I was. A .45 isn't built for range and the slug ripped a groove in the pavement and screamed off down the block. The guy let out a startled yell and tore back toward the car with the other guy yelling for him to hurry. He damn near made it, then one of the ricochets took him through the legs and he went down with a scream.

The other guy didn't wait. He jammed the gas down and wrenched the wheel over as hard as he could and the guy shrieking his lungs out in the gutter forgot the pain in his legs long enough to let out one final, terrified yell before the wheels of the car made a pulpy mess of his body. My hand kept squeezing the trigger until there were only the flat echoes of the blasts that were drowned out by the noise of the car's exhaust and the futile gesture as the gun held opened, empty.

And there I was standing over a dead little guy who had two holes in his back and the dried streaks of tears on his face. He didn't look tired any more. He seemed to be smiling. What was left of the one in the gutter was too sickening to look at.

I opened the cigarettes and stuck one in my

mouth. I lit it and breathed out the smoke, watching it sift through the rain. The guy couldn't hear me, but I said, 'It's a hell of a city, isn't it, feller?'

A jagged streak of lightning cut across the sky to answer me.

The police cars took two minutes getting to the spot. They converged from both ends of the street, howling to a stop under the light and the boys next to the drivers were out before the tires stopped whining.

One had a gun in his hand. He meant business with it too. It was pointed straight at my gut and he said, 'Who're you?'

I pointed my butt at the thing on the sidewalk. 'Eyewitness.'

The other cop came behind me and ran his hand over my pockets. He found the gun, yanked it out of the holster and smelled the barrel. For a second I thought he was going to clip me with it, but this cop had been around long enough to ask questions first. He asked them with his eyes.

'Look in my side pocket,' I said.

He dipped his hand in my coat and brought out my wallet. The badge was pinned to the flap with my P.I. ticket and gun license inside the cardcase. He looks them both over carefully, scrutinizing my picture then my face. 'Private Investigator, Michael Hammer.'

'That's right.'

He scowled again and handed the gun and wallet back. 'What happened?'

'This guy came in the bar back there a few minutes ago. He looked scared as hell, had two drinks and ran out. I was curious so I tagged after him.'

'In this rain you were curious,' the cop with the gun said.

'I'm a curious guy.'

The other cop looked annoyed. 'Okay, go on.'

I shrugged. 'He ran out and a Buick came after him. There were two shots from the car, the guy fell and one punk hopped out of the car to frisk him. I let loose and got the guy in the legs and the driver of the car ran over him. Purposely.'

'So you let loose!' The lad with the gun came in at me with a snarl.

The other cop shoved him back. 'Put that thing away and call the chief. I know this guy.'

It didn't go over big with the young blood. 'Hell, the guy's dead, isn't he? This punk admits shooting, don't he? Hell, how do we know there was a Buick?'

'Go take a look at the corpse over there,' the cop said patiently.

Laddie boy with the gun shoved it back on

his hip and walked across the street. He started puking after his first look and crawled back in the prowl car.

So at one o'clock in the morning Pat got there with no more fanfare than the winking red light on the top of the police car. I watched him step out and yank his collar up against the rain. The cops looked smart when he passed because there wasn't anything else to do. A killing in this neighborhood was neither important nor interesting enough to drag out the local citizenry in a downpour, so the harness bulls just stood at attention until the brass had given his nod of recognition.

The cop who had frisked me said, 'Good evening, Captain Chambers.'

Pat said hello and was led out to look over the pair of corpses. I stayed back in the shadows smoking while he bent over to look at the one on the sidewalk. When he finished his inspection he straightened up, listened to the cop a minute and wrinkled up his forehead in a perplexed frown.

My cigarette arched through the night and fizzled out in the gutter. I said, 'Hi, Pat.'

'What are you doing here, Mike?' Two cops flanked him as he walked over to me. He waved them away.

'I'm the eyewitness.'

'So I've heard.' Behind Pat the eager beaver

cop licked his lips, wondering who the hell I was and hoping I didn't sound off about his gun-waving. 'What's the whole story, Mike?'

'That's it, every bit of it. I don't know any more about it than you do.'

'Yeah.' He made a sour face. 'Look, don't screw me. Are you on a case?'

'Chum, if I was I'd say so then keep my trap closed. I'm not on a case and I don't know what the hell happened. This guy got shot, I nicked the other guy and the boy in the car finished him off.'

Pat shook his head. 'I hate coincidence. I hate it especially when you're involved. You smell out murder too well.'

'Sure, and this one stinks. You know either one of them?'

'No. They're not carrying any identification around either.'

The morgue wagon rolled up with the Medical Examiner about fifty feet in the rear. The boys hopped out and started cleaning up the mess after the verdict was given and the pictures taken. I ambled out to the middle of the street and took a look at the body that was squashed against the roadbed.

He looked like an hourglass.

Fright and pain had made a distorted death mask of his face, but the rain had scrubbed away the blood leaving him a ghostly white in contrast with the asphalt of the street. He was about forty-five and as medium as you can get. His clothes had an expensive look about them, but one shoe had a hole in the bottom and he needed a haircut bad.

The driver of the wagon splashed the light of a flash over him and gave me a toothy grin. 'He's a goodie, ain't he?'

'Yeah, a real beaut.'

'Not so much, though. You should a seen what we had last week. Whole damn trailer truck rolled over that one and we had to scrape him away from between the tires. Could a put him in a shoe box.'

'Do you sleep good nights?' I gave him my best disgusted look.

'Sure, why?' He even sounded surprised.

'Forget it. Put that light on his face again.'

The guy obliged and I had a close look this time. I walked around and had a squint from the other side then told him to knock off the light. Pat was a vague figure in a trench coat, watching me closely. He said, 'Know him?'

'I've seen him before. Small-time hardcase, I think.'

'The M.E. remembered him. He was a witness at a coroner's inquest about twelve years ago. The guy was one of Charlie Fallon's old outfit.'

I glanced at Pat then back to the corpse

again. The guy had some odd familiarity I couldn't place and it wasn't Fallon I was thinking of. Fallon died of natural causes about the same time I was opening up shop and what I knew of him came strictly from the papers.

'Nope, can't quite place him,' I said.

'We'll get him tagged. Too bad they couldn't've had the decency to carry a lodge card or something. The one on the sidewalk there only had forty cents in change and a house key in his pocket. This guy had a fin and two ones and nothing else.'

I nodded. 'A buck must have been all that first lad had then. He bought two drinks in the bar before he left.'

'Well, let's go back there and check. Maybe somebody'll know him there.'

'Nobody will,' I said.

'Never can tell.'

'Nuts. They didn't know him when he came in, I'm telling you. He just had two drinks and left.'

'Then what're you getting excited about?' He had his hands shoved down in his pockets and was watching me with eyes that were half shut.

'Skip it.'

'The hell I'll skip it. Two guys are murdered and I want to know what the hell

13

goes on. You got another wild hair up your tail, haven't you?'

'Yeah.' The way I said it brought the scowl back to his face.

'Spill it, Mike.'

'Let's go back to the bar. I'm getting so goddamn sick of the things that happen in this town I have to take a bath every time I even stick my head out the door.'

The rain stopped momentarily as if something had amazed it, then slashed down with all the fury it could muster, damning me with its millions of pellets. I took a look around me at the two rows of tenements and the dark spots on the pavement where the dead men were a minute ago and wondered how many people behind the walls and windows were alive today who wouldn't be alive tomorrow.

Pat left a moment, said something to the M.E. and one of the cops, then joined me on the sidewalk. I nudged a brace of Luckies out of the pack, handed him one and watched his face in the light. He looked teed off like he always did when he came face to face with a corpse.

I said, 'This must gripe the pants off you, Pat. There's not one blasted thing you can do to prevent trouble. Like those two back there. Alive one minute, dead the next. Nice, huh?'

The cops get here in time to clear up the mess, but they can't move until it happens. Christ, what a place to live!'

He didn't say anything until we turned into the bar. By that time most of the customers were so helplessly drunk they couldn't remember anything anyway. The bartender said a guy was in for a few minutes awhile back, but he couldn't help out. Pat gave up after five minutes and came back to me. I was sitting at the booth with my back to the bundle in the corner ready to blow up.

Pat took a long look at my face. 'What's eating you, Mike?'

I picked the bundle up and sat it on my knee. The coat came away and the kid's head lolled on my shoulder, his hair a tangled wet mop. Pat pushed his hat back on his head and tucked his lip under his teeth. 'I don't get it.'

'The dead guy . . . the one who was here first. He came in with the kid and he was crying. Oh, it was real touching. It damn near made me sick, it was so touching. A guy bawling his head off, then kissing his kid good-by and making a run for the street.

'This is why I was curious. I thought maybe the guy was so far gone he was deserting his kid. Now I know better, Pat. The guy knew he was going to die so he took his kid in here, said so long and walked right into it. Makes a

15

nice picture, doesn't it?'

'You're drawing a lot of conclusions, aren't you?'

'Let's hear you draw some better ones. Goddamn it, this makes me mad! No matter what the hell the guy did it's the kid who has to pay through the nose for it. Of all the lousy, stinking things that happen . . . '

'Ease off, Mike.'

'Sure, ease off. It sounds real easy to do. But look, if this was his kid and he cared enough to cry about it, what happens to him?'

'I presume he has a mother.'

'No doubt,' I said sarcastically. 'So far you don't know who the father is. Do we leave the kid here until something turns up?'

'Don't be stupid. There are agencies who will take care of him.'

'Great. What a hell of a night this is for the kid. His old man gets shot and he gets adopted by an agency.'

'You don't know it's his father, friend.'

'Who else would cry over a kid?'

Pat gave me a thoughtful grimace. 'If your theory holds about the guy knowing he was going to catch it, maybe he was bawling for himself instead of the kid.'

'Balls. What kind of a kill you think this is?'

'From the neighborhood and the type of

people involved I'd say it was pretty local.'

'Maybe the killer hopes you'll think just that.'

'Why?' He was getting sore now too.

'I told you he ran over his own boy deliberately, didn't I? Why the hell would he do that?'

Pat shook his head. 'I don't think he did.'

'Okay, pal, you were there and I wasn't. You saw it all.'

'Damn it, Mike, maybe it looked deliberate to you but it sounds screwball to me! It doesn't make sense. If he did swerve like you said he did, maybe he was intending to pick the guy up out of the gutter and didn't judge his distance right. When he hit him it was too late to stop.'

I said something dirty.

'All right, what's your angle?'

'The guy was shot in the legs. He might have talked and the guy in the car didn't want to be identified for murder so he put the wheels to him.'

Suddenly he grinned at me and his breath hissed out in a chuckle. 'You're on the ball. I was thinking the same thing myself and wanted to see if you were sure of yourself.'

'Go to hell,' I said.

'Yeah, right now. Let's get that kid out of here. I'll be up half the night again on this damn thing. Come on.'

'No.'

Pat stopped and turned around. 'What do you mean . . . 'no'?'

'What I said. I'll keep the kid with me . . . for now anyway. He'll only sit down there at headquarters until morning waiting for those agency people to show up.'

Maybe it's getting so I can't keep my face a blank any more, or maybe Pat had seen that same expression too often. His teeth clamped together and I knew his shoulders were bunching up under the coat. 'Mike,' he told me, 'if you got ideas about going on a kill-hunt, just get rid of them right now. I'm not going to risk my neck and position because of a lot of wild ideas you dream up.'

I said it low and slow so he had to listen hard to catch it. 'I don't like what happened to the kid, Pat. Murder doesn't just happen. It's thought about and planned out all nice and neat, and any reason that involves murder and big fat Buicks has to be a damn good one. I don't know who the kid is, but he's going to grow up knowing that the guy who killed his old man died with a nice hot slug in the middle of his intestines. If it means anything to you, consider that I'm on a case. I have me a legal right to do a lot of things including shooting a goddamn killer if I can sucker him into drawing first so it'll look like self-defense.

'So go ahead and rave. Tell me how it won't do me any good. Tell me that I'm interfering in police work and I'll tell you how sick I am of what goes on in this town. I live here, see? I got a damn good right to keep it clean even if I have to kill a few bastards to do it. There's plenty who need killing bad and if I'm electing myself to do the job you shouldn't kick. Just take a look at the papers every day and see how hot the police are when politics can make or break a cop. Take a look at your open cases like who killed Scottoriggio . . . or Binnaggio and his pal in Kansas City . . . then look at me straight and say that this town isn't wide open and I'll call you a liar.'

I had to stop and take a breath. The air in my lungs was so hot it choked me.

'It isn't nice to see guys cry, Pat. Not grown men. It's worse to see a little kid holding the bag. Somebody's going to get shot for it.'

Pat knew better than to argue about it. He looked at me steadily a long minute, then down at the kid. He nodded and his face went tight. 'There's not much I can do to stop you, Mike. Not now, anyway.'

'Not ever. Think it's okay to keep the kid?'

'Guess so. I'll call you in the morning. As

long as you're involved the D.A. is probably going to want a statement from you anyway. This time keep your mouth shut and you'll keep your license. He's got enough trouble on his hands trying to nail the big boys in the gambling racket and he's just as liable to take it out on you.'

My laugh sounded like trees rubbing together. 'He can go to hell for all I care. He got rough with me once and I bet it still hurts when he thinks about it. What's the matter with him now . . . can't he even close up a bookie joint?'

'It isn't funny, Mike.'

'It's a scream. Even the papers are laughing.'

A slow burn crept into his face. 'They should. The same guys who do the laughing are probably some of the ones who keep the books open. It's the big shots like Ed Teen who laugh the loudest and they're not laughing at the D.A. or the cops . . . they're laughing at Joe Citizen, guys like you, who take the bouncing for it. It isn't a bit funny when Teen and Lou Grindle and Fallon can go on enjoying a life of luxury until the day they die while you pay for it.'

He got it out of his system and remembered to hand me a good night before he left. I stared at the door swinging shut, my arms tight around the kid, hearing his words come back slowly with one of them getting louder every time it repeated itself.

Lou Grindle. The arm. Lou Grindle who was a flashy holdover from the old days and sold his services where they were needed. Lou Grindle, tough boy de luxe who was as much at home in the hot spots along the Stem as in a cellar club in Harlem.

Lou Grindle who was on his hands and knees in the back of Lake's joint a week ago shooting craps with the help while two of his own boys stood by holding his coat and his dough and the one who held his coat was the dead guy back in the gutter who looked like an hourglass.

I wrapped the coat around the kid and went out in the doorway where I whistled at cabs until one stopped and picked me up. The driver must have had kids of his own at home because he gave me a nasty sneer when he saw the boy in my arms.

I told him where to make his first stop and he waited until I came back. Then I had him make seven others before I got any results. A bartender with a half a bag on mistook me for one of the boys and told me I might find Lou Grindle on Fifty-seventh Street in a place called the Hop Scotch where a room was available for some heavy sugar card games once a week. I threw him a buck and went back to the cab.

I said, 'Know where the Hop Scotch is on Fifty-seventh?'

'Yeah. You goin' there now?'

'Looks that way, doesn't it?'

'Don't you think you better take that kid home, buddy? It ain't no good fer kids to be up so late.'

'Chum, there's nothing I'd like to do better, but first I got business to take care of.'

If I was drunk the cabbie might have tossed me out. As it was, he turned around in his seat to make sure I wasn't, then rolled across to Fifty-seventh.

I left the kid in the cab with a fin to keep the driver quiet and got out. The Hop Scotch was a downstairs gin mill that catered to crowds who liked dirty floor shows and a lot of noise and didn't mind footing the bill. It was hopping with drunks and half drunks who ganged up around the dance floor where a stripper was being persuaded not to stay within the limits prescribed by New York law and when they started throwing rolled-up bills out she said to hell with the law, let go her snaps and braces and gave the customers a treat when she did a two-handed pickup of all the green persuaders.

A waiter was watching the show with a grin

on his fat face and I grabbed him while he was still gone over the sight of flesh. I said, 'Where's Lou?' just like we were real pals.

'Inside. Him and the others're playin'.' His thumb made a vague motion toward the back.

I squeezed through the crowd to where a bus boy was clearing off an empty table and pulled out a chair. The boy looked at the five in my fingers and waited. 'Lou Grindle's inside. Go tell him to come out.'

He wanted the five, but he shook his head. 'Brother, nobody tells Lou nothing. You tell 'im.'

'Say it's important business and he'll come. He won't like it if he doesn't get to hear what I have to tell him.'

The guy licked his lips and reached for the five. He left the tray on the table, disappeared around a bend that led to the service bar and kitchen, came back for his tray and told me Lou was on his way.

Out on the floor another stripper was trying to earn some persuasion dough herself so the outside of the room was nice and clear with no big ears around.

Lou came around the bend, looked at the bus boy who crooked a finger my way, then came over to see who the hell I was. Lou Grindle was a dapper punk in his forties with

23

eyes like glass marbles and a head of hair that looked painted on. His tux ran in the three-figure class and if you didn't look for it you'd never know he was packing a gun low under his arm.

The edges of his eyes puckered up as he tried to place me and when he saw the same kind of a gun bulge on me as he had himself he made the mistake of taking me for a cop. His upper lip twitched in a sneer he didn't try to hide.

I kicked another chair out with my foot and said, 'Sit down, Lou.'

Lou sat down. His fingers were curled up like he wanted to take me apart at the seams. 'Make it good and make it quick,' he said. He hissed when he talked.

I made it good, all right. I said, 'One of your butt boys got himself killed tonight.'

His eyes unpuckered and got glassier. It was as close as he could come to looking normally surprised. 'Who?'

'That's what I want to find out. He was holding your coat in a crap game the other night. Remember?'

If he remembered he didn't tell me so.

I leaned forward and leaned on the table, the ends of my hand inside the lapel of my coat just in case. 'He was a medium-sized guy in expensive duds with holes in his shoes. A long time ago he worked for Charlie Fallon. Right now I'm wondering whether or not he was working for you tonight.'

Lou remembered. His face went tight and the cords in his neck pressed tight against his collar. 'Who the hell are you, Mac?'

'The name's Mike Hammer, Lou. Ask around and you'll find what it means.'

A snake wore the same expression he got just then. His eyes went even glassier and under his coat his body started sucking inward. 'A goddamn private cop!' He was looking at my fingers. They were farther inside my coat now and I could feel the cold butt of the .45.

The snake look faded and something else took its place. Something that said Lou Grindle wasn't taking chances on being as fast as he used to be. Not where he was alone, anyway. 'So what?' he snarled.

I grinned at him. The one with all the teeth showing.

'That boy of yours, the one who died . . . I put a slug through his legs and the guy who drove the car didn't want to take a chance on him being picked up so he put the wheels to him. Right after the two of 'em got finished knocking off another guy too.'

Lou's hand moved up to his pocket and plucked out a cigar. Slowly, so I could watch it happen. 'Nobody was working for me tonight.'

'Maybe not, Lou, maybe not. You better hope they weren't.'

He stopped in the middle of lighting the cigar and threw those snake eyes at me again. 'You got a few things to learn, shamus, I don't like for guys to talk tough to me.'

'Lou . . . ' His head came back an inch and I could see the hate he wore like a mask. ' . . . if I find out you had a hand in this business tonight I'm going to come back here and take that slimy face of yours and rub it in the dirt. You just try playing rough with me and you'll see your guts lying on the floor before you die. Remember what I said, Lou. I'd as soon shoot your goddamn greasy head off as look at you.'

His face went white right down to his collar. If he had lips they didn't show because they were rolled up against his teeth. The number on the floor ended and the people were coming back where they belonged, so I stood up and walked away. When I looked back he was gone and his chair was upside down against the wall.

The cab was still there with another two bucks chalked up on the meter. It was nearly three o'clock and I had told Velda I'd meet her at two-thirty. I said, 'Penn Station,' to the driver, held the kid against me to soften the jolts of the ride and paid off the driver a few minutes later.

Velda isn't the kind of woman you'd miss even in Penn Station. All you had to do was follow the eyes. She was standing by the information booth tall and cool-looking, in a light gray suit that made the black of her hair seem even deeper. Luscious. Clothes couldn't hide it. Seductive. They didn't try to hide it either. Nobody ever saw her without undressing her with their eyes, that's the kind of woman she was.

A nice partner to have in the firm. And someday . . .

I came up behind her and said, 'Hello, Velda. Sorry I'm late.'

She swung around, dropped her cigarette and let me know she thought I was what I looked like right then, an unshaven bum wringing wet. 'Can't you ever be on time, Mike?'

'Hell, you're big enough to carry your own suitcases to the platform. I got caught up in a piece of work.'

She concentrated a funny stare on me so hard that she didn't realize what I had in my arms until it squirmed. Her breath caught in her throat sharply. 'Mike . . . what . . . '

'He's a little boy, kitten. Cute, isn't he?'

Her fingers touched his face and he smiled sleepily. Velda didn't smile. She watched me with an intensity I had seen before and it was all I could do to make my face a blank. I flipped a butt out of my pack and lit it so my mouth would have a reason for being tight and screwed up on the side. 'Is this the piece of work, Mike?'

'Yeah, yeah. Look, let's get moving.'

'What are you doing with him?'

I made what was supposed to be a laugh. 'I'm minding him for his father.'

She didn't know whether to believe me or not. 'Mike . . . this Florida business can wait if there's something important.'

The speaker system was calling off that the Miami Limited was loading. For a second I debated whether or not I should tell her and decided not to. She was a hell of a woman but a woman just the same and thought too goddamn much of my skin to want to see me wrapped up in some kind of a crazy hate again. She'd been through that before. She'd be everything I ever wanted if she'd just quit making sure I stayed alive. So I said, 'Come on, you got five minutes.'

I put her on the train downstairs and made a kiss at her through the window. When she smiled with that lovely wide mouth and blew a kiss back at me I wanted to tell her to get off and forget going after a punk in Miami who had a hatful of stolen ice, but the train jerked and slipped away. I waved once more and went back upstairs and caught another cab home.

Up in the apartment I undressed the kid, stuffed the ragged overalls in the garbage pail and made him a sack on the couch. I backed up a couple of chairs to hold him in and picked him up. He didn't weigh very much. He was one of those little bundles that were probably scattered all over the city right then with nobody caring much about them. His pale hair was still limp and damp, yet still curly around the edges.

For a minute his head lolled on my shoulder, then his eyes came open. He said something in a tiny voice and I shook my head. 'No, kid, I'm not your daddy. Maybe I'll do until we find you another one, though. But at least you've seen the last of old clothes and bar rooms for a while.'

I laid him on the couch and pulled a cover up over him.

Somebody sure as hell was going to pay for this.

2

The sun was there in the morning. It was high above the apartments beaming in through the windows. My watch read a few minutes after ten and I unpiled out of bed in a hurry. The phone let loose with a startling jangle at the same time something smashed to the floor in the living room and I let out a string of curses you could have heard on the street.

If I yelled it got stuck in my throat because the kid was standing barefooted in the wreckage of a china-base table lamp reaching up for my rod on the edge of the end table. Even before I got to him he dragged it out of the clip by the trigger guard and was bringing his other hand up to it.

I must have scared the hell out of him the way I whisked him off the floor and disentangled his mitt from the gun. The safety was off and he had clamped down on the trigger while I was thanking the guy who invented the butt safety on the .45.

So with a gun in one hand and a yelling kid in the other I nudged the phone off the hook to stop the goddamn ringing and yelled hello

30

loud enough so the yowls wouldn't drown me out.

Pat said, 'Got trouble, Mike?' Then he laughed.

It wasn't funny. I told him to talk or hang up so I could get myself straightened out.

He laughed again, louder this time. 'Look, get down as soon as you can, Mike. We have your little deal lined up for you.'

'The kid's father?'

'Yeah, it was his father. Come on down and I'll tell you about it.'

'An hour. Give me an hour. Want me to bring the kid along?'

'Well . . . to tell the truth I forgot all about him. Tell you what, park him somewhere until we can notify the proper agency, will you?'

'Sure, just like that I'll dump the kid. What's the matter with you? Oh, forget it, I'll figure something out.'

I slammed the phone back and sat down with the kid on my knee. He kept reaching for the gun until I chucked it across the room in a chair. On second thought I called the doorman downstairs and told him to send up an errand boy. The kid got there about five minutes later and I told him to light out for the avenue and pick up something a year-old kid could wear and groceries he could handle.

The kid took the ten spot with a grin. 'Leave it to me, mister. Me, I got more brudders than you got fingers. I know whatta get.'

He did, too. For ten bucks you don't get much, but it was a change of clothes and between us we got the boy fed. I gave the kid five bucks and got dressed myself. On the floor downstairs was an elderly retired nurse who agreed to take the kid days as long as I kept him nights and for the service it would only cost me one arm and part of a leg.

When she took the kid over I patted his fanny while he tried to dig out one of my eyes with his thumb. 'For a client,' I said, 'you're knocking the hell out of my bank roll.' I looked at the nurse, but she had already started brushing his hair back and adjusting his coveralls. 'Take good care of him, will you?'

'Don't you worry a bit now. As a matter of fact, I'm glad to have something to do with my time.' The kid yelled and reached his hand inside my coat and when I pulled away he yelled again, this time with tears. 'Do you have something he wants?' she asked me.

'Er . . . no. We were . . . er, playing a game with my coat before. Guess he remembered.' I said so long and got out. She'd eat me out if she knew the kid wanted the rod for a toy.

Pat was at ease in his office with his feet up on the desk, comparing blown-up photos of prints in the light that filtered in the windows. When I came in he tossed them aside and waved me into a chair.

'It didn't take us long to get a line on what happened last night.'

I sat back with a fresh cigarette in my fingers and waited. Pat slid a report sheet out of a stack and held it in front of him.

'The guy's name was William Decker,' he said. 'He was an ex-con who had been released four years ago after serving a term for breaking and entering. Before his arrest he had worked for a safe and lock company in a responsible position, then, probably because of his trade, was introduced to the wrong company. He quit his job and seemed to be pretty well off at the same time a wave of safe robberies were sweeping a section of the city. None of those crimes were pinned on him, but he was suspected of it. He was caught breaking into a place and convicted.'

'Who was the bad company?' I cut in.

'Local boys. A bunch of petty gangsters, most of whom are now up the river. Anyway, after his release, he settled down and got married. His wife died less than a year after the baby was born. By the way, the kid's name is William too.

'Now . . . we might still be up in the air about this if something hadn't happened last night that turned the light on the whole thing. We put Decker's prints through at the same time another investigation was being made. A little before twelve o'clock last night we had a call to investigate a prowler seen on a fire escape of one of the better apartment buildings on Riverside Drive. The squad car that answered the call found no trace of the prowler, but when they investigated the fire escape they came across a broken window and heard a moan from inside.

'When they entered they found a woman sprawled on the floor in a pretty battered condition. Her wall safe was open and the contents gone. There was one print on the dial that the boys were able to lift and it was that of William Decker. When we pulled the card we had the answers.'

'Great.' My voice made a funny flat sound in the room.

Pat's head came up, his face expressionless. 'Sometimes you *can't* do what you want to do, Mike. You were all steamed up to go looking for a killer and now you're getting sore because it's all so cut and dried.'

'Okay, okay, finish reading. I want to hear it.'

He went back to the report. 'Like I said, his wife died and in all likelihood he started going bad again. He and two others planned a safe robbery with Decker opening the can while the others were lookouts and drove. It's our theory that Decker tried to get away with the entire haul without splitting and his partners overtook and killed him.'

'Nice theory. How'd you reach it?'

'Because it was a safe job where Decker would have to handle the thing alone . . . because he went home long enough after the job to pick up his kid . . . and because you yourself saw the man you shot frisking him for the loot before you barged in on the scene.'

'Now spell it backwards.'

'What?'

'Christ, can't you see your own loopholes? They're big enough.'

He saw them. He stuck his tongue in the corner of his cheek and squinted at the paper. 'Yeah, the only catch is the loot. It wasn't.'

'You hit it,' I agreed. 'And something else . . . if he was making a break for it he would have taken the dough along. This guy Decker knew he was damn well going to die. He walked right out into it like you'd snap your fingers.'

Pat nodded. 'I thought of that too, Mike. I think I can answer it. All Decker got in that haul was three hundred seventeen dollars and a string of cultured pearls worth about twenty bucks. I think that when he realized that was all there was to be had, he knew the others wouldn't believe him and took a powder. Tried to, at least.'

'Then where's the dough?'

Pat tapped his fingernails against his teeth. 'I think we'll find it in the same place we'll find the pearls ... if anybody's honest enough to turn it in ... and that's on top of a garbage pail somewhere.'

'Aw, nuts. Even three hundred's dough these days. He wouldn't chuck it.'

'Anger and disgust can make a person do a lot of things.'

'Then why did he let himself get knocked off?'

Pat waited a moment then said, 'I think because he realized that they might try to take out their revenge on the child.'

I flipped the butt into the waste basket. 'You sure got it wrapped up nice and tight. Who was the other guy?'

'His name was Arnold Basil. He used to work for Fallon and had a record of three stretches and fourteen arrests without convictions. We weren't able to get much of a line on him so far. We do know that after Fallon died he went to Los Angeles and while he was there got drunk and was picked up for disorderly conduct. Two of our stoolies reported having seen him around town the last month, but hadn't heard about him being mixed up in anything.'

'Did they mention him sticking close to Lou Grindle?'

Pat scowled. 'Where'd you get that?'

'Never mind. What about it?'

'They mentioned it.'

'What're you doing about it?'

'Checking.'

'That's nice.'

He threw the pencil across the desk. 'Don't get so damn sarcastic, Mike.' He caught the stare I held on him and started tapping his teeth again. 'As much as I'd like to pin something on that cheap crook, I doubt if it can be done. Lou doesn't play for peanuts and you know it. He has his protection racket and he manages to stay out of trouble.'

'You could fix that,' I said. 'Breed 'im some trouble he can't get out of.'

'Yeah, try it.'

I stood up and slapped on my hat. 'I think maybe I will just for the hell of it.'

Pat's hands were flat on the desk. 'Damn it, Mike, lay off. You're in a huff because the whole thing works out and you're not satisfied because you can't go gunning for somebody. One of these days you're going to dig up more trouble than you can handle!'

'Pat, I don't like orphan-makers. There's still the driver of that car and don't forget it.'

'I haven't. He'll be in the line-up before the week is out.'

'He'll be dead first. Mind if I look at this?' I picked up the report sheet and scanned it. When I finished remembering a couple of addresses I tossed it back.

He was looking at me carefully now, his eyes guarded. 'Mike, did you leave something out of what you've told me?'

'Nope, not a thing.'

'Then spill it.'

I turned around and looked at him. I had to put my hand in my pocket to keep it still. 'It just stinks, that's all. The guy was crying. You'd have to see him to know what he looked like and you didn't see him. Grown men don't cry like that. It stinks.'

'You're a crazy bastard,' Pat said.

'So I've been told. Does the D.A. want to see me?'

'No, you were lucky it broke so fast.'

'See you around then, Pat. I'll keep in touch with you.'

'Do that,' he said. I think he was laughing at me inside. I wasn't laughing though. There wasn't a damn thing to laugh about when you saw a guy cry, kiss his kid, then go out and make him an orphan.

Like I said, the whole thing stunk.

To high heaven.

★   ★   ★

It took me a little while to get over to the East Side. I cruised up the block where the murder happened, reached the corner and swung down to the street where Decker had lived. It was one of those shabby blocks a few years away from condemnation. The sidewalks were littered with ancient baby buggies, a horde of kids playing in the garbage on the sidewalks and people on the stoops who didn't give a damn what the kids did so long as they could yap and slop beer.

The number I had picked from Pat's report was 164, a four-story brownstone that seemed to tilt out toward the street. I parked the car and climbed out, picking my way through the swarm of kids, then went up the steps in to the vestibule. There wasn't any door, so I didn't have to ring any bells. One mailbox had SUPT scratched into the metal case under the 1-C. I walked down the dark channel of the hallway until I counted off three doors and knocked.

A guy loomed out of the darkness. He was a big guy, all right, about two inches over me with a chest like a barrel. There might have been a lot of fat under his hairy skin, but there was a lot of muscle there too.

'Whatta ya want?' The way he said it you could tell he was used to scaring people right off.

I said, 'Information, friend. What ya bet you give it to me?'

I watched his hands. They looked like they wanted to grab me. I stood balancing myself on my toes lightly so he'd get the idea that whatever he had I had enough to get away from him. Just like that he laughed. 'You're a cocky little punk.'

'You're the first guy who ever called me little, friend.'

He laughed again. 'Come on inside and have some coffee and keep your language where it belongs. I got all kinds of visitors today.'

There was another long hallway with some light at the end that turned out to be a kitchen. The big guy stood in the doorway nodding me in and I saw the priest at the table nibbling at a hard roll. The big guy said, 'Father, this is . . . uh, what's the name?'

'Mike Hammer. Hello, Father.'

The priest held out a big hand and we shook. Then the super tapped his chest with a forefinger. 'Forgot myself, I did. John Vileck's the name. Sit down and have a bite and let's hear what you got on your mind.' He took another cup and saucer off the shelf and filled it up. 'Sugar'n milk's on the table.'

When I was sugared and stirred I put my cards on the table. 'I'm a private investigator. Right now I'm trying to get a line on a guy who lived here until last night.'

Both the priest and the super exchanged glances quickly. 'You mean William Decker?' the priest asked.

'That's right.'

'May I ask who is retaining you?'

'Nobody, Father. I'm just sore, that's all. I was there when Decker was knocked off and I didn't like it. I'm on my own time and my own capital.' I tried the coffee. It was strong as acid and hot as hell.

Vileck stared at his cup, swirling it around to cool it off. 'Decker was an all-right guy. Had a nice wife, too. The cops was here last night and then morning again.'

'Today?'

He looked up at me, his teeth tight

41

together. 'Yeah, I called 'em in about an hour before you come alone. Couple cops in a patrol car. Me and the Father here went upstairs to look around and somebody'd already done a little looking on their own. The place's a wreck. Turned everything upside down.'

The priest put his cup down and leaned back in his chair. 'Perhaps you can make something of it, Mr. Hammer.'

'Maybe I can. If the police have the right idea, whoever searched Decker's place was looking for a pile of dough that he was supposed to have clipped during a robbery last night. The reason he was bumped was because he never got that dough to start with and knew his pals wouldn't believe him. He tried to get out but they nailed him anyway. Apparently they thought that when he came back to get his kid he stashed the money figuring to pick it up later.'

Vileck said, 'The bastards!' then looked across the table. 'Sorry, Father.'

The priest smiled gently. 'Mr. Hammer . . . do you know anything at all about William Decker?'

'I know he had a record. Did you?'

'Yes, he told me about that some time ago. You see, what puzzles me is the fact that William was such a straightforward fellow. He was doing his best to live a perfect life. It wasn't easy for him, but he seemed to be making a good job of it.'

Vileck nodded agreement. 'That's right, too. Me and the Father here was the only ones around here that knew he had a record. When he first moved here he made no bones about it, then he started having trouble keeping a job because guys don't like for ex-cons to be working for them. Tell you somethin' . . . Decker was as honest as they come. None of this wrong stuff for him, see? Wouldn't even cheat at cards and right on time with his rent and his bills. Never no trouble at all. What do you make of it?'

'Don't you know?'

There was genuine bewilderment in his eyes. 'For the love of me, I sure don't see nothing. He was okay all the way. Always doing things fer his kid since his wife died of cancer.'

'Then he had it tough, eh?'

'Yeah, real tough. Doctors come high and he couldn't afford much. She was supposed to have an operation and he finally got her lined up for it, but by that time it was too late and she died a few days after they cut her apart. Decker was in bad shape for a while.'

'He drink much?' I asked.

'Nope. Never had a drop all that time. He

didn't want to do nothin' that might hurt his kid. He sure was crazy about that boy. That's why he was strictly on the up and up.'

The priest had been listening, nodding occasionally. When Vileck finished he said, 'Mr. Hammer, a week ago William came to church to see me and asked me if I would keep his insurance policies. They are all made out to the child, of course, and he wanted to be sure that if ever anything happened to him the child would be well provided for.'

That one stopped me for a second. I said, 'Tell me, was he jumpy at the time? I mean, now that you look back, did he seem to have anything on his mind at all?'

'Yes, now that I look back I'd say that he was upset about something. At the time I believed it was due to his wife having died. However, his story was plausible enough. Being that he had to work, he wanted his important papers in safe hands. I never believed that he was intending to . . . to . . . '

Vileck balled his hands up and knocked his knuckles together. 'Nuts. I don't believe he done it because he was going to rob a joint. The guy was straight as they come.'

'Some things happen to make a guy go wrong,' I said. 'Did he need dough at all?'

'Sure he needed dough. He'd get in maybe two, three days a week on the docks . . . pier

51 it was, but that was just enough to cover his eats. He lived pretty close, but he got by.'

'Any friends?'

The super shrugged. 'Sometimes a guy from the docks would come up awhile. He played chess with the blind newsie down the block every Monday night. Both of 'em picked it up in the big house. Nope, can't say that he had any other friends 'cept me. I liked the guy pretty much.'

'No reason why he needed money . . . nothing like that?'

'Hell, not now. Before the wife died, sure. Not now though.'

I nodded, finished my coffee and turned to the priest. 'Father, did Decker make any tentative plans concerning the boy at all?'

'Yes, he did. It was his intention that the boy be brought up by one of our church organizations. We discussed it and he went so far as to make a will. The insurance money will take care of the lad until he finishes school, and what else Decker had was to be held in trust for his boy. This whole affair is very distressing. If only he had come to me with his problem! Always before he came to the church for advice, but this time when he needed to most he failed. Really, I . . . '

'Father, I have the boy. He's being well cared for at present and whenever you're ready I'll be glad to turn him over to you. That kid is the reason I'm in this and when I get the guy that made him an orphan they can get another grave ready in potter's field. This whole town needs its nose wiped bad. I'm sick of having to live with some of the scum that breeds here and in my own little way I'm going to do something about it.'

'Please . . . my son! I . . . '

'Don't preach to me now, Father. Maybe when it's over, but not now.'

'But surely you can't be serious.'

Vileck studied my face a second, then said, 'He is, Father. If I can help ya out, pal . . . lemme know, will ya?'

'I'll let you know,' I said. 'When you make arrangements for the boy, Father, look me up in the phone book. By the way, who was the friend of Decker's . . . the one on the docks?'

'Umm . . . think his name was Booker. No, Hooker, that's it. Hooker. Mel Hooker.'

I pushed the cup back and shoved away from the table.

'That's all then. Any chance of taking a look around the apartment?'

'Sure, go on up. Top floor, first door off the landing. And it won't do no good to ask them old biddies nothin'. They was all doing the weekly wash when whoever took the place apart was there. Once a week they get hot

46

water and their noses were all in the sinks.'

'Thanks,' I said. 'For the coffee too.'

'Don't mention it.'

'So long, Father. You'll buzz me later?'

He nodded unhappily. 'Yes, I will. Please
. . . no violence.'

I grinned at him so he'd feel better and
walked down the tunnel to the hall.

Vileck hadn't been wrong about somebody
taking the place apart. They had started at
one end of the three tiny rooms and wound
up at the other leaving a trail of wreckage
behind them that could have been sifted
through a window screen. It was one hell of a
mess. The bag of garbage beside the door that
had been waiting to get thrown out had been
scattered with a kick and when I saw it I felt
like laughing because whatever they were
looking for they didn't get. There was no
stopping place in the search to indicate that
the great *It* had been located.

For a while I prowled through the ruin of
poverty, picking up a kid's toy here and there,
a woman's bauble, a few work-worn things
that had belonged to Decker. I even did a
little probing in a few spots myself, but there
wasn't a damn thing of any value around. I
finished my butt and flipped it into the sink,
then closed the door and got out of there.

I had a nasty taste in my mouth because so

far it looked like Pat was right all along the line. Decker had gotten himself loused up with a couple of boys and pulled a job that didn't pay off. The chances were that they had cased the joint so well they wouldn't have believed him when he gave them the story of the nearly empty safe.

I sat there in the car and thought about it. In fact, I gave it a hell of a lot of thought. I thought so much about it I got playing all the angles against each other until all I could see was Decker's face with the tears rolling down his cheeks as he bent over to kiss the kid.

So I said a lot of dirty words.

The goon who drove the car was still running around loose and if I had to go after somebody it might as well be him. I stepped on the starter, dragged away from the curb and started back across town.

★   ★   ★

It was more curiosity than anything else that put me on Riverside Drive. When I finally got there I decided that it might be a good idea to cruise around a little bit and see if anybody with a pair of sharp eyes might have spotted the boys who cased the joint before they pulled the job.

I didn't have any more luck than you could

stuff in your eye. That section of town was a money district, and the people who lived there only had eyes for the dollar sign. They were all sheer-faced apartment buildings with fancy doormen doing the honors out front and big, bright Caddies hauled up close to the curb.

One of the janitors thought he remembered a Buick and a couple of men that hung around the neighborhood a week back but he couldn't be sure. For two bucks he took me through an underground alley to the back court and let me have a look around.

Hell, Decker had had it easy. Every one of the buildings had the same kind of passageway from front to back, and once you were in the rear court it was a snap to reach up and grab the bottom rung of the fire ladder. After I had my look I told the guy thanks and went back to the street.

Two doors down was the building where Decker had pulled the job so I loped in past the beefy doorman and went over the bellboard until I found LEE, MARSHA and gave the button a nudge. There was a phone set in a niche in the wall that gave the cliff dweller upstairs a chance to check the callers before unlocking the door and I had to stand with it at my ear a full minute before I heard it click.

Then heaven answered. What a voice she had. It made the kind of music song writers try to imitate and can't. All it said was, 'Yes?' and I started getting mental images of LEE, MARSHA that couldn't be sent through the mail.

I tried hard to sound like a gentleman. 'Miss Lee?'

She said it was.

'This is Mike Hammer. I'm a private investigator. Could I speak to you a few minutes?'

'Oh . . . about the robbery?'

'That's right,' I said.

'Why . . . yes. I suppose you may. Come right up.'

So I went up to heaven in a private elevator that let me out in a semi-private foyer where cloud 4D had a little brass hammer instead of a doorbell. I raised it, let it drop and a ponderous nurse with a mustache scowled me in.

And there was my angel in a big chair by the window. At least the right half of her was angel. The left half sported a very human mouse under the eye and a welt as big as a fist across her jaw.

My face must have been doing some pretty funny things trying to keep from laughing, because she tapped her fingers on the end of the chair and said, 'You had better be properly sympathetic, Mr. Hammer, or out you go.'

I couldn't hold it back and I laughed anyway, but I didn't go out. 'Half of you is the most beautiful girl I ever saw,' I grinned.

'I half thank you,' she grinned back. 'You can leave if you want to, Mrs. Ross. You'll be back at five?'

The nurse told her she would and picked up her coat. When she made sure her patient was all right she left. I was hoping she'd get herself a shave while she was out.

'Please sit down, Mr. Hammer. Can I get you a drink?'

'No, I'll get it myself. Just tell me where to find the makings.'

My angel got up and pulled the filmy housecoat around her like a veil. 'Hell, I'll get it myself. This leading the life of a cripple is a pain. Everybody treats me like an invalid. The nurse is the 'compliments of the management' hoping I don't sue them for neglecting to keep their property properly protected. She's a good cook, otherwise I would have told them to keep her.'

She walked over to a sideboard and I couldn't take my eyes off her. None of this fancy hip-swinging business; just a nice plain walk that could do more than all the fancy

51

wriggling a stripper could put out. Her legs brushing the sheer nylon of the housecoat made it crackle and cling to her body until every curve was outlined in white with pink undertones.

She had tawny brown hair that fell loosely about her shoulders, with eyes that matched perfectly, and a mouth that didn't have to go far to meet mine. Marsha must have just come from a bath, because she smelt fresh and soapy without any veneer of perfume.

When she turned around she had two glasses in her hands and she looked even prettier coming toward me than going away. Her breasts were precocious things that accentuated the width of her shoulders and the smooth contours of her stomach, rising jauntily against the nylon as though they were looking for a way out.

I thought she was too busy balancing the glasses to notice what I was doing, but I was wrong. She handed me a highball and said, 'Do I pass?'

'What?'

'Inspection. Do I pass?'

'If I could get my mouth unpuckered I'd let out a long low whistle,' I told her. 'I'm getting tired of seeing dames in clothes that make them look like a tulip having a hard time coming up. With all the women wearing crew cuts with curled ends these days it's a pleasure to see one with hair for a change.'

'That's a left-handed compliment if ever I heard one. What a lover you'd make.'

I looked at her a long time. 'Don't fool yourself.'

She looked at me just as long. 'I'm not.'

We raised the glasses in a silent toast and sipped the top off them. 'Now, Mr. Hammer . . . '

'Mike.'

Her lips came apart in a smile. 'Mike. It fits you perfectly. What was it you wanted to see me about?'

'First I want to know why you seem so damn familiar. Even with the shiner you remind me of somebody I've seen before.'

Her hands smoothed the front of the housecoat. 'Thank you for remembering.' She let her eyes drift to the piano that stood in the corner and the picture on top of it. I picked up my drink and walked over to it and this time I did let out a long low whistle.

It was a big shot of Marsha in a pre-Civil War dress that came up six inches above her waist before nature took over. The make-up artist had to do very little to make her the most beautiful woman I had ever seen. She had been younger when it was taken, but me . . . I'd take Marsha like she was now. Time

53

had only improved her. Almost hidden by the frame was a line that said the photo was released by the Allerton Motion Picture Company.

Marsha was familiar because I had seen her plenty of times before. So have you. Ten years ago she was an up-and-coming star in Hollywood.

'Yesteryear, those were the days,' she said.

I put the picture back and sat down opposite her so I could see her better. She was well worth looking at and she didn't have to cross her legs to attract attention, either. They were nice legs, too.

'It's a wonder I forgot you,' I said.

'Most people do. The public has a short memory.'

'How come you quit?'

'Oh, it's a sad but brief story. Perhaps you read about it. There was a man, a bit player but a charming heel if ever I saw one. He played up to me to further his own career by picking up a lot of publicity. I was madly in love with him until I found that he was making a play for my secretary in his spare time. In my foolishness I made an issue of it and he told me how he was using me. So, I became the woman scorned and said if he saw her again I'd see that he was blacklisted off every lot in Hollywood. At the time I carried enough potential importance to let me get away with it. Anyway, he told my secretary that he'd never see her after that and she promptly went out and drove her car off a cliff.

'You know Hollywood. It was bad publicity and it knocked me back plenty. Before they could tear my contract up I resigned and came back East where I stuck my savings in investments that allow me to live like I want to.'

I made a motion with my head to take in the room. The place held a fortune in well-chosen furniture and the pictures on the wall weren't any cheap copies, either. Every one of them must have cost four figures. If this was plain living, I'd like to take a crack at it myself.

I pulled out a smoke and she snapped the catch on a table lighter, holding the flame out to me. 'Now . . . you didn't come up here for the story of my life,' she said. Her eyes danced for me.

'Nope, I want to know about the robbery.'

'There's little to tell, Mike. I left here a few minutes before seven to pick up one of the Little Theater members who broke his arm in a fall, drove him home, stopped off at a friend's for a while then came in about a quarter to twelve. As I was about to turn on the lights I saw the beam of a flashlight inside here and like a fool ran right in. For a second I saw this man outlined against the window and the next thing I knew I was flat on my back. I got up and tried to scream, then he hit me again and the world turned upside down. I was still there on the floor when the police came.'

'I got that much of the story from Captain Chambers. Did they tell you the guy is dead?'

'No, they haven't gotten in touch with me at all. What happened?'

'One of his partners killed him. Ran right over him with the car.'

'Did they . . . recover the money?'

'Nope, I'm beginning to think they never will, either.'

'But . . .'

I dragged on the butt and flipped the ashes off in the tray. 'I'm willing to bet that the guy chucked the cash and your pearls on the top of some rubbish pile. He didn't come in here for any three hundred bucks. That kind of job isn't worth the trouble.'

She bit her lips and frowned at me. 'You know something, Mike, I was thinking the same thing.'

I looked at her curiously. 'Go on.'

'I think this . . . this robber knew what he was doing, but got his floors mixed. Do you know Marvin Holmes?'

'The playboy who keeps a stable of blondes?'

'That's right. He has the apartment directly above me. The rooms are laid out exactly the same and even the wall safe is in the identical spot as mine. He always keeps a small fortune on hand and he wasn't home last night either. I met him just as I was going out and he mentioned something about a night club.'

'You've been up there?'

'Several times. He's always throwing parties. I don't rate because I'm not a blonde,' she added as an afterthought.

It made sense, all right. Just to see how much sense it did make I picked Marvin Holmes' number out of the phone book and dialed it. A butler with a German accent answered, told me yes, Mr. Holmes was at home and put him on. I lied and said I was from the insurance company and wanted to know if he kept a bundle at his fingertips. The sap sounded half looped and was only too happy to tell me there was better than ten grand in his safe and tacked on that he thought the guy who opened the safe on the floor below him had made a mistake. I thanked him and hung up.

Marsha said, 'Did he . . . '

'The guy has the same idea as you, chick.

57

He thinks there was a one-floor error and for my money you're both right.'

Her shoulders made a faint gesture of resignation. 'Well, I guess there's little that can be done then. I had hoped to recover the pearls for sentimental reasons. I wore them in my first picture.'

If I grinned I couldn't have been nice to look at. My lips felt tight over my teeth and I shook my head. 'It's a dirty mess, Marsha. Two guys are dead already and there'll be another on the way soon. The guy who robbed your place left a baby behind, then went right out to get chopped down. Hell, it isn't what he took, it's why he took it. He was on the level for a long time then just like that he went bad and no guy like him is going to pull something that'll let his own kid get tossed to the dogs.

'Damn it, I was there and saw it! I watched him cry and kiss his kid good-by and go out and cash in his chips. Now I have the kid and I know what he must have felt like. Goddamn it anyway, there's a reason why these things happen and that's what I want. Maybe it's only a little reason and maybe it's a big one, but by God, I'm going to get it.'

Her eyes were square and steady on mine, a deep liquid brown that got deeper as she stared at me. 'You're a strange kind of guy,' she said. I picked up my hat and stood up. She came forward to meet me, holding her hand out. 'Mike . . . about the child . . . if I can help out with it, well I'm pretty well set up financially . . . '

I squeezed her hand. 'You know, you're a strange kind of guy yourself.'

'Thanks, Mike.'

'But I can take care of the kid okay.' She gave me a lopsided smile that made her look good even with the shiner. 'By the way . . . would you happen to have an extra picture around . . . like that one?' I nodded toward the piano.

For a long space of time she held on to my hand and ran her eyes over my face. 'What for, won't I do in person?'

I let my hat drop and it stayed on the floor. My hands ran up her arms until my fingers were digging into her shoulders and I drew her in close. She was all woman, every bit of her. Her body was taut, her breasts high and firm with all the vitality of youth, and I could feel the warm outlines of her legs as I pressed her against me. She raised herself on her toes deliberately, tantalizing, a subtle motion that I knew was an invitation not lightly given.

I wanted to kiss her, but I knew that when I did I'd want to make it so good and so hard it would hurt long enough to be remembered and now wasn't the time. Later, when her mouth was smooth and soft again.

'You'll be back, Mike?' she whispered.

She knew the answer without being told. I pushed her away and picked up my hat.

There were things in this city that could be awfully nasty.

There were things in this city that could be awfully nice too.

3

I stopped by the office that afternoon. The only one in the building to say hello was the elevator operator and he had to look twice to recognize me. It was a hell of a feeling. You live in the city your whole life, take off for six months and you are unknown when you come back. I opened the door and felt a little better when I saw the same old furniture in the same old place. The only thing that was missing was Velda. Her desk was a lonely corner in the anteroom, dusted and ready for a new occupant.

I said something dirty. I was always saying something dirty these days.

She had left a folder of correspondence she thought I might want to see on my desk. It wasn't anything important. Just a record of bills paid, my bank statements and a few letters. I closed the folder and stowed it away in a drawer. There was a fifth of good whisky still there with the wrapper on. I stripped off the paper, uncorked the bottle and looked at it. I worked the top off and smelled it. Then I put it back and shut the drawer. I felt stinking and didn't like the feeling.

Outside on Velda's desk the phone started ringing. I went out in a hurry hoping it might be her, but a rough voice said, 'You Mike Hammer?'

'Yeah, who's this?'

'Johnny Vileck. You know, the super down in Decker's building. I had a hell of a time tryin' to get you. Lucky I remembered your name.'

'What's up?' I asked.

'I was thinking over what we was speaking about this morning. Remember you asked me about Decker needin' dough?'

'Uh-huh.'

'When I went out to get the paper I got talking to the blind newsie on the corner. The old guy was pretty busted up about it. Him and Decker was pretty good friends. Anyway, one night after the old lady died, he was up there playing chess when this guy come around. He wanted to know when Decker was going to get the cash he owed. Decker paid him something and the guy left and after it he mentioned that he had to borrow a big chunk to cover the wife's operation. Mentioned three grand.'

I let it jell in my head for a minute, twisting it around until it made sense. 'Where could he get that kind of dough?'

Vileck grunted and made a shrug I

couldn't see. 'Beats me. He never borrowed nuthing and it's damn sure he didn't go to no bank.'

'Anybody in the neighborhood got it?'

'Not in this neighborhood, pal. Once somebody'll hit a number or a horse, but he ain't lending it out, you can bet. There's plenty of tough guys around here who show up with a roll sometimes, but it's flash money and they're either gone or in jail the next day. Nope, he didn't get it around here.'

'Thanks for the dope, John. If you ever need a favor, let me know.'

'Sure, pal, glad to let you know about it.'

'Look . . . did you mention this to the cops?'

'Naw. I found out after they left. Besides, they don't hear from me unless they ask. Cops is okay long as they stay outa my joint.'

I told him so long and put the receiver back. There was the reason for murder and it was a good one. Three grand worth. Now it was coming out right. Decker went into somebody for three grand and he had to bail himself out by stealing it. So he made a mistake when he raided the wrong apartment and his pals didn't believe it. They thought he was holding out. So they bump him figuring to lift a jackpot and all they got was a measly three hundred bucks and a string of pearls.

Damn it, the whole thing made me boil over! Because a guy couldn't wait to get his dough back a kid is made an orphan. My city, yeah. How many places around town was the same thing going on?

I sat down on the edge of the desk to think about it and the whole thing hit me suddenly and sharply and way back in my head I could hear that crazy music start until it was beating through my brain with a maddening frenzy that tried to drive away any sanity I had left. I cursed to myself until it was gone then went back to my desk and pulled out the bottle. This time I had a drink.

It took me all afternoon to find what I wanted. I went down to the docks and let my P.I. ticket and my badge get me inside the gates until I reached the right paymaster who had handled William Decker's card. He was a little guy in his late fifties with an oversize nose built into a face that was streaked with little purple veins.

He made me wait until he finished tallying up his report, then stuck the clipboard on a nail in the wall and swung around in his chair. He said, 'What's on your mind, buddy?'

I offered him a smoke and he waved it away to chew on a ratty cigar. 'Remember a guy named Decker?'

He grunted a yes and waited.

'He have any close friends on the docks here?'

'Might have. What'cha want to know for?'

'I heard he died. I owed him a few bucks and I want to see that it goes to his estate.'

The guy clucked and sucked his tongue a minute. He opened his desk drawer and riffled through a file of cards until he came to the one he wanted. 'Well, here's his address and he's got a kid. Got him down for two dependents, but I think his wife died awhile back.'

'I found that out. If I can dig up a pal of his maybe he'll know something more about him.'

'Yeah. Well, seems like he always shaped in with a guy named Hooker. Mel Hooker. Tall thin guy with a scar on his face. They got paid off today so they'll be in the joints 'cross the way cashing their checks. Why don'tcha go over an' try?'

I stuffed the butt in the ash tray on the desk. 'I'll do that. Give me his address in case I miss him.'

He scratched something on a pad and handed it over. I said thanks and left.

* * *

It wasn't that easy. I thought I hit every saloon on the street until a guy told me about a couple I had missed and then I found him. The place was a rattrap where they'd take the drunks that had been kicked out of other places and make them spend their last buck. You had to go down a couple of steps to reach the door and before you reached it you could smell what you were walking into.

The place was a lot bigger than I expected. They were lined up two deep at the bar and when they couldn't stand any more they sat down at the bench along the wall. One guy had passed out and was propped up against a partition with his pockets turned inside out.

Mel Hooker was down the back watching a shuffleboard game. He had half a bag on and looked it. The yellow glare of the overhead lights brought out the scar that ran from his forehead to his chin in bold relief almost as if it was still an ugly gash. I walked over and pulled out the chair beside him.

He looked at me enough to say, 'Beat it.'

'You Mel Hooker?'

'Who wants to know?' His voice had a nasty drunken snarl to it.

'How'd you like to get the other side of your face opened up, feller?'

He dropped his glass like it was shot out of his hand and tried to get up off his chair. I shoved him back without any trouble. 'Stay put, Mel. I want to talk to you.'

His breathing was noisy. 'I don't wanna talk to you,' he said.

'Tough stuff, Mel. You'll talk if I tell you to. It's about a friend of yours. He's dead. His name was William Decker.'

The flesh around the scar seemed to get whiter. Something changed in his eyes and he half twisted his head. One of the guys at the shuffleboard was taking a long time to make his play. Mel unfolded himself and nodded to an empty table over in the corner. 'Over . . . here. Make it quick.'

I got up and went back to the bar for a pair of drinks and brought them back to the table. When Mel took his his hand wasn't too steady. I let him take half of it down in one gulp before I asked, 'Who'd he owe dough to, Mel?'

He almost dropped this glass, too. In time, he recovered it and set it down very deliberately and wiped his mouth with the back of his hand. 'You a cop?'

'I'm a private investigator.'

'You're gonna be a dead investigator if you don't get the hell outa here.'

'I asked you a question.'

His tongue flicked out and whipped over his lips. 'Get this, I don't know nothing about nothing. Bill was a friend of mine but his business was his own. Now lemme alone.'

'He needed three grand, Mel. He borrowed it from somebody. He didn't get it around home so he must have got it someplace around here.'

'You're nuts.'

'You're a hell of a friend,' I said, 'one hell of a friend.'

Hooker dropped his head and stared at his hands. When he looked up his mouth was drawn back tight. His voice came out barely a whisper. 'Listen, Mac, you better quit asking questions. Bill was my friend and I'd help him if I could, but he's dead and that's that. You see this scar I got? I'd sooner have that than be dead. Now blow and lemme alone.'

He wouldn't look back at me when he left. He staggered out to the bar and through the mob around it until he reached the door, then disappeared up the stairs. I polished my drink off and waved the waiter over with another. He gave me a frozen look and snatched the buck out of my hand.

The place got too damn quiet. The weights weren't slamming on the shuffleboard and everybody at the bar seemed to have taken a sudden interest in the television set over the bar. I sat there and waited for my change, but I had the drink gone without seeing it.

This I liked. This I was waiting for because the stupid bastards should have known better. My God, did I look like some flunkey from the sticks or did the wise boys lose their memories too?

I pushed the glass back and got up. I found the men's room in the back by the smell and did what I had to do and started to wash my hands. That's how long they gave me.

The guy in the double-breasted suit in the doorway spoke out of the corner of his mouth to somebody behind him. His little pig eyes looked like he was getting ready to enjoy himself. 'He's a big one, ain't he?'

'Yeah.' The other guy stepped in and seemed to fill up the doorway.

The little guy's hand came out of his pocket with a sap about a foot long and he swung it against his knee waiting to see if I was going to puke or start bawling. The big guy took his time about slipping on the knucks. Outside the volume on the television went up so loud it blasted its way all the way back there.

I dropped the paper towel and backed off until my shoulders were up against the doors of the pot. The little guy was leering. His mouth worked until the spit rolled down his chin and his shoulder started to draw back the sap. His pal closed in on the side, only his eyes showing that there might be some human intelligence behind that stupid expression.

The goddamn bastards played right into my hands. They thought they had me nice and cold and just as they were set to carve me into a raw mess of skin I dragged out the .45 and let them look down the hole so they could see where sudden death came from.

It was the only kind of talk they knew. The little guy stared too long. He should have been watching my face. I snapped the side of the rod across his jaw and laid the flesh open to the bone. He dropped the sap and staggered into the big boy with a scream starting to come up out of his throat only to get it cut off in the middle as I pounded his teeth back into his mouth with the end of the barrel. The big guy tried to shove him out of the way. He got so mad he came right at me with his head down and I took my own damn time about kicking him in the face. He smashed into the door and lay there bubbling. So I kicked him again and he stopped bubbling. I pulled the knucks off his hand then went over and picked up the sap. The punk was vomiting on the floor, trying to claw his way under the sink. For laughs I gave him a taste of his own sap on the back of his hand and felt the bones go into splinters. He wasn't going to be using any tools for a long time.

They moved aside and let me get in to the bar. They moved aside so far you'd think I was contaminated. The bartender looked at me and his thick lips rubbed together. I dropped the knucks and the sap on the bar and waved the bartender over with my forefinger. 'I got some change coming,' I said.

He turned around and rang up a NO SALE on the register and handed me fifty-five cents.

If somebody breathed before I left I didn't hear it. I got out of there feeling like myself again and went back to the car. I only had one thing to do before I saw Pat. I checked the slip the timekeeper gave me and saw that Mel Hooker lived not too far from where Decker had lived. I got snarled up in traffic halfway there and it was dark by the time I found his address.

The place was a rooming house with the usual sign outside advertising a lone vacancy and a landlady on the bottom floor using her window for a crow's nest. She was at the door before I got up the steps waiting to smile if I was a renter or glare if I was a visitor.

She glared when I asked her if Mel Hooker had come in yet. Her finger waved up the stairs. 'Ten minutes ago and drunk. Don't you two raise no ruckus or out you both go.'

If she had been nicer I would have soothed her feelings with a bill. All she got was a sharp thanks and I went upstairs. I heard him shuffling around the room and when I knocked all sound stopped. I knocked again and he dragged across the floor and snapped the lock back. I don't know who he expected to see. It sure wasn't me.

I didn't ask to come in; I gave the door a shove and he reeled back. His face had lost its tenseness and was dull, his mouth sagging. There was a table in the middle of the room and I perched on it, watching him close the door, then turn around until he faced me!

'Christ!' he said.

'What'd you expect, Mel?' I lit a Lucky and peered at him through the smoke. 'You're a hell of a guy,' I told him. 'I guess you knew those boys would tag after me and you didn't want to stick around to see the blood.'

'Wh . . . what happened?'

I grinned at him. 'I've been messing around with bastards like that for a long time. They should have remembered my face. Now they're going to have trouble remembering what they used to look like before. Did you pull the same stunt on your friend Decker, Mel? Did you beat it when they went looking for him?'

He staggered over to a chair and collapsed

in it. 'I don't . . . know . . . whatcha talking about.'

I leaned forward on the edge of the table and spit the words out. 'I'm talking about the loan shark racket. I'm talking about a guy named William Decker who used to be your friend and needed dough bad. He couldn't get it from a legitimate source so he hit up a loan shark and got what he needed. When he couldn't pay off they put the pressure on him probably through his kid so he tries to cop a bank roll from a rich guy's safe. He miffed the job and they gave him the works. Now do you know what I'm talking about?'

Hooker said, 'Christ!' again and grabbed the arms of the chair. 'Friend, you gotta get outa here, see? You gotta leave me alone!'

'What's the matter, Mel? You were a tough guy when I met you tonight. What's getting you so soft?'

For a minute a crazy madness passed over his face, then he let out a gasp and buried his head in his hands. 'Damn it, get outa here!'

'Yeah, I'll get out. When you tell me who's banking the soaks along the docks I'll get out.'

'I . . . I can't. Oh, Lord, lemme alone, will ya!'

'They're tough, huh?' He read something in my words and his eyes came up in a series of little jerks until they were back on mine. 'Are they tougher than the guys you pushed on me?'

Mel swallowed hard. 'I didn't . . . '

'Don't crap me, friend. Those guys weren't there by accident. They weren't there just for me, either. Somebody's got a finger on you, haven't they?'

He didn't answer.

'They were there for you,' I said, 'only you saw a nice way to shake them loose on me. What gives?'

His finger moved by itself and traced the scar that lay along the side of his jaw. 'Look, I got cut up once, I did. I don't want to fool around with them guys no more. Honest. I didn't do nothing! I don't know why they was there but they was!'

'So you're in a trap too,' I said.

'No I ain't!' He shouted it. His face was a sickly white and he drooled a little bit. 'I'm clean and I don't know why they're sticking around me. Why the hell did you came butting in for?'

'Because I want to know why your pal Decker needed dough.'

'Christ, his wife was dying. He had to have it. How'd I know he couldn't pay it back!'

'Pay what back to who?'

His tongue flashed over his lips and his

mouth clammed shut.

'You have a union and a welfare fund for that, don't you?'

This time he spit on the floor.

'Who'd you steer him to, Mel?'

He didn't answer me. I got up off the edge of the table and jerked him to his feet. 'Who was it, Mel . . . or do you want to find out what happened to the tough boys back in the bar?'

The guy went limp in my hands. He didn't try to get away. He just hung there in my fist, his eyes dead. His words came out slow and flat. 'He needed the dough. We . . . thought we had a good tip on the ponies and pooled our dough.'

'So?'

'We won. It wasn't enough so we threw it back on another tip, only Bill hit up a loan shark for a few hundred to lay a bigger bet. We won that one too and I pulled out with my share. Bill thought he could get a big kill quick and right after he paid the shark back, knocked him down for another grand to add to his stake and this time he went under.'

'Okay, so he owed a grand.'

Mel's head shook sadly. 'It was bigger. You pay back one for five every week. It didn't take long to run it up into big money.'

I let him go and he sank back into the

chair. 'Now names, Mel. Who was the shark?'

I barely heard him say, 'Dixie Cooper. He hangs out in the Glass Bar on Eighth Avenue.'

I picked up my deck of smokes and stuffed them in my pocket. I walked out without closing the door and down past the landlady who still held down her post in the vestibule. She didn't say anything until Mel hobbled to the door, glanced down the stairs and shut it. Then the old biddy humphed and let me out.

The sky had clouded up again, shutting out the stars and there was a damp mist in the air. I called Pat from a candy store down the corner and nobody answered his phone at home, so I tried the office. He was there. I told him to stick around and got back in my car.

Headquarters building was like a beehive without any bees when I got there. A lone squad car stood at the curb and the elevator operator was reading a paper inside his cab. The boys on the night stand had that bored look already and half of them were piddling around trying to keep busy.

I got in the elevator and let him haul me up to Pat's floor. Down the corridor a typewriter was clicking busily and I heard Pat rummaging around the drawers of his file cabinet. When I pushed the door open he

76

said, 'Be right with you, Mike.'

So I parked and watched him work for five minutes. When he got through at the cabinet I asked him, 'How come you're working nights?'

'Don't you read the papers?'

'I didn't come up against any juicy murders.'

'Murders, hell. The D.A. has me and everybody else he can scrape together working on that gambling probe.'

'What's he struggling so hard for, it isn't an election year for him. Besides, the public's going to gamble anyway.'

Pat pulled out his chair and slid into it. 'The guy's got scruples. He has it in for Ed Teen and his outfit.'

'He's not getting Teen,' I said.

'Well, he's trying.'

'Where do you come in?'

Pat shrugged and reached for a cigarette. 'The D.A. tried to break up organized gambling in this town years ago. It flopped like all the other probes flopped . . . for lack of evidence. He's never made a successful raid on a syndicate establishment since he went after them.'

'There's a hole in the boat?'

'A what?'

'A leak.'

'Of course. Ed Teen has a pipeline right into the D.A.'s office somehow. That's why the D.A. is after his hide. It's a personal affront to him and he won't stand for it. Since he can't nail Teen down with something, he's conducting an investigation into his past. We know damn well that Teen and Grindle pulled a lot of rough stuff and if we can tie a murder on them they'll be easy to take.'

'I bet. Why doesn't he patch that leak?'

Pat did funny things with his mouth. 'He's surrounded by men he trusts and I trust and we can't find a single person who's talking out of turn. Everybody's been investigated. We even checked for dictaphones, that's how far we went. It seems impossible, but nevertheless, the leak's here. Hell, the D.A. pulls surprise raids that were cooked up an hour before and by the time he gets there not a soul's around. It's uncanny.'

'Uncanny my foot. The D.A. is fooling with guys as smart as he is himself. They've been operating longer too. Look, any chance of breaking away early tonight?'

'With this here?' He pointed toward a pile of papers on his desk. 'They all have to be classified, correlated and filed. Nope, not tonight, Mike. I'll be here for another three hours yet.'

Outside the racket of the typewriter stopped and a stubby brunette came in with a wire basket of letters. Right behind her was another brunette, but far from stubby. What the first one didn't have she had everything of and she waved it around in front of you like a flag.

Pat saw my foolish grin and when the stubby one left said, 'Miss Scobie, have you met Mike Hammer?'

I got one of those casual glances with a flicker of a smile. 'No, but I've heard the District Attorney speak of him several times.'

'Nothing good, I hope,' I said.

'No, nothing good.' She laughed at me and finished sorting out the papers on Pat's desk.

'Miss Scobie is one of the D.A.'s secretaries,' Pat said. 'For a change I have some help around here. He sent over three girls to do the manual labor.'

'I'm pretty good at that myself.' I think I was leering.

The Scobie babe gave me the full voltage from a pair of deep blue eyes. 'I've heard that too.'

'You should quit getting things second-hand.'

She packed the last of the papers in a new pile and tacked them together with a clip. When she turned around she gave me a look

Pat couldn't see but had a whole book written there in her face. 'Perhaps I should,' she said.

I could feel the skin crawl up my back just from the tone of her voice.

Pat said, 'You're a bastard. Mike. You and the women.'

'They're necessary.' I stared at the door that closed behind her.

His mouth cracked in a grin. 'Not Miss Scobie. She knows her way around the block without somebody holding her hand. Doesn't her name mean anything to you?'

'Should it?'

'Not unless you're a society follower. Her family is big stuff down in Texas. The old man had a ranch where he raised horses until they brought oil in. Then he sat back and enjoyed life. He raises racing nags now.'

'The Scobie Stables?'

'Uh-huh. Ellen's his daughter. When she was eighteen she and the old boy had a row and she packed up and left. This department job is the first one she ever had. Been here better than fifteen years. She's the gal the track hates to see around. When she makes a bet she collects.'

'What the hell's she working for then?'

'Ask her.'

'I'm asking you.'

80

Pat grinned again. 'The old man disinherited her when she wouldn't marry the son of his friend. He swore she'd never see a penny of his dough, so now she'll only bet when a Scobie horse is running and with what she knows about horses, she's hard to fool. Every time she wins she sends a telegram to the old boy stating the amount and he burns up. Don't ask her to tip you off though. She won't do it.'

'Why doesn't the D.A. use her to get an inside track on the wire rooms?'

'He did, but she's too well known now. A feature writer for one of the papers heard about the situation, and gave it a big play in a Sunday supplement a few years ago, so she's useless there.'

I leaned back in my chair and stared at the ceiling. 'Texas gal. I like the way they're built.'

'Yeah, big.' Pat grunted. 'A big one gets you every time.' His fingers rapped on the desk. 'Let's come back to earth, Mike. What's new?'

'Decker.'

'That's not new. We're still looking for the driver who ran down his buddy. They found the car, you know.'

I sat up straight.

'You didn't miss everything that night. There were two bullet holes in the back. One hit the rear window and the other went through the gas tank. The car was abandoned over in Brooklyn.'

'Stolen heap?'

'Sure, what'd you expect? The slugs came from your gun, the tires matched the imprints in the body and there wasn't a decent fingerprint anywhere.'

'Great.'

'We'll wrap it up soon. The word's out.'

'Great.'

Pat scowled at me in disgust. 'Hell, you're never satisfied.'

I shook a cigarette out and lit up. Pat pushed an ash tray over to me. I said, 'Pat, you got holes in your head if you think that this was a plain, simple job. Decker was in hock to a loan shark for a few grand and was being pressured into paying up. The guy was nuts about his kid and they probably told him the kid would catch it if he didn't come across.'

'So?'

'Christ, you aren't getting to be a cynic like the rest of the cops, are you? You want things like this to keep on happening? You like murder to dirty up the streets just because some greaseball wants his dirty money! Hell, who's to blame . . . a poor jerk like Decker or a torpedo who'll carve him up if he doesn't pay up? Answer me that.'

'There's a law against loan sharks operating in this state.'

'There's a law against gambling, too.'

Pat's face was dark with anger.

'The law has been enforced,' he snapped.

I put the emphasis on the past tense. 'It *has*? That's nice to know. Who's running the racket now?'

'Damn it, Mike, that isn't my department.'

'It should be; it caused the death of two men so far. What I want to know is, is the racket organized or not?'

'I've heard that it was,' he replied sullenly. 'Fallon used to bank it before he died. When the state cracked down on them somebody took the sharks under their wing. I don't know who.'

'Fallon? Fallon, hell, the guy's been dead since 1940 and he's still making news.'

'Well, you asked me.'

I nodded. 'Who's Dixie Cooper, Pat?'

His eyes went half shut. 'Where do you get your information from? Goddamn, you have your nose in everywhere.'

'Who is he?'

'The guy's a stoolie for the department. He has no known source of income, though he claims to be a promoter.'

'Of what?'

'Of everything. He's a guy who knows where something is that somebody else wants and collects a percentage from the buyer and seller both. At least, that's what he says.'

'Then he's full of you know what. The guy is a loan shark. He's the one Decker hit up for the money.'

'Can you prove it?'

'Uh-huh.'

'Show me and we'll take him into custody.'

I stood up and slapped on my hat. 'I'll show you,' I said. 'I'll have him screaming to talk to somebody in uniform just to keep from getting his damn arms twisted off.'

'Go easy, Mike.'

'Yeah, I'll do just that. I'll twist 'em nice and easy like he twisted Decker. I'll go easy, all right.'

Pat gave me a long look with a frown behind it. When I said so long he only nodded, and he was reaching for the phone as I shut the door.

Down the hall another door slammed shut and the stubby brunette came by, smiled at me politely and kept on going to the elevator. After she got in I went back down the corridor to the office, pushed the door open and stuck my head in. Ellen Scobie had one foot on a chair with her dress hiked up as far as it would go, straightening her stocking.

'Pretty leg,' I said.

She glanced back quickly without bothering to yank her dress down like most dames would. 'I have another just like it,' she told me. Her eyes were on full voltage again.

'Let's see.'

So she stood up in one of those magazine poses and pulled the dress up slowly without stopping until it couldn't go any further and showed me. And she was right. The other was just as pretty if you wasted a sight like that trying to compare them.

I said, 'I love brunettes.'

'You love anything.' She let the dress fall.

'Brunettes especially. Doing anything tonight?'

'Yes . . . I was going out with you, wasn't I? Something I should learn about manual labor?'

'Kid,' I said, 'I don't think you have anything to learn. Not a damn thing.'

She laughed deep in her throat and came over and took my arm. 'I'm crazy about heels,' she said. 'Let's go.'

We passed by Pat's office again and I could still hear him on the phone. His voice had a low drone with a touch of urgency in it but I couldn't hear what he was saying. When we were downstairs in the car Ellen said, 'I hope you realize that if we're seen together my boss will have you investigated from top to bottom.'

'Then you do the investigating. I have some fine anatomy.'

Her mouth clucked at me. 'You know what I mean. He's afraid to trust himself these days.'

'You can forget about me, honey. He's investigated me so often he knows how many moles I got. Who the hell's handing out the dope, anyway?'

'If I knew I'd get a promotion. Right now the office observes wartime security right down to burning everything in the wastebaskets in front of a policeman. You know what I think?'

'What?'

'Somebody sits in another building with a telescope and reads lips.'

I laughed at her. 'Did you tell the D.A. that?'

She grinned devilishly. 'Uh-huh. I said it jokingly and damned if he didn't go and pull down the blinds. Everybody hates me now.' She stopped and glanced out the windows, then looked back at me curiously. 'Where're we going?'

'To see a guy about a guy,' I said.

She leaned back against the cushions and closed her eyes. When she opened them again I was pulling into a parking lot in Fifty-second Street. The attendant took my keys and handed me a ticket. The evening was just starting to pick up and the gin mills lining the street were starting to get a play.

Ellen tugged at my hand. 'We aren't drinking very fancy tonight, are we?'

'You come down here much?'

'Oh, occasionally. I don't go much for these places. Where are we going?'

'A place called the Glass Bar. It's right down the block.'

'That fag joint,' she said with disgust. 'The last time I was there I had three women trying to paw me and a guy with me who thought it was funny.'

'Hell, I'd like to paw you myself,' I laughed.

'Oh, you will, you will.' She was real matter-of-fact about it, but not casual, not a bit. I started to get that feeling up my back again.

The Glass Bar was a phony name for a phonier place. It was all chrome and plastic, and glass was only the thing you drank out of. The bar was a circular affair up front near the door with the back half of the place given over to tables and a bandstand. A drummer was warming up his traps with a pair of cuties squirming to his jungle rhythm while a handful of queers watched with their eyes oozing lust.

87

Ellen said, 'The bar or back room?'

I tossed my hat at the redhead behind the check booth. 'Don't know yet.' The redhead handed me a pasteboard with a number on it and I asked her, 'Dixie Cooper been in yet?'

She leaned halfway out of the booth and looked across the room. 'Don't see him. Guess he must be in back. He came in about a half hour ago.'

I said thanks and took Ellen's arm. We had a quick one at the bar, then pushed through the crowd to the back room where the babes were still squirming with the drummer showing no signs of tiring. He was all eyes for the wriggling hips and the table with the queers had been abandoned for one closer to the bandstand.

Only four other tables were occupied and the kind of people sitting there weren't the kind I was looking for. Over against the wall a guy was slouched in a chair reading a late tabloid while he sipped a beer. He had a hairline that came down damn near to his eyebrows and when his mouth moved as he read his top teeth stuck out at an angle. On the other side of the table a patsy was trying to drag him into a conversation and all he was getting was a grunt now and then.

The guy with the bleached hair looked up and smiled when I edged over, then the smile froze into a disgusted grimace when he saw Ellen. I said, 'Blow, Josephine,' and he arched his eyebrows and minced off.

Buck teeth didn't even bother to look at me.

Ellen didn't wait to be invited. She plunked herself in a chair with a grin and leaned on the table waiting for the fun to start.

Buck teeth interrupted his reading long enough to say, 'Whatta you want?'

So I took the .45 out and slid it down between his eyes and the paper and let him stare at it until he went white all the way back of his ears. Then I sat down too. 'You Dixie Cooper?'

His head came around like somebody had a string on it. 'Yeah.' It was almost a whisper and his eyes wouldn't come away from the bulge under my coat.

'There was a man,' I said. 'His name was William Decker and he hit you up for a loan not long ago and he's dead now.'

Cooper licked his lips twice and tried to shake his head. 'Look . . . I . . . '

'Shut up.'

His eyes seemed to get a waxy film over them.

'Who killed him,' I said.

'Honest to God, Mac, I . . . Christ . . . I didn't kill 'im. I swear . . . '

'You little son-of-a-bitch you, when you put the squeeze on him for your lousy dough he had to pull a robbery to pay off!'

This time his eyes came away from my coat and jerked up to mine. His upper lip pared back from his teeth while his head made funny shaking motions. 'I . . . don't get it. He . . . didn't get squeezed. He paid up. I give 'im a grand and two days later he pays it back. Honest to God, I . . . '

'Wait a minute. He paid you back all that dough?'

His head bobbed. 'Yeah, yeah. All of it.'

'You know what he used it for?'

'I . . . I think he was playing the ponies.'

'He lost. That means he paid you back and his losses too. Where'd he get it?'

'How should I know? He paid me back like I told you.'

Dixie started to shake when I grinned at him. 'You know what'll happen to you if I find out you're lying?'

He must have known, all right. His buck teeth started showing gums and all. Somehow he got his lips together enough to say, 'Christ, I can prove it! He . . . he paid me off right in Bernie Herman's bar. Ask Bernie, he was there. He saw him pay me and he'll remember because I bought the house a drink. You ask him.'

I grinned again and pulled out the .45 and handed it to Ellen under the table. Dixie couldn't seem to swallow his own spit any more. I said, 'I will, pal. You better be right. If he tries to scram, put one in his leg, Ellen.'

She was a beautiful actress. She never changed her smile except to give it the deadly female touch and it wasn't because she meant it, but because she was having herself a time and was enjoying every minute of it.

I went out to the phone and looked up Bernie Herman's number and got the guy after a minute or so and he told me the same thing Dixie had. When I got back to the table they were still in the same position only Dixie had run out of spit altogether.

Ellen handed me the rod and I slipped it back under my coat. I nodded for her to get up just as a waiter decided it was about time to take our order. 'Your friend cleared you, Dixie. You better stay cleared or you'll get a slug right in those buck teeth of yours. You know that, don't you?'

A drop of sweat rolled down in his eye and he blinked, but that was all.

I said, 'Come on, kitten,' and we left him sitting there. When I passed the waiter I jerked my thumb back to the table. 'You better bring him a whiskey. Straight. Make it a double.'

He jotted it down and went over to the service bar.

Outside a colored pianist was trying hard to play loud enough to be heard over the racket of the crowd that was four deep around the bar. I pushed Ellen behind me and started elbowing a path between the mob and the booths along the side and if I didn't almost trip over a foot stuck out in the aisle I wouldn't have seen Lou Grindle parked in the booth across from a guy who looked like a Wall Street banker.

Only he wasn't a banker, but the biggest bookie in the business and his name was Ed Teen.

Lou just stopped talking and stared at me with those snake eyes of his. I said, 'Your boy's still in the morgue, Lou. Don't you guys go in for big funerals these days?'

Ed Teen smiled and the creases around his mouth turned into deep hollows. 'Friends of yours, Lou?'

'Sure, we're real old buddies, we are,' I said. 'Some day I'm gonna kick his teeth in.'

Lou didn't scare a bit. The bastard looked almost anxious for me to try it. Ellen gave me a little push from behind and we got through the crowd to the checkroom where I got my hat, then went outside to the night.

Her face was different this time. The

humor had gone out of it and she watched me as though I'd bite her. 'Lord, Mike, a joke's a joke, but don't go too far. Do you know who they were?'

'Yeah, scum. You want to hear some dirty words that fit 'em perfectly?'

'But . . . they're dangerous.'

'So I've heard. That makes it more fun. You know them?'

'Of course. My boss would give ten years off his life to get either one of them in court. Please, Mike, just go a little easy on me. I don't mind holding your gun to frighten someone like that little man back here, but those two . . . '

I slipped my arm around her shoulders and squeezed. 'Kitten, when a couple of punks like that give me the cold shivers I'll hang up. They're big because they have money and the power and guns that money can buy, but when you take their clothes off and there's no pockets to hold the money or the guns they're just two worms looking for holes to hide in.'

'Have it your way, but I need a drink. A big one and right now. My stomach is all squirmy.'

She must have been talking about the inside. I felt her stomach and it was nice and flat. She poked me with her elbow for the liberty and made me take her in a bar.

Only this one was nearly empty and the only dangerous character was a drunk arguing with the bartender about who was going to win the series. When we had our drink I asked her if she wanted another and she shook her head. 'One's enough on top of what happened tonight. I think I'd like to go home, Mike.'

She lived in the upper Sixties on the top floor of the only new building in the block. About a half-dozen brownstones had been razed to clear an area for the new structure and it stood out like a dame in a French bathing suit at an old maids' convention. It was still a pretty good neighborhood, but most of the new convertibles and sleek black sedans were lumped together in front of her place.

I got in line behind the cars at the curb and opened the door for her. 'Aren't you coming up for a midnight snack, Mike?'

'I thought I was supposed to ask that,' I laughed.

'Times have changed. Especially when you get to my age.'

So I went up.

There was an automatic elevator, marble-lined corridors under the thick maroon rugs, expensive knickknacks and antique furniture

94

all for free before you even hit the apartment itself. The layout wasn't much different inside, either. For apartment-hungry New York, this was luxury. There were six rooms with the best of everything in each as far as I could see. The living room was one of these ultra modern places with angular furniture that looked like hell until you sat in it. All along the mantel of the imitation fireplace was a collection of genuine Paul Revere pieces that ran into big dough, while the biggest of the pieces, each with its own copper label of historical data, was used beside the front windows as flowerpots.

I kind of squinted at Ellen as I glanced around. 'How much do they pay you to do secretarial work?'

Her laugh made a tinkling sound in the room. 'Not this much, I'll tell you. Three of us share this apartment, so it's not too hard to manage. The copper work you seem to admire belongs to Patty. She was working for Captain Chambers with me tonight.'

'Oh, short and fat.'

'She has certain virtues that attract men.'

'Money?'

Ellen nodded.

'Then why does she work?'

'So she can meet men, naturally.'

'Cripes, are all the babes after all the men?'

'It seems so. Now, if you'll just stay put I'll whip up a couple of sandwiches. Want something to drink?'

'Beer if you have it.'

She said she had it and went back to the kitchen. She fooled around out there for about five minutes and finally managed to get an inch of ham to stay between the bread. A lanky towheaded job in one of these shortie nightgowns must have heard the raid on the icebox, because she came out of the bedroom as Ellen came in and snatched the extra sandwich off the plate. Just as she was going to pop it in her mouth she saw me and said, 'Hi.'

I said 'Hi' back.

She said, 'Ummm,' but that was before she bit into the sandwich.

Moving her arms jerked the shortie up too far. Ellen blocked the view by handing me my beer and called back over her shoulder, 'Either go put some more clothes on or get back in bed.'

The towhead took another bite and mumbled, 'With you around I need a handicap.' She took another bite and shuffled back to the bedroom.

'See what I have to put up with?'

'I wish I had to put up with it.'

'You would.'

So we sat and finished the snack and dawdled over a beer until I said it was time to scram and she looked painfully unhappy with an expression that said I could stay if I wanted to badly enough. I told her about the kid and the arrangements I had made with the nurse, tacking on that I should have tucked him into bed long ago.

The same look she had in the office stole into her face. 'Tuck me into bed too, Mike,' she said. With the lithe grace of an animal she slid out of the chair past me and in the brief second that our eyes met I felt the heat of the passion that burned behind those deep blue irises.

Not much more than a minute could have passed. Her voice was a husky whisper calling, 'Mike . . . ' and I went to her.

There was no light except that which seeped in from the other room, a faint glow that made a bulky shadow of the bed with lesser shadows outlining the furniture against the deeper blackness of the room itself. I could hear the rhythmic sigh of her breathing, too heavy to be normal, and my hands shook when I stuck a cigarette in my mouth.

She said, 'Mike . . . ' again and struck the match.

Her hair was a smooth mass of bronze on

the pillow, her mouth full and rich, showing the shiny white edges of her teeth. There was only the sheet over her that rose and dipped between the inviting hollows of her breasts. Ellen was beautiful as only a mature woman can be beautiful. She was lustful as only a mature woman can be lustful.

'Tuck me in, Mike.'

The match burned closer to my fingers. I reached down and got the corner of the sheet in my fingers and flipped it all the way back. She lay there beautiful and naked and waiting.

'I love brunettes,' I said.

The tone of my voice told her no, not tonight, but her smile didn't fade. She just grinned impishly because she knew I'd never be able to look at her again and say no. 'You're a heel, Mike.'

The match went out. 'You told me that once tonight.'

'You're a bigger heel than I thought.' Then she laughed. When I backed out of the room she was still chuckling, but that thing was running up my back again.

I was thinking of her all the way back to my apartment and thinking of her when I put my car away. I was thinking too damn much to be careful. When I stabbed my key in the lock and turned it there was a momentary catch in

98

the tumblers before it went all the way around and I swore out loud as I rammed the door with my shoulder and hit the floor. Something swished through the air over my head and I caught an arm and pulled a squirming, fighting bundle of muscle down on top of me.

If I could have reached my rod I would have blown his guts out. His breath was in my face and I brought my knee up, but he jerked out of the way bringing his hand down again and my shoulder went numb after a split second of blinding pain. He tried again with one hand going for my throat, but I got one foot loose and kicked out and up and felt my toe smash into his groin. The cramp of the pain doubled him over on top of me, his breath sucking in like a leaky tire.

Then I got cocky. I thought I had him. I went to get up and he moved. Just once. That thing in his hand smashed against the side of my head and I started to crumple up piece by piece until there wasn't anything left except the sense to see and hear enough to know that he had crawled out of the room and was falling down the stairs outside. Then I thought about the lock on my door and how I had a guy fix it so I could tell if it had been jimmied open so I wouldn't step into any blind alleys without a gun in my hand, but because of a dame who lay naked and smiling on a bed I wouldn't share I had forgotten all about it.

And that was all.

4

I thought I was in a boat that was sinking and I tried to get over the side before it turned over on me. I clawed for the railing that wouldn't stand still while the screaming of the bells and mechanical pounding of laboring engines blasted the air with frantic insistence.

Somehow I got my eyes open and saw that I wasn't in a boat, but on the floor of my own apartment trying to grab the edge of the table. My head felt like a huge swollen thing that throbbed with a terrible fury, sending the pain shooting down to the balls of my feet. I choked on my tongue and muttered thickly, 'God . . . my head . . . my head!'

The phone didn't let up and whoever was pounding on the door wouldn't go away because they could hear me inside.

I staggered to the door first and cursed. It was still unlocked; nobody had to pound like that. The damn thing was almost too heavy for me to open with one hand.

I guess I must have looked pretty bad. The elderly nurse took one look at me and her arms tightened protectively around the kid.

He didn't scare so easily though, or maybe he was used to seeing a bloated, unshaven face. He laughed.

'Come on in,' I said.

The old lady didn't like the idea, but she came in. Mad, too. 'Mr. Hammer . . . ' she started.

'Look, get off my back. I wasn't drunk or disorderly. I damn near got my skull smashed in . . . ' I looked at the light streaming in the windows, 'last night. Right here. I'm sorry you were inconvenienced, but I'll pay for it. Goddamn that phone . . . hello, hello!'

'Mike?'

I recognized Pat's voice. 'Yeah, it's me. What's left of me.'

'What happened?' He sounded sharp and impatient.

'Nothing. I just got jumped in my own joint and nearly brained, that's all. The bastard got away.'

'Look, you get down here as fast as you can, understand? On the double.'

'Now what's up?'

'Trouble, and it's all yours, friend. Damn it, Mike, how many times do I have to remind you to keep your nose out of police business!'

'Wait a minute . . . '

'Wait my foot. Get down here before the

D.A. sends somebody after you. There's another murder and it's got your name on it.'

I hung up and told my head to go right ahead and explode if it wanted to.

Then the old lady let out a short scream and nearly broke her neck running for the kid. He was on his hands and knees reaching for my gun that lay under the table on the floor. She kicked it away and snapped him back on her lap.

Lord, what a day this was going to be!

Somebody else was at the door this time and all they had to do was rap just once more before I got it opened and they'd get a rap right in the teeth. The guy in the uniform said, 'You Michael Hammer?'

Nodding my head hurt, so I grunted that I was.

He handed me a box about two feet long and held out a pad. 'Package from the Uptown Kiddie Shop. Sign here, please.'

I scrawled my name, handed him a quarter and took the package inside. There was a stack of new baby clothes under the wrappings with a note on top addressed to me. It said,

Dear Mike:
Men are never much good at these things, so I picked up some clothes for

the little boy. Let me know if they fit all right.

Marsha

The nurse was still eyeing me suspiciously. I handed her the boy and edged back to a nice soft chair. 'Before you say anything, let me explain one thing. The kid's old man was bumped. Murdered. He's an orphan and I'm trying to find out who made him that way. Somebody doesn't like the idea and they got funny ways of telling me so, but that isn't stopping me any. Maybe this'll happen again and maybe it won't, but you'd be doing me and the kid a big favor if you'll put up with it until this mess is cleaned up. Will you?'

Her face was expressionless a moment, then broke into a smile. 'I . . . think I understand.'

'Good. Arrangements are being made now so the kid'll be taken care of permanently. It won't be long.' I patted the back of my head and winced.

'You'd better let me take a look at your scalp,' she said.

She let me hold the kid while she probed around the lump awhile. If she had found a hole to stick her finger in, I wouldn't have been at all surprised. Finally she stood back satisfied and picked the kid up. 'There doesn't seem to be anything wrong, but if I were you I'd see a doctor anyway.'

I told her I would.

'You know, Mr. Hammer, in my time I've seen a great deal of suffering. It isn't new to me, not by a long sight. All I ask is that you don't bring any of it home to the child.'

'Nothing will bother the kid. I'll see to that. He'll be all right with you then?'

'I'll take perfect care of him.' She paused and her face creased in a frown. 'This town is full of rabid dogs and there's not a dogcatcher in sight.'

'I kill mad dogs,' I said.

'Yes, I've heard that you do. Good morning, Mr. Hammer.' I handed her the box of clothes, picked the rod up from the floor and ushered her out.

My head was still booming away and I tried to fix it up with a hot shower. That helped, but a mess of bacon and eggs helped even more. It woke me up enough to remember Pat said my name was on a murder and I didn't have the sense to ask who he was talking about.

I gave it a try on the phone anyway, but they couldn't locate Pat in the building anywhere. I held the receiver down for a second, long enough to check Marsha's number in the book, then punched out her call. The nurse with the mustache answered and told me that Miss Lee had just left for a morning rehearsal of the Little Theater Group and wasn't expected back until later that afternoon.

Nuts. So now I had to go down to police headquarters and face an inquisition. My legs had more life in them by the time I reached the street, and when I had pulled up in front of the building downtown I was back to normal in a sense. At least I felt like having a beer and a butt without choking over the thought.

They were real happy to see me, they were. They looked like they hoped I wouldn't come so they could go drag me down by the neck, but now that I was there everything was malicious, tight smiles and short, sharp sentences that steered me into a little room where I was supposed to sit and sweat so I'd blab my head off when they asked me questions.

I spit on the floor, right in the middle, to be exact, and had the Lucky I wanted. The college boy with the pointed face who rated as the D.A.'s assistant glared at me but didn't have the guts to back it up with any words. He parked behind a desk and tried to look important and tough. It was a lousy act.

When I started wondering how long they

were going to let me cool my heels the corridor got noisy and I picked out Pat's voice raising Cain with somebody. The door slammed open and he stalked in with his face tight in anger.

I said, ' 'lo, Pal,' but he didn't answer.

He walked up to the desk and leaned on it until his face wasn't an inch away from the D.A.'s boy and he did a good job of keeping his hands off the guy's neck. 'Since when do you take over the duties of the Police Department? I'm still Captain of Homicide around here and when there's murder I'll handle it myself, personally, understand? I ought to knock your ears off for pulling a stunt like that!'

The boy got a blustery red and started to get up. 'See here, the District Attorney gave me full permission . . . '

'To butt into my business because a friend of mine is suspected of murder!'

'Exactly!'

Pat's voice got dangerously low. 'Get your ass out of this office before I kick hell out of you. Go on, get out. And you tell the D.A. that I'll see him in a few minutes.'

He practically ran to the door. I could see the D.A. getting a sweet version of the story, all right. I said, 'What'd he do to you, kid?'

'Crazy little bastard. He thinks because I'm

a friend of yours I'll do a little whitewashing. He got me out of the building on a phony call right after I spoke to you.'

'You're not going to be very popular with the D.A. for that.'

'I'm sick of that guy walking all over this office. They pulled a raid on a wire room last night and all they got was an empty apartment with a lot of holes in the walls and a blackboard that still showed track results and a snotty little character who said he was thinking of opening a school for handicappers. The guy was clean and there wasn't a thing the D.A. could do.'

'Sounds like a good business. Whose wire room was it?'

'Hell, who else has wire rooms in this town? The place was run by one of Ed Teen's outfit.'

'Or so your information said.'

'Yeah. So now the D.A. gets in a rile and raises hell with everyone from the mayor down. He's pulled his last rough sketch on me with this deal though. Let him try getting rough just once and the news boys are going to get a lot of fancy stuff that won't do a thing for him when election time comes.'

'Where is he now?'

'Inside waiting for you.'

'Let's see the guy then.'

'Just a minute. Tell me something straight. Did you kill a guy named Mel Hooker?' he asked.

'Oh, God!'

Pat's eyes got that squinty look. 'What's the matter?'

'Your corpse was the friend of William Decker . . . That beautiful local-type kill the police seem to be ignoring so well.'

'The police aren't ignoring anything.'

'Then they're not looking very hard. Mel and Decker were playing the ponies and Mel introduced him to a loan shark that financed his little escapades. There was a catch in it. Mel said Decker lost his shirt, but the loan shark, that Dixie Cooper guy, said Decker paid him off in full and was able to prove it.'

Pat muttered something under his breath. He nodded for me to follow him and started for the door. This time the tight smiles loosened up and nobody seemed to want to get in our way. From the way Pat was glowering it looked like he was ready to take me and anybody else apart and had already started.

Pat knocked on the door and I heard the D.A. call out for somebody to see who it was. The door opened, a pair of thick-lensed glasses did a quick focus on the two of us and the D.A. said, 'Show them in, Mr. Mertig.'

It was quite a gathering. The D.A. straddled his throne with two assistant D.A.'s flanking him, a pair of plainclothes men in the background and two more over by the window huddled together for mutual protection apparently.

'Sit down, Hammer,' the D.A. said.

Everybody watched me with the annoyed look you see when the king isn't obeyed pronto. I walked up to his desk, planted my hands on the top and leaned right down in his face. I didn't like the guy and he didn't like me, but he wasn't getting snooty now or any other time. I said, 'You call me *Mister* when you use my name. I don't want any crap from you or your boys and if you think you can make it tough for me just go ahead and try it. I came in here myself to save you the trouble of getting a false arrest charge slapped against your office and right now I'm not above walking out just to see what you'd do. It's about time you learned to be polite to your public when you're not sure of your facts.'

The D.A. started to get purple. In fact, a lot of people started to get purple. When they all got a nice livid tinge I sat down.

He made a good job of keeping his voice under control. 'We are sure of the facts . . . *Mister* Hammer.'

'Go on.'

'A certain Mel Hooker has been found dead. He was shot to death with a .45.'

'I suppose the bullet came from my gun?' I tried to make it sound as sarcastic as possible.

The purple started to fade into an unhealthy red. Unhealthy for me, I mean. 'Unfortunately, no. The bullet passed through the man and out the window. So far we haven't been able to locate it.'

I started to interrupt, but he held up his hand. 'However, you were very generous with your fingerprints. They're all over the place. The landlady identified your picture and vouched that she heard threats before you left, so it is quite a simple matter to see what followed.'

'Yeah, I went back later and shot him. I'm really that stupid.'

'Yes, you really are.' His eyes were narrow slits in his face.

'And you got rocks in your head,' I said. He started to get up but I beat him to it. I stood there looking down at him so he could see what I thought of him. 'You're a real bright boy, you are. Brother, the voters sure must be proud of you! Christ, you're ready to kick anything around because your vice racket business is getting the works. It's got you so far down you're all set to slap me in the clink

111

without having the foresight to ask me if I got an alibi or not for the time of the shooting. So it happened last night and I don't know what time and without bothering to find out I'll hand you my alibi on a platter and you can choke on it.'

I pointed to the intercom on his desk. 'Get Ellen Scobie in here.'

The D.A.'s face was wet with an angry sweat. His finger triggered the gadget and when Ellen answered he told her to come in.

Before the door opened I had a chance to look at Pat and he was shaking his head slowly trying to tell me not to go overboard so far I couldn't get back. Ellen came in, smiled at me through a puzzled frown and stood there waiting to see what was going on. From the look that passed between us, the D.A. caught on fast, but he wasn't letting me get in any prompting first. He said, 'Miss Scobie, were you with this . . . with *Mister* Hammer last night at, say eleven-thirty?'

She didn't have to think to answer that one. 'Yes, I did happen to be with him.'

'Where were you?'

'I should say that we were sitting in a bar about then. A place on Fifty-second Street.'

'That's all, Miss Scobie.'

Everybody ushered her out of the room with their eyes. When the door clicked shut the D.A.'s voice twanged like a flat banjo string. 'You may go too, *Mister* Hammer. I'm getting a little tired of your impertinence.' His face had turned a deadly white and he was speaking through his teeth. 'I wouldn't be a bit surprised if your license was revoked very shortly.'

My voice came out a hiss more than anything else. 'I'd be,' I said. 'You tried that once before and remember what happened?'

That's all I had to say and for a few seconds I was the only one who didn't stop breathing in the room. Nobody bothered to open the door for me this time. I went out myself and started down the corridor, then Pat caught up with me.

We must have been thinking the same things, because neither one of us bothered to speak until we were two blocks away in Louie's place where a quick beer cooled things down to a boil.

Pat grinned at me in the mirror behind the bar. 'You're a lucky bastard, Mike. If the press wasn't so hot on the D.A.'s heels you'd be out of business if he lost the election over it.'

'Aw, he gives me a pain. Okay, he's got it in for me, but does he have to be so goddamn stupid about it? Why didn't he do some checking first. Christ, him and his investigators are making the police look ridiculous.

I'm no chump. I got as much on the ball as any of his stooges and in my own way maybe I got as many scruples too.'

'Ease off, Mike. I'm on your side.'

'I know, but you're tied down too. Who has to get murdered before the boob will put some time in on the case? Right now you got three corpses locked together as nicely as you please and what's being done?'

'More than you think.'

I sipped the top of my beer and watched his eyes in the mirror. 'It wasn't any news that Decker and Hooker were tied up. The lab boys lifted a few prints out of his apartment. Some of them were Hooker's.'

'He have a record?'

Pat shook his head. 'During the war he had a job that required security and he was printed. We picked up the blind newspaper dealer's prints too. He had a record.'

'I know. They graduated from the same Alma Mater up the river.'

Pat grinned again. 'You know too damn much.'

'Yeah, but you do it the easy way. What else do you know?'

'You tell me, Mike.'

'What?'

'The things you have in that mind of yours, chum. I want your angle first.'

114

I ordered another round and lit a cigarette to go with it. 'Decker needed dough. His wife was undergoing an operation that cost heavy sugar and he had to get it from someplace. He and Hooker got some hot tips on the nags and they pooled their dough to make some fast money. When they found out the tips were solid ones they went in deeper. Hooker pulled out while he was ahead, but Decker wanted to make the big kill so he borrowed a grand from Dixic Cooper. According to Hooker, he lost everything and was in hock to Cooper for plenty, but when I braced the guy he proved that Decker had paid him back.

'Okay, he had to get the dough from somebody. He sure as hell didn't work for it because the docks have been too slow the past month. He had to do one of two things . . . either steal it or borrow it. It could be that when he went back to his old trade he found it so profitable he couldn't or didn't want to give it up. If that was the case then hc made a mistake and broke into the wrong apartment. He and his partners were expecting a juicy haul and if Decker spent a lot of time casing the joint a gimmick like breaking into the wrong apartment would have looked like a sorry excuse to the other two who were expecting part of the proceeds. In that case he would have tried to take a flyer and they caught up with him.'

Pat looked down into his glass. 'Then where does Hooker come in?'

'They were friends, weren't they? First Decker gets bumped for pulling a funny stunt, the driver of the car gives the second guy the works so he won't be captured and squeal, then he goes and gets Hooker because he's afraid Decker might have spilled the works to his friend.'

'I'll buy that,' Pat said. 'It's exactly the way I've had it figured.'

'You buy it and you'll be stuck,' I told him. I finished my beer and let the bartender fill it up again. Pat was making wry faces now. He was waiting for the rest of it.

I gave it to him. 'William Decker hadn't been pulling any jobs before that one. He was going straight all along the line. He must have known what might happen and got his affairs in order right down to making provisions for his kid. If Decker paid off Cooper then he borrowed the dough from somebody else and the somebody put on the squeeze play. For my money they even knew where the dough could be had and laid it out so all Decker had to do was go up the fire escape and open up the safe.

'That's where he made his mistake. He got into the wrong place and after all the briefing

116

he had who the hell would believe his story. No, Decker knew he jimmied the wrong can and didn't dare take a chance on correcting the error because Marsha Lee could have come to at any time and called the cops. In the league where he was playing they only allow you one mistake. Decker knew they would believe·that he had stashed the money thinking to come back later and get it, so he took off by himself.

'What happened was this . . . he had to go home for his kid. When they knew he had taken a powder they put it together and beat it back to his place. By that time he was gone, but they picked him up fast enough. When he knew he was trapped he kissed his kid good-by and walked out into a bullet. That boy of Grindle's searched him for the dough and when he didn't find it, the logical thought was that he hid it in his apartment. He didn't have much chance to do anything else. So, the driver of the car scooted back there and got into the place and messed it up.'

Pat's teeth were making harsh grating noises and his fingers rasped against the woodwork of the bar. 'So you're all for nailing the driver of the murder car, right?'

The way I grinned wasn't human. It tied my face up into a bunch of hard knots.

117

'Nope,' I said, 'that's your job. You can have him. I want the son-of-a-bitch who put the pressure on him. I want the guy who made somebody decent revert back to a filthy crime and I want him right between my hands so I can squeeze the juice out of him.'

'Where is he, Mike?'

'If I knew I wouldn't tell you, friend. I want him for myself. Someday I want to be able to tell that kid what his face looked like when he was dying.'

'Damn it anyway, Mike, you can stretch friendship too far sometimes.'

'No, I'll never stretch it, Pat. Just remember that I live in this town too. Besides having what few police powers the state chooses to hand me, I'm still a citizen and responsible in some small way for what happens in the city. And by God, if I'm partly responsible then I have a right to take care of an obligation like removing a lousy orphan-maker.'

'Who is he, Mike?'

'I said I didn't know.'

'But you know where to find out.'

'That's right. It isn't too hard if you want to take a chance on getting your head smashed in.'

'Like you did last night?'

'Yeah. That's something else I have to even

118

up. I don't know why or how it happened, but I got a beaut of an idea, I have.'

'Something like looking for a guy named Lou Grindle whom you called all sorts of names and threatened to shoot on sight if you found out he was responsible for Decker's death?'

My mouth fell open. 'How the hell did you get that?'

'Now you're taking me for the chump, Mike. I checked the tie-up Arnold Basil had with Grindle thoroughly, and from the way Lou acted I knew somebody had been there before me. It didn't take long to guess who it was. Lou was steamed up to beat hell and told me what happened. Let me tell you something. Don't try anything with that boy. The D.A. has men covering him every minute he's awake trying to get something on him.'

'Where was he last night then?'

A thundercloud rolled over Pat's face. 'The bastard skipped out. He pulled a fastie and skipped his apartment and never got back until eleven. In case you're thinking he had anything to do with Hooker's death, forget it. He couldn't have gotten back at that time.'

'I'm not thinking anything. I was just going to tell you he was in a place called the Glass Bar on Eighth Avenue with Ed Teen somewhere around ten. The D.A. ought to get new eyes. The old ones are going bad.'

Pat swore under his breath.

I said, 'What made you say that, Pat?'

'Say what?'

'Oh, connect Lou and Hooker.'

'Hell, I didn't connect anything. I just said . . . '

'You said something that ought to make you think a lot more, boy. Grindle and Decker and Hooker don't go together at all. They're miles apart. In fact, they're so far apart they're backing into each other from the ends.'

He set his glass down with a thump. 'Wait a minute. Don't go getting this thing screwed up with a lot of wacky ideas. Lou Grindle isn't playing with anything worth a few grand and if he is, he doesn't send out blockheads to do the job. You're way the hell out of line.'

'Okay, don't get excited.'

'Good Lord, who's getting excited? Damn it, Mike . . . '

My face was as flat as I could make it. I just sat there with the beer in my hand and stared at myself in the mirror because I started thinking of something that was like a shadow hovering in the background. I thought about it for a long time and it was still a shadow when I finished and it had a shape that was so curious I wanted to go up closer for another look.

I didn't hear Pat because his voice was so low it was almost a whisper, but he repeated it loud enough so I could hear it and he made me look at him so I wouldn't forget it. His hands were a nervous bunch of fingers that opened and shut with every word and his mouth was all teeth with sharp biting edges.

'Mike, you try pulling a smart frame that will pull Grindle into that damn murder case of yours and you and I are finished! We've worked too damn long and hard to nail that punk and his boss to have you slip over a cutie that will stink up the whole works. Don't give me the business, friend. I know you and the way you work. Anything appeals to you just as long as you can point a gun at somebody. For my money Lou Grindle is as far away from this as I am and because one of his boys tried to pick up some extra change you can't fix him for it. All right, I'll give you the benefit of the doubt and say that if you tried hard enough and lived through it you'd do it, but Lou's got Teen and a lot more behind him. He'd get out of that charge easy as pie and only leave the department open for another big laugh. When we get those two, we want them so it'll stick, and no frame is going to do it. You lay off, hear?'

I didn't answer him for a long minute, then: 'I wasn't thinking of any frame, Pat.'

Pat's hands were still jerking on the bar. 'The hell you weren't. Remember what I told you, that's all.' He swilled his beer down and fiddled with the empty glass until the bartender moved in and filled it up again. I didn't say a damn thing. I just sat. Pat's fingernails were little firecrackers going off against the wood while his coat rippled as the muscles bunched underneath the fabric.

It lasted about five minutes, then he drained the glass and shoved it back. He muttered, 'Goddamn!'

I said, 'Relax, chum.'

Then he repeated what he said the first time, told me to take it easy, and swung off the stool. I waited until he was out the door, then started to laugh. It wasn't so easy to be a cop. At least not a city cop. Or maybe it was the years that were getting him down. Six years ago you couldn't get him excited about anything, not even a murder or a naked dame with daisies in her hair.

The bartender came over and asked me if I wanted another. I said no and shoved him a quarter to make into change, then picked up a dime and walked back to the phone booth. The book listed the Little Theater as being on the edge of Greenwich Village and a babe with a low-down voice told me that Miss Lee was there and rehearsing and if I was a friend I could certainly come up.

The Little Theater was an old warehouse with a poster-decorated front that was a lousy disguise. The day had warped into a hot afternoon and the air inside the place was even hotter, wetter and bedded down with the perfumed smell of make-up. A sawed-off babe in a Roman toga let me in, locked the door to keep out the spies, then wiggled her fanny in the direction of all the noise to show me where to go. A pair of swinging doors opened and two more dames in togas came through for a smoke. They stood right in the glare of the only light in the place looking too cool to be real and lit up the smokes without seeing me there in the shadows.

Then I saw why they were so cool. One of them flipped the damn thing open and stood with her hands on her hips and she didn't have a thing on underneath it. Sawed-off said, 'Helen, we have a visitor.'

And Helen finally saw me, smiled, and said, 'How nice.'

But she didn't bother to do anything about the toga. I said, 'The play's the thing,' and sawed-off grinned a little like she wished she had thought of the open-toga deal first herself and sort of pushed me into the swinging doors.

Inside, a pair of floor fans moved the air around enough to make you think you were cool, at least. I opened my shirt and tie, then stood there for a moment getting used to the artificial dusk. All around the place were stacks of funeral-parlor chairs with clothes draped over them. Up front a rickety stage held up some more togas and a few centurions in uniform while a hairy-legged little squirt in tennis shorts screamed at them in a high falsetto as he pounded a script against an old upright piano.

It wasn't hard to find Marsha. There was a baby spot behind her outlining a hundred handfuls of lovely curves through the white cotton toga. She was the most beautiful woman in the place even with a touched-up shiner, and from where I stood I could see that there was plenty of competition.

The squirt with the hairy legs called for a ten-minute break and sawed-off called something up to Marsha I didn't catch. She tried to peer past the glare of the footlights, didn't make out too well, so came off the stage in a jump and ran all the way back to where I was.

Her hands were warm, friendly things that grabbed mine and held on. 'Did you get my package, Mike?'

'Yup. Came down to thank you personally.'

'How is the boy?'

'Fine, just fine. Don't ask me how I feel because I'll give you a stinking answer. Somebody tried to break my head open last night.'

'Mike!'

'I got a hard head.'

She moved up close and ran her hand over my hair to where the bump was and wrinkled her nose at me. 'Do you know who it was?'

'No. If I did the bastard'd be in the hospital.'

Marsha took my arm and nodded over to the side of the wall. 'Let's sit down a few minutes. I can worry better about you that way.'

'Why worry about me at all?'

The eye with the shiner was closed just enough to give it the damnedest look you ever saw. 'I could be a fool and tell you why, Mike,' she said. 'Shall I be a fool?'

If ever I had wanted to kiss a woman it was then, only she had too much make-up on and there were too many people for an audience. 'Later. Tonight, maybe,' I told her. 'Be a fool then.' I was grinning and her lips went into a smile that said a lot of things, but mostly was a promise of tonight.

When we had a pair of cigarettes going I tipped my chair back against the wall and stared at her. 'We have another murder on our hands, kitten.'

The cigarette stopped halfway to her lips and her head came around slowly. 'Another? Oh, no!'

I nodded. 'Guy named Mel Hooker. He was Decker's best friend. You know, Marsha, I think there's a hell of a lot more behind this than we thought.'

'Chain reaction,' she softly.

'Sort of. It didn't take much to start it going. Three hundred bucks and a necklace, to be exact.'

Marsha nodded, her lips between her teeth. 'My playboy friend in the other apartment was coerced into keeping his money in a bank instead of the wall safe. The management threatened to break his lease unless he co-operated. Everybody in the building knows what happened and raised a fuss about it. Apparently the idea of being beaten up by a burglar doesn't sound very appealing, especially when the burglar is wild over having made a mistake in safes.'

'You got off easy. He might have killed you.'

Her shoulders twitched convulsively. 'What are you going to do, Mike?'

'Keep looking. Make enough stink so trouble'll come looking for me. Sometimes it's easier that way.'

'Do you . . . have to?' Her eyes were soft, and her hand on my arm squeezed me gently.

'I have to, kid. I'm made that way. I hate killers.'

'But do you have to be so . . . so damned reckless about it?'

'Yeah. Yeah, I do. I don't have to be but that's the way I like it. Then I can cut them down and enjoy it.'

'Oh, Lord! Mike, please . . . '

'Look, kid, when you play with mugs you can't be coy. At first this looked all cut-and-dried-out and all there was to it was nailing a bimbo who drove a car with a hot rod in the back seat. That's the way it looked at first. Now we got names creeping into this thing, names and faces that don't belong to any cheap bimbos. There's Teen and Grindle and a guy who died a long time ago but who won't stay buried . . . his name was Charlie Fallon and I keep hearing it every time I turn around.'

Somebody said, 'Charlie Fallon?' in a voice that ended with a chuckle and I turned around, chewing on my words.

The place was getting to look like backstage of a burlesque house. The woman in the dress toga did a trick with the oversize cigarette holder and stood there smiling at us. She was medium in height only. The rest of her was over-done, but that's the way they liked them in Hollywood. Her name was Kay Cutler and she was right in there among the top movie stars and it wasn't hard to see why.

Marsha introduced us and I stood there like an idiot with one of those nobody-meets-celebrity grins all over my pan. She held my hand longer than was necessary and said, 'Surprised?'

'Hell, yes. How come all the talent in this dump?'

The two of them laughed together. Kay did another trick with the holder. 'It's a hobby that gets a lot of exciting publicity. Actually we don't play the parts for the audience. Instead we portray them so the others can use our interpretation as a model, then coach them into giving some sort of a performance. You wouldn't believe it, but the theater group makes quite a bit of money for itself. Enough to cover expenses, at least.'

'You come for free?'

She laughed and let her eyes drift to one of the centurions who was giving me some dark looks. 'Well, not exactly.'

Marsha poked me in the back so I'd quit leering. I said, 'You mentioned Charlie Fallon before. Where'd you hear of him?'

'If he's the one I'm thinking of a lot of people knew him. Was he the gangster?'

'That's right.'

'He was a fan-letter writer. God, how that man turned them out! Even the extras used to get notes and flowers from the old goat. I bet I've had twenty or more.'

'That was a long time ago,' I reminded her.

She smiled until the dimples showed in her cheeks. 'You aren't supposed to mention the passage of time so lightly. I still claim to be in my early thirties.'

'What are you?'

I got the dimples again. 'I'm a liar,' she said. 'Marsha, didn't you ever get mail from that character?'

'Perhaps. At the time I didn't handle my own correspondence and it was all sorted out for me.' She paused and squinted a little. 'Come to think of it, yes. I did. I remember talking about it to someone one day.'

I pulled on the butt and let the smoke out slowly. 'He was like that. The guy made plenty and didn't know how to spend it, so he threw it away on the girlies. I wonder if he ever followed it up?'

'Never,' Kay stated flatly. 'When he was still news some of the columnists kept up with his latest crushes and slipped in a publicity line now and then, but nobody ever saw him around the Coast. By the way, what's so important about him now?'

'I wish I knew. For a dead man he's sure not forgotten.'

'Mike is a detective, Kay,' Marsha said bluntly. 'There have been a couple of murders and Mike's conducting an investigation.'

'And not getting far,' I added.

'Really?' Her eyebrows went up and she cocked the holder between her teeth and gave me a look that was sexy right down to her sandals. 'A detective. You sound exciting.'

'You're not going to sound at all if you don't get back to your warrior, lady,' Marsha cut in. 'Now scram.'

Kay faked a pout at her and said so long to me after another long hand-clasp. When she was across the room Marsha slipped her arm through mine. 'Kay's a wonderful gal, but if you have it and it wears pants she wants it.'

'Good old Kay,' I said.

'Luckily, I know her too well.'

'Any more around like that?'

'Well, if it's a celebrity you'd like to meet, I can take you backstage and introduce you to a pair of Hollywood starlets, a television sensation, the country's biggest comic and . . .'

'Never mind,' I said. 'You're enough for me.'

She gave me another one of those squeezes with a laugh thrown in and I wanted to kiss her again. The kid with an arm in a sling who tapped her on the shoulder as he murmured, 'Two minutes more, Marsha,' must have read my mind, because his eyes went limp and sad.

Marsha nodded as he walked off and I pointed my cigarette at his back. 'The kid's got a crush on you.'

She watched him a moment, then glanced at me. 'I know it. He's only nineteen and I'm afraid he has stars in his eyes. A month ago he was in love with Helen O'Roark and was so far down in the dumps when he found out she was married he almost starved himself to death. He's the one I took to the hospital the night the Decker fellow broke into my apartment.'

'What happened to him?'

'He was setting up props and fell off the ladder.'

Down at the end of the hall hairy legs in short pants was banging on the piano again screaming for everyone to get back on the stage. Togas started to unravel from the floor, chairs and the scenery and if I had a dozen more pairs of eyes I could have enjoyed myself. Those babes didn't give a damn what they showed and I seemed to be the only one there who appreciated the view. The overhead lights went out and the stage spots came on and I was doing good watching the silhouettes until Marsha said, 'I'm getting jealous, Mike.'

It wasn't so much what she said as the way she said it that made me jerk around. And there she was leaning on the stack of chairs like a nymph under a waterfall with her own toga wide open down the middle and an impish little grin playing with her mouth. She was barely a reflection of light and shadow, a vague white statue of warm, live flesh that moved with her breathing, then the toga came shut slowly before I could move and she was out of reach.

'You don't have to be jealous of anybody,' I said.

She smiled again, and in the darkness her hand touched mine briefly and the cigarette fell out of my fingers to the floor where it lay like a hot red eye. Then she was gone and all I could think about was tonight.

5

After the Little Theater the glare of the sun was almost blinding. I fired up another butt and climbed back into the car where I finished smoking it before I had myself in line again. All the while I kept seeing Marsha in that white toga until it was branded into my brain so deeply that it blotted out everything else. Marsha and Kay and Helen of Troy or something in a lot of white togas drifting through the haze like beautiful ghosts.

Like the ghost of a killer I was after. I threw the butt out the window and hit the starter.

I let my hands and my eyes drive me through traffic while the rest of me sat and thought. It should have been so damn easy. Three guys dead and a killer running loose looking for his lousy split of a robbery that didn't happen. Decker dead on the sidewalk. Arnold Basil dead in the gutter. Hooker dead in his own room and me damn near dead on the floor. Sure it was easy, just like an illiterate doing acrostics.

Then where the hell was the big puzzle? Was it because Basil had been Lou Grindle's boy, or because Fallon's name kept cropping up? I jammed the horn down at the guy in front of me and yelled as I pulled around him. He gave me a scared grimace and plenty of room and I shot by him swearing at the little things that piled up one after the other.

Then I grinned because that was where the puzzle was. In all the little things.

Like the boys who tried to take me when I was putting the buzz on Hooker.

Like the money that Decker had picked up from somewhere to pay off Dixie Cooper.

Like Decker putting his affairs in order before he walked out and got himself bumped.

Now I knew where I was going and what I wanted to do, so I got off the avenue onto a street and headed west until I could smell the river and see the trucks pulling into their docks for the night and hear the mixture of tongues as the longshoremen streamed out of the yards.

The nearest of them were still ten minutes away when I pulled up outside the hole-in-the-wall saloon and there weren't any early birds inside when I pushed the door open. The bartender was perched on a stool watching the television and his hand automatically went out for a glass as he heard me slide up to the bar.

I didn't let him waste his beer. I said,

'Remember me, buddy?'

He had a frown all set and his mouth shaped to tell me off when his memory came back with a jolt. 'Yeah.' His frown had a twisted look now.

I leaned on the bar so my coat hung loose enough for him to see the leather of the gun sling and he knew I wasn't kidding around. 'Who were they, buddy?'

'Look, I . . .'

'Maybe I ought to ask it different. Maybe I ought to ask it with the nose of a gun shoved down your throat. You can get it that way if you want.'

He choked up a little and his eyes kept darting toward the door hoping someone would come in. He licked his lips to bring the words out and said, 'I . . . don't know . . . who the hell they were.'

'You like it the hard way, don't you? Now just once I'm going to tell you something and I want an answer. Scarface Hooker is dead. He was shot last night and because you know who they were you might be sitting on top of a powder keg. In case you're not sure, let me tell you that you are right now . . . with me. I'm going to bust you wide open or leave you for those babies to handle.'

The guy started to sweat. It formed in little cold drops along the ridges of his forehead and rolled down his cheeks. He made a swipe with the back of his hand across his mouth and swallowed hard. 'They was private detectives.'

'They were like hell.'

'Look, I'm telling ya, I saw their badges.'

'Tell me some more.'

'They come in here looking for Hooker. They said he was working against the union and pulling a lot of rough stuff. Hell, how'd I know? I'm a union man myself. If that's what he was doing he shoulda got beat up. They showed me their badges and said they was working for the union so I played along.'

'Ever see them before?'

'No.'

'Anybody else see them?'

'Yeah.'

'Goddamn it, say something! Don't give me one word.'

'One guy says they was uptown boys. They was roughs . . . strongarm boys. The little guy . . . I heard the other one call him Nocky.'

'What else?'

'That's all. I swear to God I don't know no more.'

I slid my elbows off the bar and gave him a tight grin. 'Okay, friend, you did fine. Let me give you a word of advice. If either of those boys come in here again you pick up the phone and call the nearest precinct station.'

'Sure. I'll ask 'em to blow my crazy head off, too.'

'They might do it before you reach the phone, mister. Those lads were after Hooker and it might have been them who got to him. They won't like anybody who can put the finger on 'em. Remember what I told you.'

He started to sweat again. All along his neck the cords were standing out against the layer of fat. He didn't look a bit happy. A couple of longshoremen pushed in through the door and lined up at the rail and he had one hell of a time trying to keep the glasses under the beer tap. He didn't want to look up when I left, but he had to and I could feel his eyes on my back.

So they were private dicks and one's name was Nocky. Anybody could pick up a badge to flash if he wanted to, but there was just the chance that they were the real thing, so the first pay station I came to I changed two bucks into nickels and started dialing all the agencies I knew of.

None of them picked up the description, but one of them did hear of a Nocky something-or-other but was sure it was a nickname. He couldn't give me any further information so I tried a couple of precincts uptown where I had an in at the desk. A

Sergeant Bellew came on and told me the name was familiar, but that was all. He had the idea that the guy was a private dick too but couldn't be sure.

On the off-chance that Pat might know, I called his office. He picked up his phone on the first ring and his voice had a snap to it that wasn't too nice. I said, 'It's Mike, Pat. What's eating you now?'

'Plenty. Listen, I'm pretty busy now and . . .'

'Nuts. You're not that busy.'

'Damn it, Mike, what is it now?'

'Ever hear of a private cop called Nocky? It's a nickname.'

'No.'

'Can you check on it for me?'

'Hell no!' His voice had an explosive crack to it. 'I can't do a damn thing except obey orders. The D.A.'s working up another stink ever since this afternoon and he's got us nuts up here.'

'What happened, another raid go sour?'

'Ah, they all go sour. He closed down a wire room and pulled in a couple of punks when he was looking for something big. Ed Teen came down with a lawyer and a bondsman and got them both out within the hour.'

'No kidding? So Ed's taking a personal

interest in what goes on now.'

'Yeah. He doesn't want 'em to talk before he does a little coaching first. You know, I think we're on to something this time. We had to pull a Gestapo act and check on our own men, but I think we have that leak located.'

'How does it look?'

'Lousy. He's a first-grade detective and up to his ears in hock. He's one of three who have been in on every deal so far and money might be a powerful persuader to get him to pass a sign along somehow.'

'Have you picked up the tip-off yet?'

'Nope. If he's doing it he's got a damn good system. Keep shut about this. The only reason I mentioned it is because I may need you soon. The guy knows all the other cops and I may have to stick a plant along the line to see who's picking up the flash from him.'

'Okay, I'll be around any time you need me. If you run into anything on that Nocky character, let me know.'

'Sure, Mike. Wish I could help you out now, but we're all tied up.'

I said so long and hung up. I still had a handful of nickels to go so I made a blind stab at a barroom number downtown and asked if Cookie Harkin was there. I had to wait while the guy looked and after a minute or so a voice said, 'Cookie speaking.'

'Mike Hammer.'

'Hey, boy. Long time no see. How's tricks?'

'Good enough. You still got wide-open ears?'

'Sure. See all, hear all and say plenty if the pay's right. Why?'

'Ever hear of a private dick named Nocky? He's a wise runt who has an oversize partner. Supposedly a couple of tough boys from somewhere uptown.'

I didn't get any answer for a minute, so I said, 'Well?'

'Wait a minute, Mike. You know what you're asking about, don't you?' He spoke in next to a whisper. I heard him pull the door of the booth closed before he said anything else. 'What're you working on?'

'Murder, friend.'

'Brother!'

'Who is he?'

'I'll have to do a little checking around first. I think I know who you mean, all right. I'll see what I can do, but if it's the guy I think it is, I'm not sticking my neck out too far, understand?'

'Sure, do what you can. I'll pay you for it.'

'Forget the pay. All I want is some inside stuff I can pass along for what it's worth. You know my angle.'

'How long will it take?'

'Gimme a coupla hours. Suppose I meet you at the Tucker Bar. It's a dive, but you can get away with anything in there.'

It was good enough. I told him I'd be there and put the rest of the nickels back in my pocket. They make a big lump and a lot of noise so I went across town to an Automat and spent them all on a supper I needed bad.

It was dark when I finished and had started to rain again.

The Tucker Bar was built under a neon sign that put out more light in advertising than was used up inside. It was off on a side street in a place nobody smart went to even on a slumming party, but it was a place where people who knew people could be found and gotten drunk enough to spill over a little excess information if the questions were put right.

I saw Cookie in the back room edging through the tables with a drink in his hand, stopping at a table here and there to say hello. He was small and skinny with a big nose, bigger ears and loose pockets that could spill out the right kind of dough when he needed it. The guy looked and acted like a cheap hood when he was the head legman for one of the biggest of the syndicated columnists. I waited at the bar nursing a beer until the act on the dance floor was finished. A couple of strippers were trying to see how fast they could shed their clothes in time to the same music. They got down to bare facts in a minute's time and there was a lot of noise around the ringside. The rest of the crowd was having a hard time trying to see what they were paying for.

There was a singer and a solo pianist after that before the management decided to let the customers go back to drinking. I picked up my glass and squeezed through the bunch standing under the arch that led to the back room and worked my way to the table where Cookie was sitting.

He had two chicks with him, a pair of phony blondes with big bosoms and painted faces and he was showing them a coin trick so they had to lean forward to see what he was doing and he could leer down their necklines. He was having himself a great time. The blondes were drinking champagne. They were having a great time too.

I said, 'Hello, ape man.'

He looked up and grinned from one big ear to another until he looked like a clam just opened. 'How do ya like that, my old pal, Mike Hammer! What're you doin' down here where people are?'

'Looking for people.'

'Well, sit right down, sit right down. Here's

one all made to order for you. Meet Tolly and Joan.'

I said, 'Hi,' and pulled out the fourth chair.

'Mike's a friend of mine from way back, kids. A real good skate.' He nodded at the blonde who was giving me the eye already. 'You take Tolly, Mike. Joan and me's already struck up a conversation. She's a French maid from Brooklyn who works for the Devoe family. Wait'll you catch her accent. She sure fooled them. Gawd, what a family of jerks they are!'

I caught his expression and the slight wink that went with it. Tomorrow the stuff Joan was handing out would turn up in print and hell would get raised in the Devoe household. She gave us a demonstration of her accent with giggles and launched into a spiel of how the old man had tried to make her and how she refused and I almost wanted to ask her how she got the mink cape that was draped over the back of her chair on a maid's salary.

Tolly turned out to be the better of the two. She was a juicy eyeful with a lot of skin showing and nothing on under the dress she wore just to be conventional. She told me she had been posing for an artist down in the Village until she caught him using a camera instead of a paint-brush. She found he was peddling the prints and made him kick in with a fifty-fifty cut or get the pants knocked off him by an ex-boy friend in the Bronx, and now she was living off the cream of the land.

'Your artist friend sure mixes pleasure with business, honey,' I told her. 'Hell, I wouldn't mind seeing you undraped a bit.'

She snapped open her purse and tossed me a wallet-sized print with a laugh. 'Get right to it.' She had a body that would make a statue drool, and with the poses the artist got her into it was easy to see why she wasn't hurting for dough. She let me look at it a little while, asked me if I wanted to dance and laughed when I said maybe later, but not right then.

Finally we got up and danced while Cookie sat and yapped with the French maid from Brooklyn. Tolly didn't have any trouble giving me the business because the mob on the dance floor had us pressed together like the ham in a sandwich.

Every bit of her was pressed against every bit of me and her mouth was right next to my ear. Every once in a while she'd stick her tongue out and send something chasing down my spine. 'I like you, Mike,' she said.

I gave her a little squeeze until her eyes half closed and she said something through her teeth. I slapped her fanny for it. We got back to the table and played kneesies while we talked until the girls decided to hit the powder room.

As they walked away Cookie said, 'Cute kids, hey?'

'Real cute. Where the devil do you find them?'

'I get around. I don't look like much, but I get around. With a pair like them on my arms it's a ticket to anyplace I want to go so long as a guy's taking up the tickets.'

I picked a smoke out of my pack and handed one to him. 'What about our deal?'

His eyes crawled up my arm to my face. 'I know them. The boys are hurting right now. You do that?'

'Uh-huh.'

'What a mess. The little one wants your guts.'

'Who are they?'

'Private dicks. That's what the little piece of paper says in their wallets. They're hoods who'll do anything for some cash.'

'If they're cops they aren't making any money unless they're hired to protect somebody.'

'They are. You know anything about the rackets, Mike?'

'A little.'

'The town's divided into sections, see. Like

the bookies. They pay off to the local big boy who pays off to Ed Teen.'

The cigarette froze in my fingers. 'Where's Teen in this?'

'He's not, but one of his local boys is the mug who uses your two playmates for a bodyguard. His name is Toady Link. Ever hear of him?'

'Yeah.'

'Then you didn't hear much. He keeps his nose clean. The bodyguards are to keep the small-timers moving and not to protect him. As bookies go, the guy's okay. Now how about coming across with something I can sell.'

I squashed the butt out and started on another. Cookie's ears were pinned and he leaned across the table with a grin like we were telling dirty stories. I said, 'There was a little murder the other night. Then there was another. In the beginning they looked little, but now they're starting to look pretty big. I haven't got a damn thing I can tell you . . . yet. When it happens you'll get it quick. How's that?'

'Fair enough. Who got killed?'

'A guy named William Decker, Arnold Basil, then the next day Decker's friend Mel Hooker.'

'I read about that.'

'You'll be reading more about it. Where'll I find this Toady Link?'

Cookie rattled off a couple of addresses where I might pick him up and I let them soak in so I wouldn't forget them. 'Just one thing, Mike,' he added, 'you don't know from nothing, see? Keep me out of it. I stay away from them boys. My racket takes dough but no rough stuff, and when it comes to rods or brass knucks you can count me out. I don't want none of them hoods after my hide.'

'Don't worry,' I said. I stood up and threw a fin on the table to cover some of Tolly's champagne.

Cookie's eyebrows went up to his hairline. 'You aren't going now, are you? Hell, what about Tolly? She's got a yen for you already and I can't make out with two dames.'

'Sure you can. Nothing to it.'

'Aw, Mike, what a guy you are, and after I hand you such a sweet dish too.'

My mouth twisted into a lopsided smile. 'I can get all the dishes I want without having them handed to me. Tell Tolly that maybe I'll look her up someday. She interests me strangely.'

He didn't say anything, but he looked disappointed. He sat there wiggling those big ears and I cleared out of the place before the blonde came back and twisted my arm into staying.

Dames.

★   ★   ★

It was turning into a night just like that first one. The sidewalks and pavements were one big wet splash reflecting the garish lights of the streets and throwing them back at you. I pulled my raincoat out of the back and slipped into it, then climbed behind the wheel.

My watch read a few minutes after nine and it was tonight. Marsha said tonight. But there were other things first and Marsha could wait. It would be all the better for the waiting.

So I got in line behind the other cars and headed uptown. On the edge of the Bronx I turned off and looked for the bar that was one of the addresses Cookie had given me and found it in the middle of the block. I left the engine going while I asked around inside, but neither the bartender nor the manager had seen the eminent Mr. Link so far that night. They obliged with his home address and I thanked them politely even though I already had it.

Toady Link was at home.

Maybe it would be better to say he was

148

occupying his Bronx residence. That's the kind of a place it was. All fieldstone and picture windows on a walled-in half-acre of land that would have brought a quarter-million at auction. There were lights on all three floors of the joint and nobody to be seen inside. If it weren't for the new Packard squatting on the drive I would have figured the lights to be burglar protection.

I slid my own heap in at the curb and walked up the gravel to the house and punched the bell. Inside there was a faraway sound of chimes and about a minute later the door opened on a chain and a face looked at me waiting to see what I wanted.

You could see why he was called Toady. It was a big face, bigger around the jowls than it was on top with a pair of protruding eyes that seemed to have trouble staying in their sockets.

I said, 'Hello, Toady. Do I get asked in?'

Even his voice was like a damned frog. 'What do you want?'

'You maybe.'

The frog face cracked into a wide-mouthed smile, a real nasty smile and the chain came off the lock. He had a gun in his hand, a big fat revolver with a hole in the end big enough to get your finger into. 'Who the hell are you, bub?'

I took it easy getting my wallet out and flipped it back so he could see the tin. I shouldn't have bothered. His eyes never came off mine at all. I said, 'Mike Hammer. Private Investigator, Toady. I think you ought to know me.'

'I should?'

'Two of your boys should. They tried to take me.'

'If you're looking for them . . .'

'I'm not. I'm looking for you. About a murder.'

The smile got fatter and wider and the hole in the gun looked even bigger when he pointed it at my head. 'Get in here,' he said.

I did like he said. I stood there in the hall while he locked the door behind me and I could feel the muzzle of that rod about an inch behind my spine. Then he used it to steer me through the foyer into an outsized living room.

That much I didn't mind. But when he lowered the pile of fat he called a body into a chair and left me standing there on the carpet I got a little bit sore. 'Let's put the heater away, Toady.'

'Let's hear more about this murder first. I don't like people to throw murder in my face, Mr. Investigator. Not even lousy private cops.'

Goddamn, that fat face of his was making me madder every second I had to look at it.

'You ever been shot, fat boy?' I asked him. His face got red up to his hairline.

'I've been shot, fat boy,' I said. 'Not just once, either. Put that rod away or I'm going to give you a chance to use it. You'll have time to pump out just one slug and if it misses you're going to hear the nastiest noise you ever heard.'

I let my hand come up so my fingertips were inside my coat. When he didn't make a move to stop me I knew I had him and he knew it too. Fat boy didn't like the idea of hearing a nasty noise a bit. He let the gun drop on the chair beside him and cursed me with those bug eyes of his for finding out he was as yellow as they come.

It was better that way. Now I liked standing in the middle of the room. I could look down at the fat slob and poke at him with a spear until he told me what I wanted to hear. I said, 'Remember William Decker?'

His eyelids closed slowly and opened the same way. His head nodded once, squeezing the fat out under his chin.

'Do you know he's dead?'

'You son-of-a-bitch, don't try tagging me with that!' Now he was a real frog with a real croak.

'He played the ponies, Toady. You were the guy who picked up his bets.'

'So what! I pick up a lot of bets.'

'I thought you didn't fool around with small-time stuff.'

'Balls, he wasn't small-time. He laid 'em big as anybody else. How'd I know how he was operating? Look, you . . . '

'Shut up and answer questions. You're lucky I'm not a city cop or you'd be doing your talking with a light in your face. Where'd Decker get the dough to lay?'

He relaxed into a sullen frown, his pudgy hands balled into tight fists. 'He borrowed it, that's where.'

'From Dixie Cooper if you've forgotten.' He looked at me and if the name meant anything I couldn't read it in his face. 'How much did Decker drop to you?'

'Hell, he went in the hole for a few grand, but don't go trying to prove it. I don't keep books.'

'So you killed him.'

'Goddamn you!' He came out of the chair and stood there shaking from head to foot. 'I gave him that dough back so he could pay off his loan! Understand that? I hate them creeps who can't stand a loss. The guy was ready to pull the dutch act so I gave him back his dough so's he could pay off!'

He stood there staring at me with his eyes hanging out of that livid face of his sucking in his breath with a wheezy rasp. 'You're lying, Toady,' I said. 'You're lying through your teeth.' My hands twisted in the lapels of his coat and I pulled him in close so I could spit on him if I felt like it. 'Where were you when Decker was killed?'

His hands fought with mine to keep me from choking him. 'Here! I was . . . right here! Let go of me!'

'What about your boys . . . Nocky and that other gorilla?'

'I don't know where they were. I . . . didn't have anything to do with that! Goddamn, that's what I get for being a sucker! I should've let them work on the bastard. I should've kept his dough and kicked him out!'

'Maybe they did work over somebody. They had Decker's buddy all lined up for a shellacking until he shook 'em off on me. I thought I taught 'em to keep their noses out of trouble, but I guess I didn't teach 'em hard enough. The guy they were going to give the business to died with a bullet in him the same night. I hear tell those boys work for you, and they weren't out after the guy on their own.'

'You . . . you're crazy!'

'Am I? Who put them on Hooker . . . you?'

'Hooker?' He worked his head into a frown that wouldn't stick.

'Don't play innocent, damn it. You know who I'm talking about. Mel Hooker. The guy who teamed up with Decker to play the nags.'

An oversize tongue made a quick pass over his lips. 'He . . . yeah, I know. Hooker. Nocky and him got in a fight. It was when he picked up his dough and cleared out. He was drunk, see? He started shooting off his mouth about how it was all crooked and he talked enough to keep some dough from coming across the board. That's how it was. Nocky tried to throw him out and he nearly brained him.'

'So your boy picked him off?'

'No, no. He wouldn't do that. He was plenty mad, that's why he was laying for him. He didn't knock anybody off. I don't go for that. Ask anybody, they'll tell you I don't go for rough stuff.'

I gave him a shove to get him away from me. 'For a bookie you're a big-hearted son-of-a-bitch. You're one in a million and, brother, you better be telling the truth, because if you aren't you're going to get a lot of that fat sweated off you. Where's these two mugs?'

'How the hell do I know?'

I didn't play with him this time. I backhanded him across the mouth and did it again when he stumbled away and tried to grab the gun on the chair. His big belly shook so hard he swayed off balance and I gave it to him again. Then he just about fell into the chair and with the rod right under his hand he didn't have the guts to make a play for it.

I asked him again. 'Where are they, Toady?'

'They . . . have rooms over the . . . Rialto Restaurant.'

'Names, Pal.'

'Nocky . . . he's Arthur Cole. The other one's Glenn Fisher.' He had to squeeze the words out between lips that were no more than a thin red gash in his face. The marks of my fingers were across his cheek, making it puff out even farther. I could tell that he was hoping I'd turn my back, even for a second. The crazy madness in his eyes made them bulge so far his eyelids couldn't cover them.

I turned my back. I did it when I picked up the phone, but there was a mirror right in front of me and I could stand there and watch him hate me while I thumbed through the directory until I found the number listed under 'Cole' and dialed it.

The phone rang, all right, but nobody answered it. Then I called the Rialto Restaurant and went through two waiters before the manager came on and told me that the boys didn't live there any more. They had packed their bags about an hour before, climbed into a cab and scrammed. Yeah, they

155

were all paid up and the management was glad to be rid of them.

I hung up and turned around. 'They beat it, Toady.'

Link just sat.

'Where'd they go?'

His shoulders hunched into a shrug.

'I have a feeling you're going to die pretty soon, Toady,' I said. And after I said it I looked at him until it sank all the way in and put his eyes back in place so the eyelids could get over them. I picked up the gun that lay beside him, flipped out the cylinder and punched the shells into my hand. They were .44's with copper-covered noses that could rip a guy in half. I tossed the empty rod back on the chair beside him and walked out of the room.

Somehow the night smelled cleaner after Toady. The rain was a light mist washing the stink of the swamp away. It shaded part of the monstrous castle the ugly frog sat in as though it were ashamed of it. I looked back at the lights and I could see why they were all on. They were the guy's only friends.

When I got back in my car I drove down to the corner, swung around and came back up the street. Before I got as far as the house the Packard came roaring out of the drive and skidded halfway across the road before it straightened out and went tearing off down the street. I had to laugh because Toady wasn't going anyplace at all. Not driving like that he wasn't. Toady was so goddamn mad he had to take it out on something and tonight the car took the beating.

I would have kept right on going myself if he hadn't left the door wide open so that the light made a streaming yellow invitation down the gravel. I jammed on the brakes and left the car sitting, the motor turning over and picked up the invitation.

The house was Toady's attempt at respectability, but it was only an attempt. The upstairs lights were turned on from switches at the foot of the stairs and only one set of prints showed in the dust that lay over the staircase. There were three bedrooms, two baths and a sitting room on the top floor, a full apartment-sized layout on the second and the only places that had been used were one bedroom and a shower stall. Everything else was neat and dormant, with the dust-mop marks last week's cleaning woman had left. Downstairs the kitchen was a mess of dirty dishes and littered newspapers. The pantry was stocked to take care of a hundred people who never came and the only things in the guest closet were Toady's hat and coat that he hadn't bothered to wear when he dashed out.

I rummaged around in the library and the study without touching anything then went down the cellar and had a drink of private stock at his bar. It was a big place with knotty pine walls rimmed with a couple hundred beer steins that were supposed to give it the atmosphere of a beer garden. Off to one side was the poolroom with the balls neatly racked and gathering more dust. He even had a cigarette machine down there. The butts were on the house and all you had to do was yank the lever, so I had a pack of Luckies on Toady too.

There were two other doors that led off the poolroom. One went into the furnace room and I stepped into a goddamned rattrap that nearly took my toes off. The other was a storeroom and I almost backed out of it when the white cloths that shrouded the stockpile of junk took shape. I found the light switch and turned it on. Instead of an overhead going on, a red light blossomed out over a sink on the end of the wall, turning everything a deep crimson.

The place was a darkroom. Or at least it had been. The stuff hadn't been touched since it was stored here. A big professional camera was folded up under wraps with a lot of movie-screen-type backdrops and a couple of wrought-iron benches. The processing chemicals and film plates had rotted away on a shelf next to a box that held the gummy remains of tubes of retouching paints. Off in the corner was a screwy machine of some sort that had its seams all carefully dustproofed with masking tape.

I put the covers back in place and turned the light off. When I closed the door I couldn't help thinking that Toady certainly tried hard to work up a hobby. In a way I couldn't blame him a bit. For friends all that repulsive bastard had was a lot of toys and dust. The louse was rich as sin with nobody to spend his money on.

I left the door open like I found it and climbed in under the wheel of my heap. I sat there feeling a little finger probing at my mind, trying to jar something into it that should already be there and the finger was still probing away when I got back to Manhattan and started down Riverside Drive.

So damn many little things and none of them added up. Some place between a tenement slum that had belonged to Decker and Toady's dismal swamp castle a killer was whistling his way along the street while I sat trying to figure out what a finger nudging my mind meant.

Lord, I was tired. The smoke in the car

stung my eyes and I had to open the window to let it out. What I needed was a long, natural sleep without anything at all to think and dream about, but up there in the man-built cliffs of steel and stone was Marsha and she said she'd wait for me. The back of my head started to hurt again and even the thought of maybe sleeping with somebody who had been a movie star didn't make it go away.

But I went up.

And she was still waiting, too.

Marsha said, 'You're late, Mike.'

'I know, I'm sorry.' She picked the hat out of my hand and waited while I peeled off my coat. When she had them stowed in the closet she hooked her arm under mine and took me inside.

There were drinks all set up and waiting beside a bowl that had held ice but was now all water. The tall red candles had been lit, burned down a few inches, then had been blown out.

'I thought you would have been here earlier. For supper perhaps.'

She handed me a cigarette from a long narrow box and followed it with a lighter. When I had my lungs full of smoke I leaned back with my head pillowed against the chair and looked at her close up. She had on a light green dress that swirled up her body, over her shoulder and came down again to a thin leather belt at her waist. The swelling around her eye had gone down and in the soft light of the room the slight purple discoloration almost looked good.

I watched her a second and grinned. 'Now I'm nearly sorry I didn't. You're nice to look at, kitten.'

'Just half?'

'No. All this time. From top to bottom too.'

Her eyes burned softly under long lashes. 'I like it when you say it, Mike. You're used to saying it too, aren't you?'

'Only to beautiful women.'

'And you've seen plenty of them.' The laugh was in her voice now.

I said, 'You've got the wrong slant, kid. Pretty is what you mean. Pretty and beautiful are two different things. Only a few women are pretty, but even one who's not so hot to look at can be beautiful. A lot of guys make mistakes when they turn down a beautiful woman for one who's just pretty.'

Her eyebrows went up in the slightest show of surprise, letting the fires of her irises leap into plain view. 'I didn't know you were a philosopher, Mike.'

'There're a lot of things you don't know about me.'

She uncurled from the chair and picked up the glasses from the table. 'Should I?'

'Uh-uh. They're all bad.' I got that look again, the one with the smile around the edges, then she brought in some fresh ice from the kitchen and made a pair of highballs. The one she gave me went down cold and easy, nestling there at the bottom of my stomach with a pleasant, creeping kind of warmth that tiptoed silently throughout my body until it was the nicest thing in the world to just sit there with my eyes half shut and listen to the rain drum against the windows.

Marsha's hand went to the switch on the record player, flooding the room with the soft tones of the 'Blue Danube.' She filled the glasses again, then drifted to the floor at my feet, laying her head back against my knees. 'Nice?' she asked me.

'Wonderful. I'm right in the mood to enjoy it.'

'You still . . . '

'That's right. Still.' I closed my eyes all the way for a minute. 'Sometimes I think I'm standing still too. It's never been like this before.'

Her hand found mine and pulled it down to her cheek. I thought I felt her lips brush my fingers, but I wasn't sure. 'Do you have the boy yet?'

162

'Yeah, he's in good hands. Tomorrow or maybe the next day they'll come for him. He'll be all right.'

'I wish there was something I could do. Are you sure there isn't? Could I keep him for you?'

'He'd be too much for you. Hell, he's only a little over a year old. I have a nurse for him. She's old, but reliable.'

'Then let me take him out for a walk or something. I really do want to help, Mike, honest.'

I ran my fingers through the sheen of her hair and across the soft lines of her face. This time I knew it when her lips parted in a kiss on my palm.

'I wish you could, Marsha. I need help. I need something. This whole thing is getting away from me.'

'Would it help to tell me about it?'

'Maybe.'

'Then tell me.'

So I told her. I sat there staring at the ceiling with Marsha on the floor and her head on my knees and I told her about it. I lined up everything from beginning to end and tried to put them together in the right order.

When you strung them out like that it didn't take long to tell. They made a nice neat pile of facts, one on top of the other, but there was nothing there to hold them together. One little push scattered them all over the place. Before I finished my jaws ached from holding my teeth together so tightly.

'Being so mad won't help you think,' Marsha said.

'I gotta be mad. Goddamn, you can't go at a thing like this unless you are mad. I never knew much about kids, but when I held the Decker boy in my hands I could see why a guy would give his insides to keep his kid alive. Right there is the thing that screws everything up. Decker knew he was going to die and didn't try to do a single thing about it. Three days before, he knew it was going to happen too. He got all his affairs put right and waited. God knows what he thought about in those three days.'

'It couldn't have been nice.'

'Oh, I don't know. I don't get it at all.' I rubbed my face disgustedly. 'Decker and Hooker tie in with Toady Link and he ties in with Grindle and Teen and it was one of Grindle's boys who shot Decker. There's a connection there if you want to look for one.'

'I'm sorry, Mike.'

'You don't have to be.'

'But I am. In a way it started with me. I keep thinking of the boy.'

'It would have been the same if Decker had broken into the other apartment. The guy knew he was going to die ... but why? Whether or not he got what he was after he was still planning to die!'

Marsha lifted her face and turned around. 'Couldn't it have been ... a precaution? Perhaps he *was* planning to run out with the money. In that case he would know there *was* a possibility that they might catch up with him. As it was, it turned out to be the same thing. He knew they'd never believe his story about the wrong apartment so he ran anyway, bringing about the same results.'

My eyes felt hot and heavy. 'It's crazy as hell. It's a mess no matter how I look at it, but someplace there's an answer and it's lost in my head. I keep trying to work it loose and it won't come. Every time I stop to think about it I can feel it sitting here and if the damn thing was human it would laugh at me. Now I can't even think any more.'

'Tired, darling?'

'Yeah.'

I looked at her and she looked at me and we were both thinking the same thing. Then her head dropped slowly and her smile had a touch of sadness in it.

'I'm a fool, aren't I?' she said.

'You're no fool, Marsha.'

'Mike . . . have you ever been in love?'

I didn't know how to answer that so I just nodded.

'Was it nice?'

'I thought so.' I was hoping she wouldn't ask me any more. Even after five years it hurt to think about it.

'Are you . . . now?' Her voice was low, almost inaudible. I caught the brief flicker of her eyes as she glanced at my face.

I shrugged. I didn't know what to tell her.

She smiled at her hands and I smiled with her. 'That's good,' she laughed. Her eyes went bright and happy and she tossed her head so that her hair fell in a glittering dark halo around her shoulders. 'I had tonight all planned. I was going to be a fool anyway and make you want me so that you'd keep wanting me.'

'It's been like that.'

She came up off the floor slowly, gracefully, reaching for my hand to pull me out of the chair. Her mouth was warmer than it should have been. Her body was supple and lovely, like a fluid filling in the gaps between us. I ran my fingers through her hair, pulling her face away while still wanting to keep her crushed against me.

'Why, Marsha?' I asked. 'Why me? You know what I'm like. I'm not fancy and I'm not famous and I work for my dough. I'm not in your class at all.'

She looked up at me with an expression you don't try to describe. A sleepy expression that wasn't a bit tired. Her hands slid up my back and tightened as she leaned against me. 'Let me be a woman, Mike. I don't want those things you say you're not. I've had them. I want all the things you are. You're big and not so handsome, but there's a devil inside you that makes you exciting and tough, yet enough of an angel to make you tender when you have to be.'

My hands wanted to squeeze right through her waist until they met and I had to let her go or she would have felt the way they were shaking. I turned around and reached for the bottle and glass on the table and while I was pouring one there was a click and the light dimmed to a pale glow.

Behind me I heard her say softly, 'Mike . . . you never told me whether I was . . . just pretty or beautiful.'

I turned around and was going to tell her that she was the most lovely thing I had ever seen, but her hands did something to her belt and the fold of the dress that came up over one shoulder dropped away leaving her standing there with one hand on the lamp like a half-nude vision and the words got stuck in my throat.

Then the light disappeared altogether and I could only drink the drink quickly, because although the vision was gone it was walking toward me across the night and somewhere on the path there was another whisper of fabric and she was there in my hands without anything to keep her from being a woman now, an invisible, naked dream throwing a mantle of desire around us both that had too great a strength to break and must be burned through by a fire that leaped and danced and towered in a blazing crescendo that could only be dampened and never extinguished.

And when the mantle was thrown back I left the dream there in the dark, warm and soft, breathing quickly to tell me that it was a dream that would come back on other nights too, disturbing and at the same time satisfying.

She was beautiful. She was pretty, too.

She was in my mind all the way home.

6

At a quarter past ten I got up, dressed and made myself some breakfast. Right in the middle of it the phone rang and when I answered it the operator told me to hold on for a call from Miami. Velda's husky voice was a pleasure to hear again. She said, 'Mike?'

And I said, 'Hello, sweetheart. How's everything?'

'Fine. At least it's partly fine. Our boy got out on a plane, but he left all the stuff behind. The insurance investigator is here making an inventory of the stuff now.'

'Great, great. Try to promote yourself a bonus if you can.'

'That wouldn't be hard,' she laughed. 'He's already made a pass. Mike, miss me?'

I felt like a heel, but I wasn't lying when I said, 'Hell yes, I miss you.'

'I don't mean as a business partner.'

'Neither do I, kitten.'

'You won't have to miss me long. I'm taking the afternoon train out.'

My fingers started batting out dots and dashes on the table. I wanted her back but not too soon. I didn't want anybody else climbing all over me. 'You stay there,' I told her. 'Stay on that guy's tail. You're still on salary from the company and if you can get a line on him now they'll cut us in for more business later. They're as interested in him as they are in recovering the stuff.'

'But, Mike, the Miami police are doing all they can.'

'Where'd he hop to?'

'Some place in Cuba. That's where they lost him.'

'Okay, get over to Cuba then. Take a week and if it's no dice forget it and come on home.'

She didn't say anything for a few seconds. 'Mike . . . is something wrong up there?'

'Don't be silly.'

'You sound like it. If you're sending me off . . . '

'Look, kid,' I cut her off, 'you'd know about it if anything was wrong. I just got up and I'm kind of sleepy yet. Be a good girl and stay on that case, will you?'

'All right. Love me?'

'You'll never know,' I said.

She laughed again and hung up. She knew. Women always know.

I went back and finished my breakfast, had a smoke then turned on the faucet in the bathroom sink to bring the hot water up.

While I shaved I turned on the radio and picked up the commentator who was just dropping affairs in Washington to get back to New York and as far as he was concerned the only major problem of the day was the District Attorney's newest successes in the gambling probe. At some time last night a series of raids had been carried out successfully and the police dragnet had brought in some twenty-five persons charged with bookmaking. He gave no details, but hinted that the police were expecting to nail the kingpins in the near future.

When I finished shaving I opened my door and took the tabloid out of the knob to see what the press had to say about it. The front page carried the pictures of those gathered in the roundup with appropriate captions while the inside double spread had a layout showing where the bookies had been operating.

The editorial was the only column that mentioned Ed Teen at all. It brought out the fact that Teen's personal staff of lawyers were going to bat for the bookies. At the same time the police were finding that a lot of witnesses were reluctant to speak up when it came to identifying the boys who took their money or paid off on wins, places and shows. At the end of the column the writer came right out with the charge that Lou Grindle had an organization specially adept at keeping witnesses from talking and demanded that the police throw some light on the subject.

I went through the paper again to make sure I didn't miss anything, then folded it up and stuck it in the bottom of my chair until I got around to reading it. Then I went downstairs and knocked on the door of the other apartment and stood there with my hat in my hands until the door opened and the nurse said, 'Good morning, Mr. Hammer. Come on in.'

'I can only stay a minute. I want to see how the kid is.'

'Oh, he's a regular boy. Right now he's trying to see what's inside the radio.'

I walked in behind her to the living room where the kid was doing just that. He had the extension cord in his fists and the set teetered on the edge of the table a hair away from complete ruin. I got there first and grabbed the both of them.

The kid knew me, all right. His face was sunny with a big smile and he shoved his hand inside my coat and then chattered indignantly when I pulled it out. 'How's the breakage charge coming?'

'We won't count that,' the nurse said. 'As a

172

matter of fact, he's been much better than I expected.'

I held the kid out where I could look at him better. 'There's something different about him.'

'There ought to be. I gave him a haircut.' I put him back on the floor where he hung on my leg and jabbered at me. 'He certainly likes you,' she said.

'I guess I'm all he's got. Need anything?'

'No, we're getting along fine.'

'Okay, anything you want just get.' I bent down and ruffled the kid's hair and he tried to climb up my leg. He yelled to come with me so I had to hand him back and wave good-by from the door. He was so damn small and pathetic-looking I felt like a heel for stranding him, but I promised myself I'd see that he got a lot of attention before he was dropped into some home for orphans.

The first lunch shift was just hitting the streets when I got to Pat's office. The desk man called ahead to see if he was still in and told me to go right up. A couple of reporters were coming out of the room still jotting down notes and Pat was perched on the edge of a desk fingering a thick manila folder.

I closed the door behind me and he said, 'Hi, Mike.'

'Making news?'

'Today we're heroes. Tomorrow we'll be something else again.'

'So the D.A.'s making out. Did you find the hole?'

He turned around slowly, his face expressionless. 'No, if that cop is passing out the word then he wised up. Nothing went out on this deal at all.'

'How could he catch on?'

'He's been a cop a long time. He's been staked out often enough to spot it when he's being watched himself.'

'Did he mention it?'

'No, but his attitude has changed. He resents the implication apparently.'

'That's going to make pretty reading. Now the papers'll call for the D.A. to make a full-scale investigation of the whole department, I suppose.'

'The D.A. doesn't know a damn thing about it. You keep it to yourself too. I'm handling the matter myself. If it is the guy there's no sense smearing the whole department. We still aren't sure of it, you know.'

He tossed the folder on top of the filing cabinet and sat down behind the desk with a sigh. There were tired lines around his eyes and mouth, little lines that had been showing up a lot lately.

I said, 'What came of the roundup?'

'Oh, hell, Mike.' He glanced at me with open disgust, then realized that I wasn't handing him a dig. 'Nothing came of it. So we closed down a couple of rooms. We got a hatful of small-timers who will probably walk right out of it or draw minimum sentences. Teen's a smart operator. His lawyers are even smarter. Those boys know all the angles there are to know and if there are any new ones they think them up.

'Teen's a real cutie. You know what I think? He's letting us take some of his boys just to keep the D.A. happy and get a chance to put in a bigger fix.'

'I don't get it,' I said.

'Look, Teen pays for protection. That is, if it takes money to keep his racket covered. If it takes muscle he uses Lou Grindle. But supposing it does take dough . . . then all the chiselers, petty politicians and maybe even the big shots who are taking his dough are going to want more to keep his personal fix in because things are getting tougher. Okay, he pays off, and the more those guys rake in the deeper in they are too. Suddenly they realize that they can't afford to let Teen get taken or they'll go along with him, so they work overtime to keep the louse clean.'

'Nice.'

'Isn't it though?' he sat there tapping his

fingers on the desk, then: 'Mike, for all you've heard, read and seen of Ed Teen, do you know what we actually have on him?'

'Tell me.'

'Nothing. Not one damn thing. Plenty of suspicions, but you don't take suspicions to court. We know everything he's hooked up with and we can't prove a single part of it. I've been upside down for a month backtracking over his life trying to tie him into something that happened a long time ago and for all I've found you could stuff it in your ear.' Pat buried his face in his hands and rubbed his eyes.

'Have you had time to do anything about Decker and Hooker?'

At least it made him smile a little. 'I haven't been upside down *that* long, Pal,' he said. 'I was going to call you on that. Routine investigation turned up something on Hooker. For the last four months he made bank deposits of close to a thousand bucks each time. They apparently came in on the same date and were all for the same amount, though he spent a little of each wad before he deposited it. That sort of ties in with your story about him hitting the winning ponies.'

I rolled a cigarette between my fingers slowly then stuck it in my mouth. 'How often were the deposits made?'

'Weekly. Regular as pie.'

'And Decker?'

'Clean. I had four men cover every minute of his time as far back as they could go. As far as we could find out he didn't even associate with any shady characters. The kind of people who vouched for him were the kind who knew what they were talking about too. Incidentally, I talked to his parish priest personally. He's made all the arrangements for the boy and cleared them with the authorities, so he'll pick him up at the end of the week.'

He stopped and watched my face a moment. The silence was so thick you could slice it with a knife. 'All right, now what are you thinking, Mike?'

I let a lazy cloud of smoke sift up toward the ceiling. 'It might scare you,' I said.

The tired lines got deeper when his mouth clamped shut. 'Yeah? Scare me then.'

'Maybe you've been closer to nailing Teen than you thought, chum.'

His fingers stopped their incessant tapping.

'After Decker was killed a lot of awfully funny things started to happen. Before they didn't seem to make much sense, but just because you can't actually see what's holding them together doesn't mean that they're not there. Wouldn't it be a scream if the guy who killed Decker could lead you to Teen?'

'Yeah, I'd laugh myself sick.' Now Pat's eyes were just thin shiny slits in his head.

I said, 'Those bank deposits of Hooker's weren't wins. Hooker was being paid off to do something. You got any idea what it was?'

'No,' sullenly.

'I'd say he was being paid to see that a certain guy was put in a certain spot where he was up the creek.'

'Damn it, Mike, quit talking in riddles!'

'Pat, I can't. It's still a puzzle to me, too, but I can tell you this. You've been routine on this case all along. It's been too small-time to open up on but I think you'd damn well better open up on it right now because you're sitting on top of the thing that can blow Teen and his racket all to hell. I don't know how or why . . . yet. But I know it's there and before very long I'm going to find the string that's holding it together. As far as Ed Teen's concerned I don't care what happens to him, only someplace in there is the guy who made an orphan out of a nice little kid and he's the one I want. You can take it for what it's worth or I can go it alone. Just don't shove the Decker kill down at the bottom of the page and hope something turns up on it because you think grabbing Teen is more important.'

He started to come up out of his chair and

his face was strictly cop without tired lines any more. He got all set to give me the business, then, like turning on the light, the scowl and the tired lines went away and he sat back smiling a little with that excited, happy look I hadn't seen him wear for so long.

'What's it about, Mike?'

'I think the Decker murder got away from somebody. It was supposed to be nice and clean and didn't happen that way.'

'What else?'

'A lot of scrambled facts that are going to get put right fast if you help out. Then I'll give it to you so there's sense to it.'

'You know, you're damn lucky I know what makes you tick, Mike. If you were anybody else I'd hammer out every last bit of information you have. I'm only sorry you didn't get on the force while you were still young enough.'

'I don't like the hours. The pay either.'

'No,' he grinned, 'you'd sooner work for free and get me all hopped up whenever you feel like it. You and the D.A. Okay, spill it. What do you need?'

'A pair of private detectives named Arthur Cole and Glenn Fisher.'

He jotted the names down and stared at them blankly a second. 'Nocky . . . ?'

'That's Cole.'

'You should have given me their names before.'

'I didn't know them before.'

He reached out and flipped the switch on the intercom. 'Tell Sergeant McMillan to come in a moment, please.'

A voice rasped that it would and while we waited Pat went to the filing cabinet and pawed through the drawers until he had what he wanted. He tossed the stuff in my lap as a thick-set plain-clothesman came in chewing on a dead cigar.

Pat said, 'Sergeant, this is Mike Hammer.'

The cop shifted his cigar and held out his hand. I said, 'Glad to know you.'

'Same here. Heard lots about you, Mike.'

'Sergeant McMillan has the inside information on the uptown boys,' Pat said. He turned to the plain-clothesman with, 'What do you know about two supposedly private detectives named Cole and Fisher?'

'Plenty. Fisher lost his license about a month ago. What do you want to know?'

Pat raised his eyebrows at me. 'Background stuff,' I said.

'The guys are hoods, plain and simple. Especially Fisher. You ever see them?'

I nodded. Pat pointed to the folder in my lap and I pulled out a couple of candid shots taken during a strike-breaking melee on the docks. My boys were right there in the foreground swinging billies.

The cop said, 'They're troublemakers. About a year ago somebody with a little pull had them tagged with badges so what they did would be a little bit legal. Neither one of 'em have records, but they've been pulled in a few times for minor offenses. Brawling mostly. They'll work for anybody who pays off. You want me to put out a call for 'em, Captain?'

'What about it, Mike?' Pat asked.

'It wouldn't be a bad idea, but you won't find them in New York. Stick them on the teletype and see if they aren't holing up in another city. You might try alerting the railroad dicks to keep an eye out for them. They skipped out last night and might still be traveling. Cole has a broken hand and Fisher's face is a mess. They ought to be easy to identify.'

'You want to do that, sergeant?'

He nodded at Pat. 'I have everything I need. They shouldn't be too hard to trace.' He said so long to me and went back the way he came.

Pat picked the photo up and studied it. 'What's with these two?'

'They worked for Toady Link.' Pat's head came up quickly. 'They were on to Hooker for some reason until I started buzzing the guy, then they went into me. I didn't get the pitch in time or Hooker might still be alive. Last night I paid a visit to our friend Link and he was happy to tell me who the boys were.'

'Mike, damn it . . .'

'If you're wondering how I found out who they were when the cops didn't know . . . I have a friend who gets around. With blondes.'

'I'm not wondering that at all! I'm wondering how the hell I could have been so negligent or stupid, whatever you want to call it.' He grinned wryly. 'I used to be a bright boy. A year ago I would have seen the connection or let you talk me into something a lot sooner. Everything you do is tying right in with this Teen affair. Did you know that we had Link slated to go through the mill this week?'

'No.'

'Well, we had. He and four others. While the D.A.'s been getting pushed around he's been doing one hell of a job on the organization's working men. Toady's about a month away from a man-sized stretch up the river. Every move you make you step on my toes.'

'Why didn't you pick it up sooner?'

'Because it's no novelty to be tied up with

Teen or Grindle, especially when there's money or murder concerned. Some of the help those two employ have turned up on more than one offense. It wasn't too difficult to suppose that Basil was just out for extra cash when he went in on that robbery and shot Decker afterward.'

'Are you positive that he's the one who did the shooting?'

'As positive as the paraffin test. Of course, he may have discharged the bullet prior to the killing, but if he did I don't know where. If this Decker thing has even the slightest tie-up with the boys we want then we'll get to it.'

'Hang on, Pat. I'm not saying that it has.'

'I'll damn soon find out.'

I tried to be unconcerned as I pulled on my smoke. 'How about letting me find out for you. So far Decker has been my party.'

'Nix, Mike. I know what you want. All you have in your head is the idea that you want to tangle with that killer. Not this time. Taking that one guy out of play could screw up this whole thing so nicely we'll be left with nothing at all.'

'Okay, pal,' I grinned, 'go right to it. Just try to get an identification out of me. Just try it.'

'Mike . . .'

'Aw, nuts, Pat. I'm as critical to this thing

as those two mugs are. It was me who saw them and me who pushed them around. Without my say-so you don't have a thing to haul them in on. You're taking all the gravy for yourself . . . or at least you're trying to.'

'What do you want, Mike?'

'I want three or four days to make my own play. Things are just beginning to look up. I'd like a file on Toady Link too.'

'That's impossible. The D.A. has it classified top secret. That's out.'

'Can't *you* get it, kid?'

'Nope. That would mean an explanation and I'm not giving blue boy a chance to climb up my back again.'

'Well, hell . . . do you know anything about the guy at all?'

He leaned back in the chair and shook his head slowly. 'Probably no more than you know, Mike. I haven't done anything more than listen in and supply a little information I had when Toady's name came up. The D.A. had his own men doing the legwork.'

I looked out the window and while I watched the people on the roofs across the street Pat studied my face and studied it hard. I could feel his eyes crawl across me and make everything I was thinking into thoughts and words of his own.

He said, 'You're thinking Toady Link's the

last step in the chain, aren't you?'

I nodded.

'Spell it out for me.'

So I spelled it out. I said, 'Big-money boys like to splurge. They say they go for wine, women and song but whoever said it forgot to add the ponies too. Go out to the races and take a look around. Take a peek at the limousines and convertibles and the bank rolls that own them.'

'So?'

'So there was a big-money boy named Marvin Holmes who likes his blondes fast and furious and very much on hand. He spends his dough like water and keeps plenty of it locked up in a safe on his wall. He plays the nags through a bookie named Toady Link and doesn't like the way the ponies run so he won't pay off his bet. He's too big to push around, but Link can't take a welch so he looks around for a way to get his dough. Somebody tips him about a former safe expert named Decker, but the guy is honest and wants to stay that way. Okay, so Toady waits until the guy needs dough. He finds out who his friend is . . . a guy named Mel Hooker, and pays him to steer Decker his way. They use a rigged-up deal to make it look like they're winning a pot and everybody is happy. Then Decker goes in over his head.

He borrows from a loan shark to make the big kill and loses everything. That's where the pressure starts. He's not a big shot and he's got a kid and he's an easy mark to push around. He knows what happens on this loan-shark deal and he's scared, so when Toady comes up with the proposition of opening a safe . . . a simple little thing like that . . . Decker grabs it, takes a pay-off from Link to keep the shark off his neck and goes to it.

'It would have been fine if Decker had hit the right apartment, but he made a mistake he couldn't afford. He had to take a powder. Maybe he had even planned on taking a powder and arranged for his kid to be taken care of if things didn't go right. I don't know about that. He had something planned anyway. The only trouble was that he didn't plan well enough, or the guys who went out with him in the job were too sharp. They had him cold. Basil shot him then went over him for the dough. He must have yelled out that Decker was clean just before I started shooting. When he went down the driver couldn't afford to let him be taken alive and ran over him.

'Just take it from there . . . he already knew where Decker lived and thought that maybe when he went back for his kid he stashed the dough he was supposed to have. The guy searched the place and couldn't find it. Then he got the idea that maybe Basil had been too hurried when he searched Decker's corpse . . . but I had been right there and figured that I wouldn't overlook picking up a pile from a corpse if I got the chance. So while I was out my apartment was searched and I came back in time to catch the guy at it. I was in too damn much of a hurry and he beat the hell out of me.

'Now let's suppose it *was* Toady. Two guys are dead and he can be right in line for the hot seat if somebody gets panicky and talks. After all, Hooker didn't know the details of the kill so he could have thought that Toady was getting him out of the way to keep him from talking. That puts him in the same spot and he's scared stiff. Evidently he did have one run-in with the tough boys before and carried the scar around on his face to prove it.

'So Hooker spots two of Toady's boys and gets the jumps. They're sticking around waiting for the right spot to stick him. When Hooker got confidential with me they must have thought that Mel was asking for protection or trying to get rid of what I knew so they tried to take me. They muffed that one and went back to get Hooker. They

187

didn't muff that one.

'Up to there Toady didn't have too much to worry about, but when I showed my face he got scared. Just before that he packed his boys out of town because he couldn't afford to have them around, so if we can get them back we ought to finger Toady without any trouble at all. Not the least little bit of trouble.'

There was a silence that lasted for a full minute and I could hear Pat breathing and my own watch ticking. Pat said, 'That's supposing you got all this dealt out right.'

'Uh-huh.'

'We can find out soon enough.' He picked up the phone and said, 'Give me an outside line, please,' and while he waited riffled through the phone book. I heard the dial tone come on and Pat fingered out a number. The phone ringing on the other end made a faraway hum. Then it stopped. 'I'd like to speak to Mr. Holmes,' Pat said. 'This is Captain Chambers, Homicide, speaking.'

He sat there and frowned at the wall while he listened, then put the receiver back too carefully. 'He's gone, Mike. He left for South America with one of his blondes yesterday morning.'

'That's great,' I said. My voice didn't sound like me at all.

Pat's mouth got tight around the corners. 'That's perfect. It proves your point. The guy isn't too big to push around after all. Somebody's scared him right out of the city. You called every goddamn move right on the nose.'

'I hope so.'

I guess he didn't like the way I said it.

'It looks good to me.'

'It looks too good. I wish we had the murder weapons to back it up.'

'Metal doesn't rot out that fast. If we get those two we'll get the gun and we'll get Toady too. It doesn't matter which one we get him for.'

'Maybe. I'd like to know who drove the car that night.'

'Toady certainly wouldn't do it himself.'

I stopped watching the people on the roof across the way and turned my face toward Pat. 'I'm thinking that he did, Pat. If it was the kind of haul he expected he wasn't going to let it go through a few hands before it got back to him. Yeah, feller, I think I'll tag Toady with this one.'

'Not you, Mike . . . *we'll* tag him for it. The police. The public. Justice. You know.'

'Want to bet?'

Suddenly he wasn't my friend any more. His eyes were too gray and his face was too bland and I was the guy in the chair who was going to keep answering questions until he was done with me. Or that's what he thought.

I said, 'A few minutes ago I asked you if you'd like to nail the whole batch of them at once.'

'So there's more to it?'

'There could be. Lots more. Only if I get a couple extra days first.'

Something you might call a smile threw a shadow around his mouth. 'You know what will happen to me if you mess things up?'

'Do you know what might happen to me?'

'You might get yourself killed.'

'Yeah.'

'Okay, Mike, you got your three days. God help you if you get in a jam because I won't.'

He was lying both times and I knew it. I'd no more get three days than he'd give me a boot when I needed a hand, but I played it like I didn't catch the drift and got up out of my chair. He was sitting there with the same expression when I closed the door, but his hand had already started to reach for the phone.

I went down the corridor to where a bunch of typewriters were banging out a madhouse symphony and asked one of the stenos where I could find Ellen Scobie. She told me that she had gone out to lunch at noon and was expected back that afternoon, but I might still find her in the Nelson Steak House if I got over there right away.

It took me about ten minutes to make the four blocks and there was Ellen in the back looking more luscious than the oversize T-bone steak she was gnawing on.

She saw me and waved and I wondered what it was going to cost to get hold of that file on Toady Link.

It made nice wondering.

7

She was all in black, but without Ellen inside it the dress would have been nothing. The sun had kissed her skin into a light toast color, dotting the corner of her eyes with freckles. Her hair swept back and down, caressing her bare shoulders whenever she moved her head.

She said, 'Hello, man.'

I slid in across the table. 'Did you eat yourself out of company?'

'Long ago. My poor working friends had to get back to the office.'

'What about you?'

'You are enjoying the sight of a woman enjoying the benefits of working overtime when the city budget doesn't allow for unauthorized pay. They had to give me the time off. Want something to eat?'

A waitress sneaked up behind me and poised her pencil over her pad. 'I'll have a beer and a sandwich. Ham. Plenty of mustard and anything else you can squeeze on.'

Ellen made a motion for another coffee and went back to the remains of the steak. I had my sandwich and beer without benefit of small talk until we were both finished and relaxing over a smoke.

She was nice to look at. Not because she was pretty all over, but because there was something alive about everything she did. Now she was propped in the corner of the booth with one leg half up on the bench grinning because the girl across the way was talking her head off to keep her partner's attention. The guy was trying, but his eyes kept sliding over to Ellen every few seconds.

I said, 'Give the kid a break, will you?'

She laughed lightly, way down in her throat, then leaned on the table and cupped her chin in her hands. 'I feel real wicked when I do things like that.'

'Your friends must love you.'

'Ooh,' her mouth made a pouty little circle, ' . . . they do. The men, I mean. Like you, Mike. You came in here especially to see me. You find me so attractive that you can't stay away.' She laughed again.

'Yeah,' I said. 'I even dream about you.'

'Like hell.'

'No kidding, I mean it.'

'I can picture you going out of your way for a woman. I'd give my right arm to hear you say that in a different tone of voice, though. There's something about you that fascinates me. Now that we have the love-making over with, what do I have that you want?'

I shouldn't have let my eyes do what they did.

'Besides that, I mean,' she said.

'Your boss has a certain file on Toady Link. I want a look at it.'

Her hands came together to cover her eyes. 'I should have known. I spend every waking hour making myself pretty for you, hoping that you'll pop in on me and when you do you ask me to climb up a cloud.'

'Well?'

'It's . . . well, it's almost impossible, Mike.'

'Why?'

Her eyes drifted away from mine reluctantly. 'Mike, I . . . '

'It isn't exactly secret information with me, Ellen. Pat told me about the D.A. getting ready to wrap Link up in a gray suit.'

'Then he should have told you that those files are locked and under guard. He doesn't trust anybody.'

'He trusts you.'

'And if I get caught doing a thing like that I'll not only lose this job and never be able to get another one, but I'll get a gray suit too. I don't like the color.' She reached out and plucked a Lucky from my pack and toyed with it before accepting the light I held out.

'I only want a look at it, kid. I don't want to steal the stuff and I won't pass the information along to anybody.'

'Please, Mike.'

I bent the match in my fingers and threw it on my plate. 'Okay, okay. Maybe I'm asking too damn much. You know what the score is as well as I do. Everything is so almighty secret with the D.A. that he doesn't know what he has himself. If he'd open up on what he knows he'd get a little more action out of the public. Right now he's trying to squelch the big-time gambling in the city and what happens? Everybody thinks it's funny. By God, if they had a look behind the scenes at what's been going on because of the same gambling they condone they'd think twice about it. They ought to take a look at a corpse with some holes punched in it. They ought to take a look at some widows crying at a funeral or a kid who was made an orphan crying for his father who's one of the corpses.'

The cigarette had burned down in her fingers without being touched, the long ash drooping wearily, ready to fall. Ellen's eyes were bright and smoky at the same time — languid eyes that hid the thoughts behind them.

'I'll get it for you, Mike.'

I waited and saw the richness of her lips grow richer with a smile.

'But it'll cost you,' she said.

I didn't get it for a second. 'Cost me what?'
'You.'

And that thing on my spine started crawling around again.

She reached out for my hand and covered it with hers. 'Mike . . . you're only incidental in the picture this time. It's the only way I'll ever be able to get you and it's worth it even if I have to buy you. But it's because of what you said that I'm doing it.'

There was something new about her, something I hadn't noticed before. I said, 'You'll never have to buy me, Ellen.'

It was a long minute before I could take my eyes off her face and get rid of the thing chasing up my back. The waitress dropped the check on the table and I put down a bill to cover them both and told her to keep the change. When we came out of the booth together the guy across the room looked at me enviously and Ellen longingly. His lunch date looked relieved.

We went back to the street and got as far as the bar on the corner. Ellen stopped me and nodded toward the door. 'Wait here for me. I can't go back upstairs or somebody's likely to think it peculiar.'

'Then how are you going to get the file out?'

'Patty — my short and stout roommate, if

196

you remember — is on this afternoon. I'll call her and have her take them when she leaves this evening. The way my luck runs, if I took them any earlier he'd pick just this day to want to see them.'

'That's smart,' I agreed. 'You know her well enough so there won't be a hitch, don't you?'

She made an impatient gesture with her hand. 'Patty owes me more favors than I can count. I've never asked her for anything before and I might as well start now. I'll be back in about ten minutes. Stay at the bar and wait for me, will you?'

'Sure. Then what?'

'Then you're going to take me to the races. Little Ellen cleans up today.'

I gave her my fattest smile and jingled a pocketful of coins. 'Pat told me about that. You're not going to be selfish about the thing, are you?'

'I think we're both going to have a profitable day, Mike,' she said impishly. She wasn't talking about money, either. I watched her cross the street and admired her legs until she was out of sight, then went into the bar and ordered a beer.

The television was tuned to the game in Brooklyn and the bets were flowing heavy and fast. I stayed out of the general argument and put my beer away. A tall skinny guy came in and stood next to me and did the same thing himself. A kid came in peddling papers and I bought one before the bartender told him to scram and quit annoying the customers.

But it didn't do any good. The guys on my left were arguing batting averages and one poked me to get my opinion. I said he was right and the other guy started jawing again and appealed to the tall skinny guy. He shrugged and tapped his ear, then took a hearing aid out of his shirt pocket and made indications that it wasn't working. He was lucky. They turned back to me again, spotted my paper and I handed it over to settle the argument. The one guy still wouldn't give in and I was about to become the backstop of a beautiful brawl.

But Ellen walked in just then and baseball switched to sex in whispers. I got her out so they could see her going away and really have something to talk about.

She cuddled up under my arm all the way back to the car and climbed in next to me looking cool and lovely and very pleased with herself. When I had about as much silence as I could take I asked, 'Did it work out?'

'Patty was glad to help out. She was a little nervous about it, but she said she'd wait until everyone had cleared out and put it in her brief case. She's taking some work home with her tonight and it shouldn't be hard to do at all.'

'Good girl.'

'Don't I deserve a kiss for effort?' She timed it as the light turned red.

Her mouth wasn't as cool as it looked. It was warm, a nice soft, live warmth with a delicate spicy sweetness that was excited into a heady wine by the tip of her tongue.

Then the car behind me blasted that the light was green again and I had to put my cup of wine down not fully tasted.

★ ★ ★

I hit three winners that afternoon. The two of us crowded the railing and yelled our heads off to push the nags home and when the last one slowed up in the stretch my heart slowed up with it because I had a parlay riding on his nose that was up in four figures. Fifty yards from the finish the jock laid on the whip and he crossed the line leading by a nostril.

Ellen shook my arm. 'You can open your eyes now. He won.'

I checked the board to make sure and there it was in big square print. I looked at the tickets that had gotten rolled up in the palm of my hand. 'I'll never do that again! How the hell do the guys who bet all their lives stand this stuff! You know what I just won?'

'About four thousand dollars, didn't you?'

'Yeah, and before this I worked for a living.' I smoothed out the pasteboards with my thumb and forefinger. 'You ought to be a millionaire, kitten.'

'I'm afraid not.'

'Why? You cleaned up today, didn't you?'

'Oh, I did very well.'

'So?'

'I don't like the color of the money.'

'It's green, isn't it? You got a better color than that?'

'I have a cleaner kind of green,' she said. Her body seemed to stiffen with a tension of some sort, drawing her hands into tight little fists. 'You know why I like to see the Scobie horses win. It's the only way and the best way I can get back at my father. Just because of me he tries to run them under other colors, but I always learn about it before the races. He pays me a living whether he wants to or not and it hurts him right where he should be hurt. However, it's still money that came from him, even if it was indirectly given, and I don't want any part of it.'

'Well, if you're going to throw it away, I'll take it.'

'It doesn't get thrown away. You'll see where it goes.'

We walked back to the ticket window and picked up a neat little pile of brand-new bills. They felt crisp as new lettuce and smelled even better. I folded mine into my wallet and stowed it away with a fond pat on the leather and started thinking of a lot of things that needed buying bad. Ellen threw hers in the wallet as if it happened every day. Thinking about it like that put a nasty buzz in my head.

'Why can't somebody follow you play for play? If anybody used your system and put a really big bundle down the odds would go skittering all over the place.'

She gave me a faint smile and took my hand going up the ramp to the gate. 'It doesn't work that way, Mike. All Scobie horses don't win by a long sight. It just happens that I know the ones that will win. It isn't that I'm a clever handicapper either. Dad has a trainer working for him who taught me all I know about horses. Whenever a winner is coming up I'm notified about it and place my bets.'

'That's all there is to it?'

'That's all. Once the papers did a piece about it and according to them I did all the picking and choosing. I let them get the idea just to infuriate the old boy. It worked out fine.'

'You're a screwball,' I said. She looked

hurt. 'But you're nice,' I added. She squeezed my arm and rubbed her face against my shoulder.

On the way back to the city the four G's in my pocket started burning through and it was all I could do to keep it there and let it burn. I wanted to stop off at the fanciest place we could find and celebrate with a drink, but Ellen shook her head and made me drive over to the East Side, pointing out the directions every few minutes.

Everything was going fine until we got stuck behind a truck and I had a chance to see where we were. Then everything wasn't so fine at all. There was a run-down bar with the glass cracked across the center facing the sidewalk. The door opened and a guy walked out, and before it shut again the familiarity of it came back with a rush and I could smell the rain and the beer-soaked sawdust and almost see a soggy little guy kissing his kid good-by.

My throat went dry all of a sudden and I breathed a curse before I wrenched the wheel and sent the heap screaming around the truck to get the hell out of the neighborhood.

We went straight ahead for six blocks, then Ellen said, 'Turn right at the next street and stop near the corner.'

I did as I was told and parked between a

beer truck and a dilapidated sedan. She opened the door and stepped out, looking back at me expectantly. 'Coming, Mike?'

I said okay and got out myself.

Then she walked me into a settlement house that was a resurrected barn or something. The whole business took about five minutes. I got introduced to a pair of nice old ladies, a clergyman and a cop who was having a cup of tea with the old ladies. Everybody was all smiles and joy and when Ellen gave one of the women a juicy wad of bills I thought they were going to cry.

Ellen, it seemed, practically supported the establishment.

I had a chance to look through the door at a mob of raggedy kids playing in the gym and I got rid of a quarter of the bundle of my wallet. I avoided a lot of thanks and got back to the car as fast as I could and looked at Ellen like I hadn't seen her before.

'Boy, am I a big-hearted slob,' I said.

She laughed once and leaned over and kissed me. This time I had a long sip of the wine before she took my cup away. 'It was worth it at that,' I mused.

'You know something, Mike . . . you're not such a heel. I mean, such a *very* big heel.'

I told her not to come to any hasty conclusions and backed the car out. It was a quarter to six and both of us were pretty hungry, so I drove up Broadway to a lot, left the car and walked back to a place that put out good food as well as good dinner music. While we waited for our orders Ellen bummed a nickel from me and went back to the phone booth to call Patty.

I could hardly wait for her to sit down again. 'Get her?'

'Uh-huh. Everything's all set. Most of the office crew have left already. She'll leave the stuff at the house for us.'

'Could we meet her somewhere? It would save time.'

'Too risky. I'd rather not. Patty seemed a little jittery on the phone and I doubt if she'd like it either. I only hope they can be put back as easily as they're taken out.'

'You won't have any trouble.' Maybe I didn't put enough conviction in my voice, because she just looked at me and bent down to her salad. I said, 'Now quit worrying. There won't be anything there that I couldn't find out if I had the time to look for it.'

'All right, Mike, it's just that I've never done anything like that before. I won't worry.'

She wrinkled her nose at me and dug into her supper.

It was eight-ten when we left the place. A thunderhead was moving up over Jersey blotting out the stars, replacing them with the dull glow of sheet lightning. I let Ellen pick up a couple quarts of beer while I rolled the car out and met her on the corner. She hopped in as the first sprinkle of rain tapped on the roof.

Sidewalks that were just damp a moment before took on a black sheen of water and drained it off into the gutter. Even with the wipers swatting furiously like a batter gone mad I could hardly see out. The car in front of me was a wavering shadow with one sick red eye, the neon signs and window fronts on either side just a ghostly parade of colors.

It was another night like that first one. The kind that made you run anywhere just to get away from it. You could see the vague shapes that were people huddled under marquees and jammed into doorways, the braver making the short dash to waiting cabs and wishing they hadn't.

By the time we reached Ellen's apartment it had slacked off into a steady downpour without the electrical fury that turned the night into a noisy, deafening day.

A doorman with an oversize umbrella led Ellen into the foyer and came back for me. Once we were out of it we could laugh. I was only making sloshing noises with my shoes but Ellen had gotten rained on down the back and her dress was plastered against her skin like a postage stamp. Going up in the elevator she stood with her back against the wall and edged sidewise after making me walk ahead of her.

I was going to knock first, but she poked her key in the lock and waved me inside.

'Nobody home?'

'Don't be silly. Tonight's date night . . . or haven't you noticed the couples arm in arm dashing for shelter.'

'Yeah.' I kicked my shoes off and carried them out to the kitchen. Ellen dumped the beer on the table and showed me where the glasses were.

'Pour me, Mike. I'll be back as soon as I get these wet things off.'

'Hurry up.'

She grinned at me and waltzed out while I was uncorking the bottles. I just finished topping the glasses off when she waltzed right back in again wrapped up in a huge terrycloth bathrobe, rubbing the rain out of her hair with a towel.

I handed her a glass and we clinked them in a toast we didn't speak. I drank without taking my eyes from hers, watching the deep blue swirl into a smoky gray that seemed to come up from the depths of a fire.

It got to be a little more than I could take.

She knew it when I said, 'Let's look at the files, Ellen.'

'All right.' She tucked the bottle under her arm and I trailed after her into the living room. A large console set took up a corner of the room and she pulled it away from the wall and worked her hand into the opening.

'Your private safe?'

'For intimate letters, precious nylons and anything else a nosy cleaning woman might take home with her.'

She pulled out another of those manila folders held together with a thick rubber band and handed it to me. My hand started to shake when I worked the band off it. The thing snapped and flew across the room.

I took it sitting down. I reached in and pulled out a stack of official reports, four photographs and more affidavits than I could count. I spread them out across the coffee table and scanned them to see what I could pick up, laying the discards on top of the empty folder. When I tried to do it carefully I got impatient, and when I went faster I got clumsy and knocked the whole batch on the floor. Ellen picked them up and sorted them out again and I went on from there.

I was cursing myself and the whole damn

mess long before I was finished because it was ending in a blank, a goddamn stone wall with nothing there but a fat ha-ha and to hell with you, bub. My hand went out of its own accord and spilled everything all across the room while Ellen let out a little scream and stepped back with her hand to her mouth.

'Mike!'

'I'm sorry, kid. It's a dud. Goddamn it, there's not a thing in there!'

'Oh, Mike . . . it can't be! The D.A. has been working on that a month!'

'Sure, trying to tangle Link up in that lousy gambling probe of his. So he proves he's a bookie. Hell, anybody can tell you that. All he had to do was go in and lay a bet with the guy himself. I'll say he's worked a month on it. Link doesn't stand a chance of getting out of this little web, but for all the time he'll draw for it, it will be worth it.'

I scooped up a couple of the reports and slammed them with my fingers. 'Look at this stuff. Two official reports that give any kind of background on the guy at all and those were turned in while Roberts was the D.A. What was going on in all the years until a month ago?'

Ellen glanced at the reports curiously and took them out of my hand, tapping the rubber-stamped number in the upper right-hand corner with her finger. 'This is a code number, Mike. These reports are part of a series.'

'Where are the rest of them then?'

'Either in the archives or destroyed. I won't say so for certain, but it's more likely that they were discarded. I've been with the department long enough to have seen more than one new office holder make a clean sweep of everything including what was in the files.'

'Damn!'

'I'll check on it the first thing in the morning, Mike. There's a possibility that they're stored away someplace.'

'Nuts on tomorrow morning. There isn't that much time to waste. There has to be another way.'

She folded the sheets up carefully, running her nail along the edges. 'I can't think of anything else unless you want to contact Roberts. He might remember something about the man.'

'That's an idea. Where does he live?'

'I don't know . . . but I can find out.' She looked at me pensively. 'Does it have to be tonight?'

'Tonight.'

I caught up with her before she reached the

phone. I put my arms around her and breathed the fragrance that was her hair. 'I'm sorry, kitten.'

Ellen let her head fall back on my shoulder and looked up at me. 'It's all right, Mike, I understand.'

She had to make three separate calls to locate Roberts' number. It was an address in Flushing and when she had it she handed me the phone to do the calling. It was a toll call, so I put it through the operator and listened to it ring on the other end. When I was about ready to hang up a woman came on and said, 'Hello, this is Mrs. Roberts.'

'Can I speak to Mr. Roberts, please?'

'I'm sorry, but he isn't home right now. Can I take a message?'

Somebody had bottled up all my luck and thrown it down the drain. I said, 'No, but can you tell me when he'll be back?'

'Not until tomorrow sometime. I expect him about noon.'

'Well, thanks. I'll call him then. 'By.'

I tried not to slam the receiver back in its cradle. I tried to sit on myself to keep from exploding and if it hadn't been for Ellen chuckling to herself from the depths of the couch I would have kicked something across the room. I spun around to tell her to shut up, but when a woman looks at you the way she was doing you don't say anything at all. You just stand there and look back because a toast-colored body that is all soft, molded curves and smooth hollows makes a picture to take your breath away, especially when it is framed against the thick texture of white terrycloth.

She laughed again and said, 'You're trapped, Mike.'

I wanted to tell her that I wasn't trapped at all, but there wasn't any room for words in my throat. I walked across the room and stood there staring at her, watching her come up off the couch into my arms to prove that she was real and not just a picture after all.

The cup was full this time, the wine mellow and sweet, and she was writhing in my arms fighting to breathe, yet not wanting me to stop holding her. I heard her say, 'Mike . . . I'm sorry you're trapped, but I'm glad . . . glad.' And I kissed her mouth shut again letting the rain slashing against the window pitch the tempo, hearing it rise and rise in a crescendo of fury, shrieking at me because the minutes were things not to be wasted.

It took all I had to shove her away. 'Texas gal, don't make it rough for me. Not now.'

She opened her eyes slowly, her fingers kneading my back. 'I can't even buy you, can I?'

'You know better than that, sugar. Let me finish what I have to do first.'

'If I let you get away you'll never come back, Mike. There are too many others waiting for you. Every week, every month there will be someone new.'

'You know too much.'

'I know I'm a Texas gal who likes a Texas man.'

My grin was a little flat. 'I'm a city boy, kid.'

'An accident of birth. Everything else about you is Texas. Even a woman doesn't come first with you.'

She stretched up on her toes, not far because she didn't have to go far, and kissed me lightly. 'Sometimes Texas men do come back. That's why there are always more Texas men.' She smiled.

'Don't forget to take those files in,' I reminded her. Then there was nothing more to say.

I went back to the rain and the night, looking up just once to see her silhouetted against the window waving to me. She didn't see me, but I waved back to her. She would have liked it if she'd known what I was thinking.

On the way back I stopped off for a drink and a sandwich and tried to think it out. I wanted to be sure of what I was doing before I stuck my neck out. I spent an hour going over the whole thing, tying it into Toady Link and no matter how I looked at it the picture was complete.

At least I tried to tell myself that it was.

I said it over and over to myself the same way I told Pat, but I couldn't get it out of my mind that some place something didn't fit. It was only a little thing, but it's the little things that hold bigger things together. I sat there and told myself that it was Toady who drove the murder car and Toady who gave the orders to Arnold Basil because he couldn't afford to trust anybody else to do the job right. I told myself that it was Toady who engineered Hooker's death and tried to engineer mine.

Yet the more I told myself the more that little voice inside my head would laugh and poke its finger into some forgotten recess and try to jar loose one face that would make me see what the picture was really like.

I gave up in disgust, paid my bill and walked out.

I walked right into trouble, too. Pat was slouched up against the wall outside my apartment with the friendliness gone completely from his face.

He didn't even give me a chance to say

hello. He held out his hand with an abruptness I wasn't used to. 'Let's have your gun, Mike.'

I didn't argue with him. He packed it open, checked the chamber and the slide, then smelled the barrel.

'You already know when I shot it last,' I said.

'I do?' It didn't sound like a question at all.

It started down low around my belly, that squeamish feeling when something is right there ready to pop in your face. 'Quit being a jerk. What's the act for?'

He came away from the door frame with a scowl. 'Goddamn it, Mike, play it straight if you have to play it at all!'

I said a couple of words.

'You've had it, Mike,' he told me. He put it flat and simple as if I knew just what he meant.

'You could tell me about it.'

'Look, Mike, I'm a cop. You were my friend and all that, but I'm not getting down on my knees to anybody. I did everything but threaten you to lay off and what happened? You did it your way anyhow. It doesn't go, feller. It's finished, washed up. I hated to see it happen, but it was just a matter of time. I thought you were smart enough to understand. I was wrong.'

'That isn't telling me about it.'

'Cut it, Mike. Toady's dead. He was shot with a .45,' he said.

'And I'm tagged.'

'That's right,' Pat nodded. 'You're tagged.'

8

Sometimes you get mad and sometimes you don't. If there was any of that crazy anger in me it had all been drained out up there in Ellen's apartment. Now it's making sense, I thought. Now it's where it should be.

Pat dropped my gun in his pocket. 'Let's go, Mike.'

So I went as far as the front door and watched the rain wash through under the sill. Before Pat opened the door I said, 'You're sure about this, aren't you?'

He *was* sure. Two minutes ago he had been as sure of it as the day he was born and now he wasn't sure of it at all. His mouth hardened into a gash that pushed his eyes halfway shut with some uncontrollable emotion until they seemed to focus on something right behind me.

I didn't want him to answer me before he knew. 'I didn't kill him, Pat. I was hoping I would, but somebody beat me to it.'

'The M.E. sets the time of death around four o'clock last night.' His voice asked for an explanation.

I said, 'You should have told me, Pat. I was

real busy then. Real busy.'

His hand came away from the door. 'You mean you can prove it?'

'I mean just that.'

'Mike . . . if you're lying . . . '

'I've never been that stupid. You ought to know that.'

'I ought to know a lot of things. I ought to know where you were every minute of last night.'

'You know how to find out.'

'Show me.'

I didn't like the way he was looking at me at all. Maybe I'm not so good at lying any more, and I was lying my head off. Last night I was busy as hell sleeping and there wasn't one single way I could prove it. If I tried to tell him the truth it would take a month to talk my way clear.

I said, 'Come on,' and headed for the phone in the lobby. I shoved a dime in the slot and dialed a number, hoping that I could put enough across with a few words to say what I wanted. He stood right there at my elbow ready to take the phone away as soon as I got my party and ask the question himself.

I couldn't mistake her voice. It was like seeing her again with the lava green of her dress flowing from her waist.

'This is Mike, Marsha. A policeman . . . wants to ask you something. Mind?'

That was as far as I could get. Pat had the phone while she was still trying to figure it out. He gave me a hard smile and turned to the phone. 'Captain Chambers speaking. I understand you can account for Mr. Hammer's whereabouts last night. Is that correct?'

Her voice was music pouring out of the receiver. Pat glanced at me sharply, curiously, then muttered his thanks and hung up. He still didn't quite know what to make of it. 'So you spent the night with the lady.'

I said a beautiful thanks to Marsha under my breath. 'That's not for publication, Pat.'

'You better stop tomcatting around when Velda gets back, friend.'

'It makes a good alibi.'

'Yeah, I'd like to see the guy who'd sooner kill Toady than sleep with a chick like that. Okay, Mike, you got yourself an alibi. I have a screwy notion that I shouldn't believe it, but Link isn't Decker and if you're in this there'll be hell to pay and I'll find out about it soon enough.'

I handed him a butt and flipped a light with my thumbnail. 'Can I hear about the deal or is it secret info like everything else?'

'There's not much to it. Somebody walked in and killed him.'

'Just like that?'

'He was in bed asleep. He got it right through the head and whoever killed him went through the place like a cyclone. I'm going back there now if you want to come along.'

'Blue boy there?'

'The D.A. doesn't know about it yet. He's out with the vice squad again,' Pat said tiredly.

'You checked the bullet, didn't you?'

Pat squirmed a little. 'I didn't wait for the report. I was so goddamned positive it was you that I came right over. Besides, you could have switched barrels if you felt like it. I've seen the extras you have.'

'Thanks. I'm a real great guy.'

'Quit rubbing it in.'

'Who found the body?'

'As far as we know, the police were the first on the scene. A telegraph boy with a message for Toady saw the door open and went to shut it. Enough stuff was kicked around inside to give him the idea there was a robbery. He was sure of it when he rang the bell and nobody answered. He called the police and they found the body.'

'Got any idea what they were looking for . . . or if they found it?'

Pat threw the butt at the floor. 'No. Come

on, take a look at it yourself. Maybe it'll make you feel better.'

What was left of Toady wouldn't make anybody feel better. Death had taken the roundness from his body and made an oblong slab of it. He lay there on his back with his eyes closed and his mouth open, a huge, fat frog as unlovely dead as he was alive. Right in the center of his forehead was the hole. It was a purplish-black hole with scorched edges flecked by powder burns. Whoever held the gun held it mighty close. If there was a back to his head it was smashed into the pillow.

Outside on the street a couple more prowl cars screamed to a stop and feet came pounding into the house. A lone newshawk was sounding off about the rights of the press and being told to shut up. Pat left me there with a plain-clothesman while he got things organized and started the cops going through the rooms in a methodical search for anything that might be a lead.

When I had enough of Toady I went downstairs and followed Pat around, watching him paw through the wreckage of the living room. 'Somebody didn't make a lot of noise, did they?'

I got a sharp grin. 'Brother, this place was really searched.'

I picked up a maple armchair and looked at

it closely. There wasn't a scratch on it. There weren't any scratches on anything for that matter. For all the jumble that it seemed to be, the room had been carefully and methodically torn apart and the pieces put down nice and gently. You could even see some order in the way it was done. The slits in the seat cushions were evenly cut all in the same place. Anything that could be unscrewed or pulled out was unscrewed or pulled out. Books were scattered all over the floor, some with the back linings ripped right out of them.

Pat had one in his hand and waved it at me. 'It wasn't very big if they went looking for it here.'

I thought I said something to myself, but I said it out loud and Pat's head swiveled around at me. 'What?'

I didn't tell him the second time. I shook my head, knowing the leer I was wearing had pulled my face out of shape and if Pat had good eyes he could read what I was thinking without looking any farther than my eyes. He might have done it if a cop hadn't come up to tell him about the junk in the basement, and he left me standing in the middle of the room right where Toady had made me stand, only this time I wasn't after Toady's hide any more because he wasn't the end at all.

Another cop came in looking for Pat. I told him he was downstairs and would be right back. The cop spread out the stuff in his hand and flashed it at me. 'Look at the pin-ups I found.' He gave a short laugh. 'I guess he didn't go for this new stuff. Don't blame him. I like the pre-war crop better myself.'

'Let's see them.'

He handed them over to me as he looked through them.

Half of them were regular studio stills and the rest were enlargements of snapshots taken during stage shows. Every one of them was personally autographed to Charlie Fallon with love and sometimes kisses from some of the biggest stars in Hollywood.

When he was done with the pictuers the cop let me look at a couple of loose-leaf pads that had scrawled notations of appointments to be made for more photos of more lovelies and the list of private phone numbers he had accumulated would have made any Broadway columnist drool. Every so often there was a reminder after a name . . . *introduction to F.*

And there it was again. Fallon. No matter where I turned the name came up. Fallon, Fallon, Fallon. Arnold Basil was an old Fallon boy. All the dames knew Fallon, Toady had some connection with Fallon. Damn it, the guy was supposed to be dead!

I didn't wait for Pat to come back. I told the cop to tell him I'd left and would call up tomorrow. Before I got to the door the reporter who was trying to make the most of being first on the scene tried to corner me for a story and I shook my head no. He dropped me for the cop and got the same story.

Something had gentled the rain, taking the madness out of it. The curious were there in a tight knot at the gate shrinking together under umbrellas and raincoats to gape at the death place and speculate among themselves. I managed to push myself through to the outer fringes of the crowd with about a minute to spare. Just as I broke clear the D.A. came in from the other side with his boys doing the blocking. His face was blacker than the night itself and I knew right away that somebody had crossed him up on another deal. His boat still had a hole in the bottom and if it leaked any more he was going to get swamped.

If it hadn't been so late I would have called Marsha to kiss her hand for pulling me out of a spot, but tonight I didn't want to see anybody or speak to anybody. I wanted to stretch out in bed and think. I wanted to start at the beginning and chew my way through it slowly until I found the tough hunk that didn't chew so easily and put it through the grinder.

Then I'd have my killer.

Two blocks down a hackie tooted his horn at me and I ran for the door he held open. I gave him my address and settled back into the seat. The guy was one of those Dodger fans who couldn't keep quiet about how the bums were doing and talked my ear off until I climbed out in front of my apartment and handed over a couple of bucks.

I got all the way upstairs and there they were again. Two of them this time. One was big as a house and the other wasn't much smaller. The little guy closed in with a badge flashing in his palm while the other one stood by ready to take me if I didn't act right. Both of them kept one hand in their pockets just to let me know that the play was theirs all the way.

The guy said, 'Police, buddy,' and stowed the badge back in his pants.

'What do you want with me?'

'You'll find out. Get moving.'

The other one said, 'Wait a minute,' and yanked my gun out of the holster. Under his flat smile his teeth were yellowed from too much smoking. 'You're supposed to have a bad temper. Guns and guys with bad tempers don't go together.'

'Neither do badges without those leather wallets a cop keeps them in.'

I caught the quick look that passed between them, but I caught the nose of a gun in my back at the same time. The big guy smiled again. 'Wise guy. You wanta do it the hard way.'

'That rod'll make a big boom in here. A nice quiet joint like this people'll want to know what all the noise is about.'

The gun pressed in a little deeper. 'Maybe. You won't hear it, buddy. Move.'

Those two were real pros. Not the kind of hoods who pick up some extra change with nickel-plated rods either. These were delivery boys, the real McCoy. They knew just where to stand so I couldn't move in and just how to look so nobody would get the pitch. One had a pint bottle of whisky outlined in his inside jacket pocket to pour over me so I'd smell like a drunk in case they had to carry me out. And they had that look. Somebody had given the orders to bump me fast if I tried to get rough.

That look was enough for me. Besides, I was curious myself.

We got downstairs and big boy said, 'Where's your car?'

I pointed it out. He snapped his fingers for my keys and got them. The other one did something with his hand and a car down the block pulled away from the curb and shot by us without looking over.

It didn't take much to see what was going to happen. I was getting a one-way ride in my own car. After I was delivered someplace first. I wasn't supposed to know about it. I was supposed to be a real good boy and act nice and polite so they wouldn't have any trouble with me. I was supposed to be a goddamn fool and let myself get killed with no fuss at all while a couple of pros congratulated themselves on their technique.

My head started banging with that insane music that was all kettle-drums and shrill flutes blended together in wild discord until my hands shook with the madness of it. What kind of a simple jerk did they take me for? Maybe they thought they were the only ones who were pros in this game. Maybe they thought this had never happened before and if it had I wouldn't be ready for it to happen again.

By God, if they played this the way a pro would play it they were going to get one hell of a jolt. I had a .32 hammerless automatic in a boot between the seat and the door right where I could get at it if I had to.

They played it that way too. Big boy said, 'You drive, shamus. Take it nice and easy or we'll take it for you.' He held the door open so I could get in and was right there beside me when I slid under the wheel. He didn't crowd me. Not him, he was an old-timer. He kept plenty of room between us, sitting jammed into the corner with his arm on the sill. His other arm was in his lap pointing my own gun at me. The little guy didn't say much. He climbed in back and leaned on the seat behind my head like he was talking to me confidentially. But it was the gun he had pressed against my neck that was doing all the talking.

We took a long ride that night. We were three happy people taking a cruise out to the shore. To keep everybody happy I switched on the radio and picked up a disk jockey and made a habit of lighting my cigarettes from the dashboard lighter so they'd get used to seeing my arms move around.

My pal beside me was calling the turns and someplace before we came to Islip he said, 'Slow down.' Up ahead a macadam road intersected the highway. 'Go right until I tell you to turn.'

I swung around the corner and followed the black strip of road. It lasted a half-mile, butting against an oiled-top dirt road that went the rest of the way. We made a few more turns after that and I started to smell the ocean coming in strong with the wind. The houses had thinned out until they were only black shapes on spindly legs every quarter-mile or so. The road curved gently away from the shore line, threading its way through the knee-high sawgrass that bent with the breeze and whisked against the fender of the car with an insidious hissing sound.

Nobody had to tell me to stop. I saw the shaded lights of the house and the bulk of the sedan against its side and I eased on the brakes. Big boy looked pleased with himself and the pressure of the gun on my neck relaxed. The guy behind me got out and stood by the door while the other one tucked the keys in his pocket and came up stepping on my shadow.

'You got the idea good,' he told me. 'Let's keep it that way. Inside and take it slow.'

I practically crawled. The boys stayed behind me and to the right and left, beautiful spots in case I tried to run for it. Either one of them could have cut me down before I got two feet. I picked the last smoke out of my pack and dropped the empty wrapper. Shortie was even smart enough to pick that up. I didn't have a match and nobody offered me one, so I let it droop there between my lips. It was a little too soon to start worrying. This wasn't the time nor the place. A body doesn't hide so easy and neither does a car. When we went we'd go together. I could almost draw a picture of the way it would happen.

The door opened and the guy was a thin dark shadow against the light. I said, 'Hello, scrimey.'

I should have kept my mouth shut. Lou Grindle backhanded me across the mouth so that my teeth went right through my lips. Two guns hit me in the spine at the same time ramming me right into him and I couldn't have gotten away with it in a million years but I tried anyway. I hooked him down as low as I could then felt my knuckles rip open when I got him in the mouth.

Neither of the guys behind me dared risk a shot, but they did just as well. One of them brought a gun barrel around as hard as he could. There wasn't even any pain to it, just a loud click that grew into a thunderous wave of sound that threw me flat on the floor and rolled over me.

The pain didn't come until later. It wasn't there in my head where I thought it would be. It was all over, a hundred agonizing points of torture where the toe of a shoe had ripped through my clothes and torn into the skin. Something dripped slowly and steadily like a leaky faucet. Every movement sent the pain shooting up from my feet and if screaming wouldn't have only made it worse I would have screamed. I got one eye open. The other was covered by a puffy mass of flesh on my cheekbone that kept it shut.

Somebody said, 'He's awake.'

'He'll get it worse this time.'

'I'll tell you when.' The voice was so decisive that nobody gave it to me worse.

I managed to focus the one good eye then. It was pointed at the floor looking at my feet. They were together at attention strapped to the rungs of a chair. My arms weren't there at all so I guess that they were tied someplace behind the same chair. And the drip wasn't from the faucet at all.

It was from something on my face that used to be a nose.

Somehow, I dragged myself straight up. It didn't hurt so bad then. When the fuzziness went away I squinted my one good eye against the light and saw them sitting around like vultures waiting for the victim to die. The two boys with the rods over by the door and Lou Grindle holding a bloody towel to his mouth.

And Ed Teen perched on the edge of the leather armchair with his chin propped on a cane. He still looked like a banker, even to the gray homburg.

He stared at me very thoughtfully for a minute. 'Feel pretty bad?'

'Guess.' The one word almost choked me.

'It wasn't necessary, you know. We just wanted to talk to you. Everything would have been quite friendly.' He smiled. 'Now we have to tie you down until we're finished talking.'

Lou threw the towel at me. 'Christ, quit stalling around with him. I'll make him talk in a hurry.'

'Shut up.' Ed didn't even stop smiling. 'You're lucky I'm here. Lou is rather impulsive.'

I didn't answer him.

He said, 'It was too bad you had to kill Toady, Mr. Hammer. He was very valuable to me.'

I got the words out. 'You're nuts.'

He pushed himself up off the cane and leaned back in the chair. 'Don't bother with explanations. I'm not the police. If you killed him that's your business. What I want is what's my business. Where is it?'

My lips felt too thick to put any conviction in my voice. 'I don't know what the hell you're talking about.'

'Remind him, Lou.'

Then he sat back chewing on a cigar and watched it. Lou didn't use his foot this time. The wet towel around his fist was enough. He was good at the job, but I had taken so much the first time that even the half-consciousness I had left went fast.

I tried to stay that way and couldn't. My head twitched and Teen said metallically, 'Now do you remember?'

I only had to shake my head once and that fist clubbed it again. It went on and on and on until there was no pain at all and I could laugh when he talked to me and try to smile when the delivery boy in the corner got sick and turned his head away to puke.

Ed rapped the cane on the floor. 'Enough. That's enough. He can't feel it any more. Let him sit and think about it a few minutes.'

Lou was glad to do that. He was breathing hard through his mouth and his chin was covered with blood. He went over and sat down at the table to massage his hand. Lou was very happy.

The cane kept up a rhythm on the floor. 'This is only the beginning you know. There's absolutely no necessity for it.'

I managed to say, 'I didn't . . . kill Link.'

'It doesn't matter whether you did or not. I want what you took from his apartment.'

Lou started to cough and spat blood on the floor. He gagged, put his hand to his mouth and pushed a couple of teeth into his palm with his tongue. When he brought his head up his eyes bored into mine like deadly little black bullets. 'I'm going to kill that son-of-a-bitch!'

'You sit there and shut up. You'll do what I say.'

He was on his feet with his hands apart fighting to keep himself from tearing Teen's throat out with his fingers. Ed wasn't so easy to scare. The snub-nosed gun in his hand said so.

Lou's face was livid with rage. 'Damn you anyway. Damn you and Fallon and Link and the whole stinking mess of you!'

'You're lisping, Lou. Sit down.' Lou sat down and stared at his teeth some more. He was proud of those teeth. They were so nice and shiny.

They lay where they were dropped on the table and seemed to fascinate him. He kept feeling his gums as though he couldn't believe it, cursing his heart out in black rage. Ed's gun never left him for a second. Right then Lou was in a killing rage and ready to take it out on anybody.

He kept saying over and over, 'Goddamn every one of 'em! Goddamn 'em all!' His mouth drew back baring the gap in his teeth and he slammed the table with his fist. 'Goddamn, this wouldn't've happened if you'd let me do it my way! I would've killed

Fallon and that lousy whore he kept and Link and this wouldn't've happened!' I got the eyes this time. They came around slow and evilly. 'I'll kill you for it, too.'

'You'll get new teeth, Lou,' Ed said pleasantly. Everything he said was pleasant.

Grindle gagged again and walked out of the room. Water started to run in a bowl somewhere and he made sloshing noises as he washed out his mouth. Ed smiled gently. 'You hit him where he hurts the most ... in his vanity.'

'Where does it hurt you the most, Ed?'

'A lot of people would like to know that.'

'I know.' I tried to grin at him. My face wouldn't wrinkle. 'It's going to hurt you in two places. Especially when they shave the hair off your head and leg.'

'I think,' he told me, 'that when Lou comes back I'll let him do you up right.'

'You mean ... like old times when Fallon pulled the strings ... with cigar butts and pliers?'

His nostrils flared briefly. 'If you have to say something at all, tell me where it is.'

'Where what is?'

The water was still running inside. Without turning his head Ed called, 'Johnny. Give it to him.'

The big guy came over. Under his shirt his

234

stomach made peculiar rolling motions. His techniques stunk. His fist made a solid chunk against my chin and I went out like a light. They poured cold water over me so I'd wake up and watch it happen all over again.

It started to get longer between rounds. I would come only partially back out of that jet-black land of nowhere and hang there limply. The big guy's voice was a hoarse croak. 'He's done, Ed. I don't think he knows what you're talking about.'

'He knows.' His cane tapped the floor again. 'Give him another dousing.'

I got the water treatment again. It washed the blood out of my eyes so I could see again and the shock of it cleared my mind enough to think.

Ed knew when I was awake. He had a cigar lit and gazed at the cherry-red end of it speculatively. 'You can hear me?'

I nodded that I could.

'Then understand something. I shall ask you just once more. Remember this, if you're dead you can't use what you have.'

'Tell . . . me what the hell . . . you want.'

Only for a second did his eyes go to the pair leaning on the window sill. If they weren't there I would have had it, but whatever I was supposed to know was too much for their big ears. 'You know very well what I mean. You've been trouble from the very first moment. I know you too well, Mr. Hammer. You're only a private investigator, but you've killed people before. In your own way you're quite as ruthless as I am . . . but not quite as smart. That's why I'm sitting here and you're sitting there. Keep what you have. I've no doubt that it's hidden some place you alone can get it, and after you're dead nobody else will find it. Not in my time at least. Johnny . . . go see what's keeping Lou.'

The guy walked inside and came right back. 'He's lying down. He puked on the bed.'

'Let him stay there then. Untie this man.'

The straps came off my hands and legs, but I couldn't get up. They let me sit there until the circulation came back, and with it the flame that licked at my body. When I could move Johnny hauled me to my feet.

'What'll I do with him, Ed?'

'That's entirely up to you. Martin, drive me back to the city. I've had enough of this.'

The little guy saluted with his two fingers and waited until Ed had picked up his topper. He made a beautiful flunky. He opened the door and probably even helped him down the steps. I heard the car purr into life and drag back on the road.

Johnny let go my coat collar and jammed the gun in my back. 'You heard what the man said.' He started me off with a push to the door.

The long walk. The last ride. The boys call it a lot of things. You sit there in the car with your head spinning around and around thinking of all the ways to get out and every time you think of one there's a gun staring you in the face. You sweat and try to swallow. All your joints feel shaky and though you want a cigarette more than anything in the world you know you'll never be able to hold one in your mouth. You sweat some more. Your mouth wants to scream for help when you see somebody walking along the street. A gun pokes you to keep quiet. There's a cop on the corner under the arc light. A prayer gets stuck in your throat. He'll recognize them . . . he'll see the glint of their guns . . . his hand will go up and stop the car and you'll be safe. But he looks the other way when the car passes by and you wonder what happened to your prayer. Then you stop sweating because your body is dried out and your tongue is a thick rasp working across your lips. You think of a lot of things, but mostly you think of how fast you're going to stop living.

I remembered how I thought of all those things the first time. Now it was different. I was beat to hell and too far gone to fight. I had the strength to drive and that was all. Johnny sat there in his corner watching me and he still had my own gun.

This time I wanted a cigarette and he gave me one. I used the dash lighter again. I finished that and he gave me another while he laughed at the way my hand shook when I tried to get it in my mouth. He laughed at the way I kept rolling the window up first to get warm then down to get cooled off. He laughed at the way I made the turns he told me to take, creeping around them so I'd have seconds longer to live.

When he told me to stop he laughed again because my arms seemed to relax and hang limply at my sides.

He took his eyes off me for one second while he searched for the door handle and he never laughed again.

I shot him through the head five times with the .32 I had pulled out of the boot and kicked him out in the road after I took my gun from his hand. When I backed around the lights of the car swept over him in time to catch one final involuntary twitch and Johnny was getting his first taste of hell.

The gray haze of morning was beginning to show in the sky behind me when I reached the shack again. It was barely enough to show me the road through the grass and outline the car against the house. I killed the engine, backed into the sand and opened the door.

This time the car wasn't any big sedan. It was the same coupé that had brought the boys to get me then pulled away at their signal. I knew who was in there. The little guy Ed called Martin had come back for Lou.

I made a circuit of the house and stopped under the bedroom window. Lou was cursing the guy, telling him to stop shaking him. I straightened up to look in, but there was no light and the curtains made an effective blind. Somebody started running the water and there was more talk I couldn't catch. It faded away until it was in the back of the house and I grabbed at the chance.

I hugged the wall climbing up on the porch, squeezing myself into the shadows. The wood had rotted too soft to have any squeak left in it but I wasn't taking any chances. I got down low with the gun in one hand and reached up for the knob with the other.

Somebody had oiled it not so long ago. It turned noiselessly and I gave the door a shove. The guy with the oilcan was nice people. He had oiled the hinges too.

My breath stuck in my lungs until I was inside with the door closed behind me, then I let it out in a low hiss and tried to breathe normally. The blood was pounding through my body making noise enough to be heard throughout the house. My legs wanted to drag me down instead of pushing me forward and the .45 became too heavy to hold steadily.

I had to fight against the letdown that was sweeping over my body. It couldn't come now! The answer was there in Lou's bloody mouth waiting to be squeezed out. I started to weave a little bit and reached out to grab the wall and hang on. My hand hit the door of a closet and slammed it shut.

Silence.

A cold, black silence.

A tentative voice calling, 'Johnny?'

I couldn't fake an answer. My knees started to go.

Again, 'Johnny, damn it!'

Lou cursed and a tongue of flame lashed out of a doorway.

There was no faking about the way I hit the floor. Lou had heard too many men fall like that before. It was real, but only because my legs wouldn't hold me any longer. I still had the .45 in my mitt and I let the feet come my way just so far before I squeezed the trigger.

The blasting roar of the gun echoed and shattered on the walls. I rolled until I hit something and stopped, my free hand clawing my one good eye to keep it open. The remnants of a scream were still in the air and the pin points of light were two guns punching holes in the woodwork searching for me. I got my hand around the leg of an end table and let it go. The thing bounced on the floor and split under the impact of the bullets. They were shouting at each other now, calling each other fools for wasting shots. So they stopped wasting shots. They thought I was hit and waited me out.

Somebody was breathing awfully funny. It made a peculiar racket when you took time to listen to it. I could hear them changing position, getting set. I went as quietly as I could and changed position myself.

It had to come soon. A few more minutes and the light would come through the curtains and they could see better than I could. It went on like a kid's game, that incessant crawling, the fear that you'd be caught, the deliberate motions of stealth that were so hard to make.

The funny breathing was real close. I could reach out and touch it. It was there on the other side of the chair. It heard me too, but it didn't change its tone. From across the room came the slightest sound and a whisper from only five feet away. 'He's over there.'

Orange flame streaked across the room and the sound jolted my ears even before the scream and the hoarse curse. The answer was two shots that pounded into the floor and a heavy thud as a body toppled over.

Lou's voice said, 'I got the son-of-a-bitch.' He still lisped.

He moved out past the chair and I saw him framed in the window.

I said, 'You got your own man, Lou.'

Lou did too many things at once. He tried to drop, shoot and curse me at the same time. He got two of them done. He dropped because I shot him. His gun went off because a dead hand pulled the trigger. He didn't curse because my bullet went up through his mouth into his brain taking the big answer with it.

There was nothing left there for me at all.

Outside the gray haze had brightened into morning, very early morning. It took me a long time to get back to the car, and much, much longer to get to the highway.

Fate allowed me a little bit of luck. It gave me a hitchhiker stranded between towns. I picked him up and told him I'd been in a fight and that he could drive.

The hiker was glad to. He felt sorry for me. I felt sorry for myself too.

9

We were on a side street just off Ninth
Avenue and the guy beside me was pulling
my arm to wake me up. He tugged and
twisted until I thought the damn thing would
come off. I got the one eye open and looked
at him.

'You sure were dead to the world, brother.
Took me a half-hour to get you out of it.'

'What time is it?'

'Eight-thirty. Feel pretty rotten?'

'Lousy.'

'Want me to call somebody?'

'No.'

'Well, look, I have to catch a bus. You think
you're going to be all right? If you're not I'll
stick around awhile.'

'Thanks . . . I'll make out.'

'Okay, it's up to you. Sure appreciate the
ride. Wish I could do something for you.'

'You can. Go get me a pack of butts.
Luckies.'

He waved away the quarter I handed him
and walked down to the corner to the
newsstand. He came back with the pack
opened, stuck one in my mouth and lit it.

'You take care now. Better go home and sleep it off.'

I said I would and sat there smoking the butt until a cop came along slapping tickets on car windows. I edged over behind the wheel, kicked the starter in and got out of there.

Traffic wasn't a problem like it usually was. I was glad to get behind a slow-paced truck and stay there. Every bone and muscle in my body ached and I couldn't have given the wheel a hard wrench if I wanted to. I got around the corner somehow and the truck crossed over to get in the lane going through the Holland Tunnel. I dropped out of position, squeezed through the intersection as the light changed and got on the street that led up to police headquarters.

Both sides of the street were lined with people going to work. They all seemed so happy. They walked alone or in couples, thousands of feet and legs making a blur of motion. I envied them the sleep they had had. I envied their normal unswollen faces. I envied a lot of things until I took time to think about it. At least I was alive. That was something.

The street in front of the red brick building was a parade ground of uniformed patrolmen. Some were walking off to their beats and others were climbing in squad cars. The plain-clothesmen went off in pairs, separating at the corner with loud so longs. Right in front of the main entrance three black sedans with official markings were drawn up at the curb with their drivers reading tabloids behind the wheel. Directly across from them a pair of squad cars pulled out and the tan coupé in front of me nosed into the space they left. I followed in behind him, did a better job of parking than he did and was up against the bumper of the car behind me so the guy would have room to maneuver.

I guess the jerk got his license wholesale. He tried to saw his way in without looking behind him and I had to lean on the horn to warn him off. Maybe I should have planted a red flag or something. He ignored the horn completely and slammed into me so hard I wrapped my chest around the wheel.

That did it. That was as much as I could take. I opened the door with my elbow and got out to give him hell. You'd think with all the cops around one of them would have jumped him, but that's how it goes. The guy was getting out of his heap with a startled apology written all over him. He took a look at my face and forgot what he was going to say. His mouth hung open and he just looked.

I said, 'You deaf or something? What the

devil do you think a horn's for?'

His mouth started to say something, but he was too confused to get it out. I took another good look at him and I could see why. He was the guy who stood next to me in the bar the afternoon before with the busted headset. He was making motions at his ears and tapping the microphone or whatever it was. I was too disgusted to pay any attention to him and waved him off. He still smacked the bumper twice again before he got himself parked.

This was starting off to be a beautiful day too.

When I got in the building I started to attract a little attention. A cop I know pretty well passed right by me with no more than a cursory glance. One asked me if I was there to register a complaint and looked surprised when I shook my head no. The place was a jumble of activity with men going in and out of the line-up room, getting their orders at the desk or scrambling to get off on a case.

Too much was popping in the morning to hope Pat would be in his office, so I waited my turn at the information desk and told the cop at the switchboard that I wanted to see Captain Chambers.

He said, 'Name?'

And I said, 'Hammer, Michael Hammer.'

Then his hand paused with the plug in it

and he said, 'Well, I'll be damned.'

He tried about ten extensions before he got Pat, said Yes, sir a few times and yanked the plug out. 'He'll be right down. Wait here for him.'

By the clock I waited exactly one minute and ten seconds. Pat came out of the elevator at a half-run and when he saw me his face did tricks until it settled down in a frown.

'What happened to you?'

'I got took, pal. Took good, too.'

He didn't ask me any more questions. He looked down at his shoes a second then put it to me hard and fast. 'You're under arrest, Mike.'

'What?'

'Come on upstairs.'

The elevator was waiting. We got on and went up. We got off at the right floor and I started to walk toward his office automatically, but he put out his hand and stopped me.

'This way, Mike.'

'Say, what's going on?'

He wouldn't look at me. 'We've had men covering your apartment, your office and all your known places of entertainment since six this morning. The D.A. has a warrant out for your arrest and there's not a damn thing you can do about it.'

'Sorry. I should have stayed home. What's the charge?'

We paused outside a stained-oak door. 'Guess.'

'I give up.'

'The D.A. looked for Link's personal file last night and found it missing. He was here when Ellen Scobie tried to put it back this morning. You have two girls on the carpet right this minute who are going to lose their jobs and probably have charges preferred against them too. You're going in there yourself and take one hell of a rap and this time there's no way out. You finished yourself, Mike. You'll never learn, but you're finished.'

I dropped my hands in my pockets and made like I was grinning at him.

'You're getting old, son. You're getting set in your ways. For the last two years all you've done is warn me about this, that, and the next thing. We used to play a pretty good game, you and me, now you're starting to play it cautious and for a cop who handles homicide that's no damn good at all.'

Then just for the hell of it that little finger that was probing my brain deliberately knocked a couple of pieces together that made lovely, beautiful sense and I remembered something Ellen had told me not so long ago. I twisted it around, revamped it a little and I was holding something the D.A. was going to pay for in a lot of pride. Yep, a whole lot of pride.

I reached for the knob myself. 'Let's go, chum. Me and the D.A. have some business to transact.'

'Wait a minute. What are you pulling?'

'I'm not pulling a thing, Pat. Not a thing. I'm just going to trade him a little bit.'

Everything was just like it was the last time. Almost.

There was the D.A. behind his desk with his boys on either side. There were the detectives in the background, the cop at the door, the little guy taking notes and me walking across the room.

Ellen and her roommate were the exceptions this time. They sat side by side in straight-back chairs at the side of the big desk and they were crying their eyes out.

If my face hadn't been what it was there would have been a formal announcement made. As it was, everybody gave me a kind of horrified stare and Ellen turned around in her seat. She stopped crying abruptly and put her hand to her mouth to stifle a scream.

I said, 'Take it easy, kid.'

Her teeth went into her lip and she buried her face in her hands.

The District Attorney was very sarcastic this time. 'Good morning, *Mister* Hammer.'

'I'm glad you remembered,' I told him.

Any other time his face would have changed color. Not now. He liked this cat-and-mouse stuff. He had waited a long time for it and now he was going to enjoy every minute of it while he had an audience to appreciate it. 'I suppose you know why you're here?' He leaned back in his chair and folded his arms across his chest. The two assistants did the same thing.

'I've heard about it.'

'Shall I read the charges?'

'Don't bother.' My legs were starting to go again. I pulled a chair across the floor and sat down. 'Start reading me off any time you feel like it,' I said. 'Get it all off your chest at once so you'll be able to listen to somebody else except your yes-men for a change.'

The two assistants came to indignant attention in their seats.

It was so funny I actually got a grin through.

The D.A. didn't think it was so funny. 'I don't intend to take any of your nonsense, *Mister* Hammer. I've had about all I can stand of it.'

'Okay, you know what you can do. Charge me with conspiracy and theft, toss me in the pokey and I catch hell at the trial. So I'll go up.'

'You won't be alone.' He glanced meaningly at the two women. There were no tears left in Ellen any more, but her friend was sobbing bitterly.

I said, 'Did you stop to think why the three of us bothered to take a worthless file out of here?'

'Does it matter?'

Ellen had nudged her companion and the crying stopped. I took the deck of cigarettes out of my pocket and fiddled with it to keep my hands busy. The white of the wrapper flashed the light back at the sun until attention seemed to be focused on it rather than me.

'It matters,' I said. 'As the charge will state, it was a deliberate conspiracy all right, perpetrated by three citizens in good standing who saw a way to accomplish something that an elected official couldn't manage. The papers will have a field day burying you.'

He smiled. The damn fool smiled at me! 'Don't bother going through that song and dance again.'

He was getting ready to throw the book in my face when Pat spoke from the back of the room. His voice held a strained note, but it had a lot of power behind it. 'Maybe you

251

better hear what he has to say.'

'Say it then.' The smile faded into a grimace of anger. 'It had better be good, because the next time you say anything will be to a judge and jury.'

'It's good. You'll enjoy hearing about it. We,' and I emphasized that 'we,' 'found the hole in the boat.'

I heard Pat gasp and take a step nearer.

'Ellen suggested it to you at one time and the full possibilities of the thing never occurred to you. We know how information is getting out of this office.'

The D.A.'s eyes were bright little beads searching my face for the lie. They crinkled up around the edges when he knew I was telling the truth and sought out Pat for advice. None came so he said, 'How?'

Now I had the ball on his goal line and I wasn't giving it up. 'I won't bother you with the details of how we did it, but I can tell you how it was being done.'

'Damn it . . . How!'

I gave him his smile back. On me it must have looked good. 'Uh-uh. We trade. You're talking to three clams unless you drop all those charges. Not only drop 'em, but forget about 'em.'

What else could he do? I caught Pat's reflection in the window glass behind the

D.A.'s head and he was grinning like an idiot. The D.A. tapped his fingers on the desk-top, his cheeks working. When he looked up he took in the room with one quick glance. 'We'll finish this privately if you gentlemen don't mind. You may stay, Captain Chambers.'

As far as the two assistants were concerned, it was the supreme insult. They hid their tempers nicely though and followed the others out. I laughed behind their backs and the thing that was working at the D.A.'s cheeks turned into a short laugh. 'You know, there are times when I hate your guts. It happens that it's all the time. However, I admire your precocity in a way. You're a thorn in my skin, but even a thorn can be used to advantage at times. If what you have to say is true, consider the charges dropped completely.'

'Thanks,' I said. The women couldn't say anything. They were too stunned. 'I understand you have a man in the department who is suspected of carrying information outside.'

He frowned at Pat. 'That is correct. We're quite sure of it. What we don't know is his method of notifying anyone else.'

'It isn't hard. There's a guy with a tin ear who stands across the street. He wears a hearing aid that doesn't work. He reads lips.

A good dummy can read lips at thirty feet without any trouble at all. Your man gets to the street, moves his mouth silently like he's chewing gum or something, but actually calls off a time and place, gets in a car and goes off on a raid. Meanwhile the guy had time to reach a phone and pass the word. Those places are set up for a quick scramble and are moved out before you get there. It's all really very simple.'

'Is he there now?'

'He was when I came in.'

The D.A. muttered a damn and grabbed the phone.

You know how long it took? About three minutes. He started to blab the second they had him inside the building. The voice on the phone got real excited and the D.A. slammed the phone back. His face had happy, happy smeared all over it and he barely had time to say thanks again and tell the women that their efforts were appreciated before he was out the door.

I got to Ellen and tried to put my arms around her. She put her hands on my chest and pushed me away. 'Please, Mike, not now. I . . . I'm much too upset. It was . . . horrible before you came.'

'Can I call you later?'

'Yes . . . all right.'

I let go of her and she hurried out, dabbing at her mouth with a damp handkerchief.

'Well,' Pat said, 'you're a smart bastard anyway. You certainly made life miserable for them for a while even if you did get them off the hook in the end.'

He held the door open and came out behind me. We walked down the corridor to his office without saying anything and when we were inside he waved me into a chair I needed worse than ever and slumped into his own in back of the desk.

Pat let me get a smoke going. He let me have one long drag, then: 'I'm not the D.A., Mike. You don't have anything to trade with me so let's have it straight. That business with the dummy outside was strictly an accident. If the D.A. wasn't so damn eager to grab Teen and Grindle he would have seen it. Two good questions would have put you right back on the spot again.'

'And I still would have had something to trade.'

'Like what?'

'Lou Grindle is dead. I killed him a few hours before I walked in here. Not only that, but two of his boys are dead. I got one and Lou bumped the other by mistake thinking he was me.'

'Mike . . . ' Pat was drumming his fists on

the arms of the chair.

'Shut up and listen. Teen had me picked up. He thought I killed Link and took something from the apartment. It was kidnaping and I was within the law when I shot them so don't worry about it. There's a body in the road out near Islip someplace and the local police ought to have it by now. The other two are in a house I can locate for you on a map and you better hop to it before they get turned up.

'Ed Teen gave the orders to bump me but you can bet your tail you aren't picking him up for it. He probably had an alibi all set for an emergency anyway, and now that he no doubt knows what happened he'll insure it.'

'Why the hell didn't you tell me this earlier? Good Lord, we can break any alibi he has if he's involved!'

'You're talking simple again, friend. I'd like to see you break his alibi. Whoever stands up for him has a chance of being dead if he talks. All you can offer is a jail cell. Nope, you won't put anything down on Teen. He's been through this mill before.'

Pat slammed his head with his open palm. 'So you waste an hour playing games with the D.A. Damn, you should have said something.'

'Yeah, I had plenty of time to talk. You would have heard all about it if you didn't give me that under arrest business.'

'I wish I knew what was going on, Mike.'

'That makes two of us.'

He dragged out a map of the Island and handed it to me. I penciled in the roads and marked the approximate spot where the house was and handed it back. Pat had the thing on the wires immediately. Downstairs somebody checked with the police in Islip and verified the finding of the body on the road.

I said, 'Pat . . . '

He covered up the mouthpiece of the phone and looked at me.

'Go through the motions of finding Lou's body before you hand the story to the D.A., will you?'

The phone went back into its cradle slowly. 'What's the score, Mike?'

'I think I know how we can get Teen.'

'That's not a good reason at all.' His voice was soft, dangerous.

'You tell him now and I'll get the treatment again, Pat. Look . . . you've been working this from the wrong angle. You would have gotten there, but it would have taken longer. I'm hot now. I can't stop while I'm hot. You said I could have three days.'

'The picture's changed.'

'Nix . . . it's just hanging a little crooked,

that's all. With all your cops and all your equipment, you're still chasing after shadows.'

'You know it all, is that it?'

'No . . . but I got the shadows chasing me now. I know something I shouldn't know. I wish to God I knew where and how I picked it up. I've been wandering through this thing picking up a piece here and there and it should have ended when Toady died. I thought he was the one I was after.'

'He was.'

Pat said it so flatly that I almost missed it.

'What'd you say?'

'He drove the car when Decker was killed.'

It was like a wave washing up the beach, then receding back into itself, the way my body was suddenly flushed before it was drained completely dry. I couldn't get my hands unclenched. They were the only live part of me, balled up in my lap doing the cursing my throat wanted to do. The killer was supposed to be mine, goddamn it. I promised the kid and I promised myself. He wasn't supposed to die in bed never knowing why he died. He should have gone with his tongue hanging out and turning black while I choked the guts out of him!

'How do you know?'

'Cole and Fisher were apprehended in Philadelphia. They decided to shoot it out

258

and lost. Cole lived long enough to say a few things.'

'What things?'

'You were right about Hooker and Decker. Toady gave the orders to get Mel. He was going to put Cole and Fisher out with Decker, changed his mind and went himself instead. That was all they knew.'

'You mean they were supposed to bump Decker?'

'No . . . just go with him when they pulled the job.'

I got up slowly. I put my hat back on and dropped my butt in the ash tray on the desk. 'Okay, Pat, get Teen your own way. I still want you to give me a break with the D.A. I want to get some sleep. I need it bad.'

'If Grindle's dead he'll stay dead. Make yourself scarce. When you wake up give me a ring. I'll hold things as long as I can.'

'Thanks.'

'And Mike . . . '

'Yeah?'

'Do something about your face. You look like hell.'

'I'll cut it off at the neck and get a new one,' I said.

Pat said seriously, 'I wish you would.'

10

I had company again. I had a whole hall full of company. Everybody was coming to see me. I was the most popular guy in town and everybody was standing in front of my door dying to get a look at me. One of my company gasped in a huge breath of air before she said, 'Oh . . . oh, thank heavens, there he is.'

The super's wife was a big fat woman no corset could contain properly and with all that air in her she looked ready to burst. But she was smiling as she recognized my walk and then the smile froze on her face. The super stopped poking a key in the lock on my door, pushed through the small knot and he froze too.

Then there was Marsha. She shoved them all out of the way. The laugh she had ready for me twisted to dismay and she said, 'Mike!'

'Hello, sugar.'

'Oh, Mike, I knew something happened to you!' She ran into my arms and the tears welled into her eyes. Her fingers touched my cheek gently and I felt them tremble. 'Darling, darling . . . what was it . . . '

'Oh, I'll tell you about it sometime. What's all the excitement about?'

She choked and gasped the words out. 'I kept calling you and calling you all last night and this morning. I . . . thought something happened . . . like that last time in your apartment. Oh, Mike . . .'

'It's all right now, honey. I'll be back to normal soon.'

'I . . . came up and you didn't answer. I told the superintendent you might be hurt . . . and he . . . he was going to look. Mike, you scared me so.'

The super was nodding, licking his lips. The others crowded in for a last look at me before going back to their apartments. His wife said, 'You scared us all, Mr. Hammer. We were sure you were dead or something.'

'I almost was. Anyway, thanks for thinking of me. Now if you don't mind, I'd just like to be left alone for a while. I'm not feeling any too hot.'

'Is there anything . . .'

'No, nothing, thanks.' I took out my key and opened the door. I had to prop myself against the jamb for a minute before I could go in. Marsha grabbed my arm and held me steady, then guided me inside to a chair and helped me down.

The day had been too long . . . too much

to it. A guy can't take days like that one and stay on his feet. I let my head fall back and closed my eyes. Marsha sobbed softly as she untied my shoes and slid them off. The aches and pains came back, a muted throbbing at first, taking hold slowly and biting deeper with each pulse beat.

Marsha had my tie off and was unbuttoning my shirt when the knock came. It didn't make any difference any more who it was. I heard her open the door, heard the murmur of voices and the high babble of a child's voice in the background.

'Mike . . . it's a nurse.'

'The superintendent asked me to look in on you,' the other voice said.

'I'm all right.'

Her voice became very efficient. 'I doubt it. Will you watch the child, please? Thank you.' Her hand slipped under my arm. 'You'll do better lying down.'

I couldn't argue with her. She had an answer for everything. Marsha was on the couch still crying, playing with the kid. I got up and went to the bedroom. She had me undressed and in bed before I realized it. The sting of the iodine and the cold compresses on my face jerked me out of immediate sleep and I heard her telling Marsha to call a doctor. It seemed like only seconds before he was there, squeezing with hands that had forgotten how to be gentle, then gone as quickly as he had come. I could hear the two women discussing me quietly, deciding to stay until I had awakened. The kid squealed at something and it was the last thing I heard.

There were only snatches of dreams after that, vague faces that had an odd familiarity and incomprehensible mutterings about things I didn't understand. It took me away from the painful present and threw me into a timeless zone of light and warmth where my body healed itself immediately. It was like being inside a huge beautiful compound where there was no trouble, no misery and no death. All that was outside the transparent walls of the compound where you could see it happen to everyone else without being touched yourself.

They were all there, Decker with his child, listening intently to what Mel Hooker had to say, and Toady Link in the background watching and nodding to make sure he said it right, his boys ready to move in if he said the wrong thing. Lou and Teen were there too, standing over the body of a man who had to be Fallon, their heads turned speculatively toward Toady. A play was going on not far away. Everybody was dressed in Roman togas. Marsha and Pat held the center of the stage with the D.A. and Ellen was standing in the open wings waiting to come on. They turned and made motions to be quiet to the dozens of others behind them . . . the women. Beautiful women. Lovely women with faces you could recognize. Women whose faces I had seen before in photographs.

When the players moved it was with deliberate slowness so you could watch every move. I stood there in the center of the compound and realized that it was all being done for my benefit without understanding why. It was a scene of impending action, the evil of it symbolized by the lone shadow of the vulture wheeling high above in a gray, dismal sky.

I waited and watched, knowing that it had all happened before and was going to happen again and this time I would see every move and understand each individual action. I tried to concentrate on the players until I realized that I wasn't the only audience they had. Someone else was there in the compound with me. She was a woman. She had no face. She was a woman in black hovering behind me. I called to her and received no answer. I tried to walk to her, but she was always the same distance away without seeming to move at all. I ran on leaden feet without getting any closer, and tiring of the chase turned back to the play.

It was over and I had missed it again.

I said something vile to the woman because she had caused me to miss it and she shrank back, disappearing into the mist.

But the play wasn't over, not quite. At first I thought they were taking a curtain call, then I realized that their faces were hideous things and in unreal voices of pure silence they were all screaming for me to stop her and bring her back. Teen and Grindle and Link were slavering in their fury as they tried to break through the transparent wall and were thrown back to the ground. Their faces were contorted and their hands curved into talons. I laughed at them and they stopped, stunned, then withdrew out of sight.

The gray and noiseless compound dissolved into sound and yellow light. I was rocked gently from side to side and a voice said, 'Mike . . . please wake up.'

I opened my one eye and the other came open with it a little bit. 'Marsha?'

'You were talking in your sleep. Are you awake, Mike?'

She looked tired. The nurse behind her looked tired too. The boy in her arms was smiling at me. 'I'm awake, honey.' I made a motion for her to pull down the shade. 'Same day?'

'No, you slept all through yesterday, all night and most of today.'

I rubbed my face. Some of the puffiness had gone down. 'Lord. What time is it?'

'Almost four-thirty. Mike . . . that Captain Chambers is on the phone. Can you answer him?'

'Yeah, I'll get it. Let me get something on.'

I struggled into my pants, swearing when I hit a raw spot. I was covered with adhesive tape and iodine, but the agony of moving was only a soreness now. I padded outside and picked up the phone. 'Hello . . . '

'Where've you been, Mike? I told you to call me.'

'Oh, shut up. I've been asleep.'

'I hope you're awake now. The D.A. found Grindle.'

'Good.'

'Now he wants you.'

'What's it this time, a homicide charge?'

'There's no charge. I explained that away. He wants Teen and he thinks you're pulling a fast one again.'

'What's the matter with that guy?'

'Put yourself in his shoes and you'll see. The guy is fighting to hang on to his job.'

'Christ, I gave him enough. What does he want . . . blood? Did he expect me to get Teen the hard way for him?'

266

'Don't be a jerk, Mike. He doesn't want Teen dead. He doesn't want a simple obit in the papers. He wants Teen in court so he can blow the whole thing wide open before the public. That's the only thing that will keep him in office.'

'What happened to the tin ear?'

'All the guy had was the telephone number of a booth in Grand Central Station. If he didn't call in every hour it meant there was trouble. We traced the number and there was nobody around. The guy worked through an intermediary who passed the information on to the right people. Both of them got paid off the same way . . . a bundle of cash by mail on the first of every month.'

'I suppose Ed Teen's laughing his head off.'

'Not exactly, but he's grinning broadly. We checked his alibi for the night before last and it's perfect. You know and I know that it's phony as hell, but nobody is breaking it down in court. According to Teen the entire thing is preposterous. He was playing cards with a group of friends right through the night.'

'Nuts. His story is as old as his racket. One good session under the lights and he'll talk.'

'You don't put him under lights.'

'There're other things you can do,' I suggested.

'You don't do that either, Mike. Teen's going around under the watchful eye of a battery of lawyers well protected by a gang of licensed strong-arm boys. You try anything smart and it'll be your neck.'

'Great. Now what's with the D.A.?'

It was a moment before he said anything. 'Mike . . . are you on the level with me?'

'You know everything I know, Pat. Why?'

'You're going to be tied up with our boy for a long time if you don't get a move on,' he said. 'And by the way, call Ellen when you have time. She wants to talk to you.'

'She there now?'

'No, she left a little while ago. I got something else for you. The playboy is back.'

'Marvin Holmes?'

'Yeah. Customs passed the word on to us but it was too late to stop him. We traced him as far as New York and lost him here. The last lead we had said he was with a foreign-looking blonde and was doing his damnedest to stay under cover.'

I let it run through my mind a minute. 'He's still scared of something.'

'It looks that way. I'm hoping to pick him up some time today. He's too well known to stay hidden long. Look, you give me a call when you have time. I have to get going now. This place is a madhouse. I wish the D.A.

would operate out of his own office for a change.'

I heard the click of his receiver cutting off the connection. Good old Pat. We still played on the same ball team. He was still worrying about me enough to want me to pick my own time and place when I had a long talk with the District Attorney.

Marsha was propped against the corner of the couch yawning. 'We have to scram, kid.'

Her mouth came shut. 'Something wrong?'

'People want to talk to me and I can't afford the time. I want to go someplace and think. I want to be where nobody'll bother me for a week if I don't feel like seeing them.'

'Well . . . we can go to my place. I won't bother you, Mike. I just want to crawl in bed and sleep forever.'

'Okay. Get your things on. I'll get dressed.'

I went back to the bedroom and finished putting on my clothes. There was a light tap on the door and I yelled come on in. The nurse opened the door and stood there holding the boy's hand. He would have been content to stay there, only he spotted the sling of the shoulder holster dangling from the dresser and made a dash for it.

This time she grabbed him before he was halfway there and dragged him back.

'I wish he liked his toys that way,' she said.

'Maybe he'll grow up to be a cop.'

I got a disapproving look for that. 'I hope not!' she paused. 'Miss Lee tells me you have to leave again.'

'That's right.'

'Then perhaps you'll do me a favor.'

'Sure.'

'They came to repaint my apartment this morning. I was wondering if you'd mind my staying here tonight.'

'Go right ahead. You'll be doing me the favor if you stay. If anybody calls tell them I'm out, you don't know where I am, nor when I'll be back. Okay?'

A frown creased her forehead. 'You . . . expect callers?' There was a tremulous note in her voice.

I laughed at her and shook my head. 'Not that kind. They'll be respectable enough.'

She sighed uncertainly and took the kid back to the living room with her. I finished tying my shoes, strapped the gun around my chest and picked my jacket off a coat hanger in the closet. My other suit was draped over the back of the chair and a quick inspection said that it wasn't worth wearing any more. I emptied out the pockets on the dresser, rolled them up in a tight ball and carried them out to the kitchen. I stuffed them into the garbage can on top of the kid's old clothes, pressed the lid down tight and shoved the can back into the corner.

Marsha was waiting for me inside trying to hide her red-rimmed eyes with some mascara. We said good-by to the nurse and the kid and picked up the elevator going down. She fell asleep almost immediately and I had a hell of a time trying to wake her up when we got to her place.

I tried shaking her, pinching her and when that didn't work I bent over and kissed her.

That worked.

She wrinkled her nose and fought her eyes open. I said, 'We're here. Come on, snap out of it.'

'You did this to me,' she smiled.

'That mustached bodyguard you got upstairs will wring my neck for it.'

Her lips crinkled in a grin. 'So that's why you came so readily. You thought you were going to be chaperoned. I'm sorry, Mike, but I'm all alone. The nurse is gone.'

I gave her a playful rap on the chin and scooted her out of the car. She took my hand and we went up together. The guy on the elevator gaped at me until I said, 'Up,' twice, then he swallowed hard and slid the door shut. It was too bad he didn't see me yesterday.

* * *

We were so far away from everything up there. The evening filtered through the blinds, the late, slanting rays of the sun forming a crosshatch pattern on the rug. She settled me back in a big chair and disappeared in the kitchen where she made all the pleasant sounds of a woman in her element. I smelled the coffee and heard the bacon and eggs sizzling in the pan. My stomach remembered how long it was since it had been filled, and churned in anticipation.

I was out there before she called me, trying to be helpful by making the toast. She said, 'Hungry?'

'Starving.'

'Me too, I finished a box of stale crackers in your place and haven't eaten since.'

That was all we said. You just don't talk when you don't leave room between bites. The coffee was hot and strong the way I like it and I finished it before I picked up a smoke.

Marsha turned the small radio on to a local station and picked up a supper orchestra and everything was perfect. It stayed that way until the band went off on the hour and a news commentator came on. It was the same boy who got all worked up over affairs in the

272

city and this time he was really running over.

He gushed through his usual routine of introducing himself to the public and said, 'Tonight has seen the end of an era. The man known to the police, the press, and the underworld as Lou Grindle has been found dead in a summer cottage near Islip, Long Island. Two men known to have been Grindle's associates were found shot to death, one in the same house and another twenty miles east of the spot. The house was the scene of violent gunplay and according to police ballistics experts, it was a bullet from Grindle's own gun that killed one of his men. An early reporter on the scene claims that the house had been used as some sort of inquisition chamber by Grindle and his men, but when questioned on the point the police refused to comment. Because of the significance of Grindle's death, the District Attorney has issued a No comment statement, but it is hinted that he is in full possession of the facts.

'Lou Grindle was a product of the racketeering of the early Twenties. Since the repeal of Prohibition he has been suspected of being a key figure in . . . '

I reached out and tuned in another station. I got a rhumba band that was all drums filling in behind a piano and let it beat through the room. But Marsha wasn't listening to it. Her mouth held a fixed position of surprise that matched the startled intensity of her eyes.

'Mike . . . that was . . . you?'

So I grinned at her. My mouth twisted up on the side and I said, 'They were going to kill me. They worked me over then took me for a ride.'

Her hands were flat on the table, pushing her up from her chair. 'Good heavens, Mike, no!' She trembled all over.

'They won't do it again, kid.'

'But . . . why, Mike?'

'I don't know. Honest to God, I don't know.'

She sat down limply and pushed her hair back from her face. 'All this . . . all this started . . . from that night . . . '

'That's right. From a loused-up robbery. You got beat to hell, I got beat to hell. A kid's an orphan. A big-shot racketeer and two of his boys are dead. Arnold Basil's dead. Toady Link is dead and so are a pair of phony private investigators who tried to shoot it out with the cops. Mel Hooker's dead. Goddamn, there won't be anybody alive before you know it!'

'Supposing they come back?'

'They won't. I'm not going to give them the chance. If anybody goes after anybody else I'll do the going.' I snubbed the butt out in my saucer. 'Mind if I use your phone?'

She told me to go ahead and came inside with me. I checked the directory again and dialed Marvin Holmes' number. It buzzed at steady intervals and just as somebody picked it up there was a knock at the door and Marsha grabbed my arm. It rattled me for a second too. Then I picked the .45 out of the holster, thumbed the safety off and handed it to her while I answered the hellos that were making a racket in my ear.

She opened the door with the gun pointed straight ahead, stared a moment then began to shake in a soft hysterical laugh. I said, 'Is Mr. Holmes there?'

It was the butler with the accent. 'If this is the police again may I say that he has not come in during the last five minutes. You are being very annoying. He is not expected back, but if he comes I will give him your message.'

I slammed the phone back the same time he did and walked over to Marsha who was still laughing crazily. The kid with his arm in a sling was trying to comfort her and shake the gun loose at the same time. I picked it out of her fingers, put it back where it belonged and shook her until she snapped out of it.

The laughing left her and she leaned

against my shoulder. 'I . . . I'm sorry, Mike. I thought . . . '

The kid said, 'Gee, Marsha . . . '

'Come on in, Jerry.' He stepped inside and shut the door. 'This is Mr. Hammer . . . Jerry O'Neill.'

Jerry said 'Hi,' but didn't make any effort to shake hands. Jerry didn't like me very much. It was easy to see why.

Marsha gave my hand a little squeeze. 'Mike, I need a drink. Do you mind?'

'Not a bit, kitten. How about you, Jerry?'

'No. No, thanks. I gotta go right away. I . . . ' he looked at Marsha hoping for some sign of jealousy, ' . . . gotta date tonight.'

She disappointed him. The stars in his eyes blinked out when she said, 'Why, that's fine, Jerry. Is there something you wanted to see me about?'

'Well,' he hesitated and shot me a look that was pure disgust, 'we were all kind of worried when you didn't show up today. We called and all that and I kinda thought, well, they didn't want me to, but I came up anyway. To make sure. Nobody was home then.'

'Oh, Jerry, I'm sorry. I was with Mr. Hammer all day.'

'I see.'

'You tell them they can stop worrying.'

'I'll do that.' He reached for the knob. 'By, Marsha.'

'Good-by, Jerry.'

He didn't say anything to me. I handed Marsha the drink. 'You shouldn't have done that. He's crazy mad in love with you.'

She sipped and stared at the amber liquid thoughtfully. 'That's why I have to do it, Mike. He's got to learn sometime.'

I raised my glass and toasted her. 'Well, I don't blame the kid much at that.'

'I wish you felt the same way,' she said.

It was a statement that needed an answer, but she didn't let me give it. She smiled, her face reflecting the fatigue of her body, finished her drink in a long draught and walked away to the bedroom. I sat down on the arm of the chair swirling the ice around in the glass. I was thinking of the kid with the busted wing, knowing how he must have felt. Some guys got everything, I thought. Others have nothing at all. I was one of the lucky ones.

Then I knew how lucky I was because she was standing in the doorway bathed in the last of the light as the sun went down into the river outside. The soft pink tones of her body softened the metallic glitter of the nylon gown that outlined her in bronze, flowing smoothly up the roundness of her thighs, melting into the curve of her stomach, then rising higher into rich contours to meet the dagger point of the neckline that dropped into the softly shaded well between her breasts.

She said simply, 'Good night, Mike,' and smiled at me because she knew she was being kissed right then better than she had ever been kissed before. The sun said good night too and drowned in the river, leaving just indistinct shadows in the room and the sound of a door closing.

I waited to hear a lock click into place.

There wasn't any.

11

I thought it would be easy to sit there with a drink in my hand and think, staring into the darkness that was a barrier against any intrusion. It wasn't easy at all. It was comfortable and restful, but it wasn't easy. I tried to tell myself that it was dark like this when Decker had come through the window and gone to the wall directly opposite me and opened the safe. I tried like hell to picture the way it started and see it through to the way it ended, but my mind wouldn't accept the continuity and kept throwing it back in jumbled heaps that made no sense. The ice in my glass clinked against the bottom four times and that didn't help either.

Someplace, and I knew it was there, was an error in the thought picture. It was a key that could unlock the whole thing and I couldn't pick it out. It was the probing finger in my brain and the voice that nagged at me constantly. It made me light one butt after another and throw them away after one drag. It got to me until I couldn't think or sit still. It made my hands want to grab something and break it into a million fragments and I would have let myself go ahead and do it if it weren't for Marsha asleep in the room, her breathing a gentle monotone coming through the door.

I wasn't the kind of guy who could sit still and wait for something to happen. I'd had enough of the darkness and myself. Maybe later I'd want it that way, but not now.

I snapped the latch on the lock that kept it open and closed the door after me as quietly as I could. Rather than go through another routine with the elevator operator I took the stairs down and got out to the street to my car without scaring anybody. I rolled down the window and let the breeze blow in my face, feeling better for it. I sat there watching the people and the cars go by, then remembered that Pat had told me Ellen had wanted me to call her.

Hell, I could do better than that. I shoved the key in the lock and hit the starter.

My finger found the bell sunk in the framework of the door and pushed. Inside a chair scraped faintly and heels clicked on the woodwork. A chain rattled on metal and the door opened.

'Hello, Texas.'

She was all bundled up in that white terrycloth robe again and she couldn't have been lovelier. Her mouth was a ripe red apple waiting to be bitten, a luscious curve of surprise over the edges of her teeth. 'I . . . didn't expect you, Mike.'

'Aren't you glad to see me?'

It was supposed to be a joke. It went flat on its face because those eyes that seemed to run through the full colors of the spectrum at times suddenly got cloudy with tears and she shook her head.

'Please come in.'

I didn't get it at all. She walked ahead of me into the living room and nodded to a chair. I sat down. She sat down in another chair, but not close. She wouldn't look directly at me either.

I said, 'What's the matter, Ellen?'

'Let's not talk about it, Mike.'

'Wait a minute . . . you *did* tell Pat that you wanted me to call, didn't you?'

'Yes, but I meant . . . oh, never mind. Please, don't say anything more about it.' Her mouth worked and she turned her head away.

That made me feel great. Like I kicked her cat or something.

'Okay, let's hear about it,' I said.

She twisted out of the chair and walked over to the radio. It was already pulled out so she didn't have to fool with it. Then she handed me another one of those manila folders.

This one had seen a lot of years. It was dirty and crisp with years. The string that held it together had rotted off leaving two stringy ends dangling from a staple. Ellen went back to her chair and sat down again. 'It's the file on Toady Link. I found it buried under tons of other stuff in the archives.'

I looked at her blankly. 'Does the D.A. know you have this?'

'No.'

'Ellen . . .'

'See if it's what you want, Mike.' Her voice held no emotion at all.

I turned up the flap only to have it come off in my hand, then reached in for the sheets of paper that were clipped together. I leaned back and took my time with these. There wasn't any hurry now. Toady was dead and his file was dead with him, but I could look in and see what his life had been like.

It was quite a life.

Toady Link had been a photographer. Apparently he had been a good one because most of the professional actresses had come to him to have their publicity pictures made. Roberts hadn't missed a trick. His reports were full of marginal notes speculating on each and every possibility and it was there that the real story came out.

Because of Toady's professional contacts he

had been contacted by Charlie Fallon. The guy was a bug on good-looking female celebrities and had paid well for pictures of them and paid better when an introduction accompanied the photographs.

But it wasn't until right after Fallon died that Toady became news in police circles. After that time there was no mention made of photography at all. Toady went right from his studio into big-time bookmaking and though he had little personal contact with Ed Teen it was known that, like the others, he paid homage and taxes to the king and whenever he took a step it was always up.

There was a lot of detail stuff there that I didn't pay any attention to, stuff that would have wrapped Toady up at any time if it had been put to use. Roberts would have used it, that much was evident by the work put in on collecting the data for the dossier. But like Ellen had said, a new broom had come in and swept everything out including months and miles of legwork.

Ellen had to speak twice before I heard her. 'Does it . . . solve anything?'

I threw them on the coffee table in disgust. 'Fallon. It solves him. He's still dead and so is Toady. Goddamn it anyway.'

'I'm sorry. I thought it would help.'

'You tried, kid. That was enough. You can

throw these things away now. What the D.A. never saw he won't miss.' I picked up my cigarettes from the table and stuffed them in my pocket. She still watched me blankly. 'I'd better be going,' I told her.

She didn't make any motion to see me out. I started to pass her and stopped. 'Texas . . . what the hell goes on? Tell me that at least, will you? It wasn't so long ago that you were doing all the passing and I thought you were a woman who knew what was going on. All right, I asked you to do me a favor and I put you in a spot. It wasn't so bad that I couldn't get you off it.'

'That's not it, Mike.' She still wouldn't look at me.

'So you're a Texas gal who likes guys that look like Texas men. Maybe I should learn to ride a horse.'

She finally looked up at me from the depths of the couch. Her eyes were blue again and not clouded. They were blue and hurt and angry all at once. 'You're a Texas man, Mike. You're the kind I dreamed of and the kind I want and the kind I'll never have, because your kind are never around long enough. They have to go out and play with guns and hurt people and get themselves killed.

'I was wrong in wanting what I did. I read

284

too many stories and listened to too many old men telling big tales. I dreamed too hard, I guess. It isn't so nice to wake up suddenly and know somebody you're all gone over is coming closer to dying every day because he likes it that way.

'No, Mike. You're exactly what I want. You're big and strong and exciting. While you're alive you're fun to be with but you won't be any fun dead. You're trouble and you'll always be that way until somebody comes along who can make bigger trouble than you.

'I'm afraid of a Texas man now. I'm going to forget all about you and stop looking for a dream. I'll wait until somebody nice and safe comes along, somebody peaceful and quiet and shy and I'll get all those foolish romanticisms out of my head and live a bored and relatively normal life.'

I planted my feet apart and looked down at her with a laugh that came up from my chest. 'And you'll always wonder what a Texas man would have been like,' I said.

The change stole over her face slowly, wiping out the bitterness. Her eyes half closed and the blue of her irises was gray again. The smile and the frown blended together like a pleasant hurt. She leaned back with a fluid animal motion, her head resting languidly against the couch. The pink tip of her tongue touched her lips that were parted in a ghost of a smile making them glisten in the light of the single lamp. Then she stretched back slowly and reached out her arms to me, and in reaching the entire front of the robe came open and she made no move to close it.

'No,' she said 'I'll find out about that first.'

We said good-by in the dim light of morning. She said good-by, Texas man, and I said so long, Texas gal, and I left without looking back because everything she had said was right and I didn't want to hear it again by looking back at her eyes. I got in the car, drove over to Central Park West and cruised along until I found a parking place. It was right near an entrance so I left it there and walked off the pavements to the grass and sat on a hill where I could see the sun coming up over the tops of the buildings in the background.

The ground still held the night dampness, letting it go slowly in a thin film of haze that was suspended in mid-air, rising higher as the sun warmed it. The whole park had a chilled eerie appearance of something make-believe. An early stroller went by on the walk, only the top half of him visible, the leash in his hand disappearing into the fog yet making all the frantic motions of having some unseen creature on its end.

When the wind blew it raised the gray curtain and separated it into angry segments that towered momentarily before filtering back into the gaps. There were other people too, half-shapes wandering through a dream world, players who didn't know they had an audience. Players buried in their own thoughts and acts on the other side of a transparent wall that shut off all sound.

I sat there scowling at it until I remembered that it was just like my dream even to the colors and the synthetic silence. It made me so uncomfortable that I turned around expecting to see the woman in black who had no face.

She was there.

She wasn't in black and she had a face, but she stopped when she saw me and turned away hurriedly just like the other one did. This one seemed a little annoyed because I blocked her favorite path.

And I knew who the woman was in the compound with me that night. She had a name and a face I hadn't seen yet. She was there in the compound trying to tell me something I should have thought of myself.

I waited until the sun had burned off the mist and made it a real world again. I went back to the daylight and searched through it looking for a little guy with big ears and a brace of dyed blondes on his arms. The sun made an arc through the sky and was on its way down without me finding him.

At three-thirty I made a call. It went through three private secretaries and a guy who rumbled when he talked. He was the last man in front of Harry Bailen, the columnist, and about as high as I was going to get.

I said, 'This is a friend of Cookie Harkin's. I got something for him that won't keep and I can't find the guy. I want his address if you have it.'

He had it, but he wasn't giving it out. 'I'm sorry, but that's private information around here.'

'So is what I got. Cookie can have it for your boss free or I can sell it to somebody else. Take your pick.'

'If you have anything newsworthy I'll be glad to pass it on to Mr. Bailen for you.'

'I bet you would, feller, only it happens that Cookie's a friend of mine and either he gets it or the boss'll get scooped and he isn't gonna like that a bit.'

The phone dimmed out a second as he covered up the mouthpiece. The rumble of his voice still came through as he talked to somebody there in the office and when he came back to me he was more sharp than before.

'Cookie Harkin lives in the Mapuah Hotel. That's M-A-P-U-A-H. Know where it is?'

'I'll find it,' I told him. 'And thanks.'

He thanked me by slamming the phone back.

I looked up the Mapuah Hotel in the directory and found it listed in a crummy neighborhood off Eighth Avenue in the upper Sixties. It was as bad as I expected, but just about the kind of a place a guy like Cookie would go for. The only rule it had was to pay the rent on time. There was a lobby with a couple of old leather chairs and a set of wicker furniture that didn't match. The clerk was a baldheaded guy who was shy a lower plate and he was bent over the desk reading a magazine.

'Where'll I find Cookie Harkin?'

'309.' He didn't look up and made no attempt at announcing me.

The only concession to modernization the place made was the automatic elevator. Probably they couldn't get anybody to run a manual job anyway. I closed the door, pushed the third button in the row and stood there counting bricks until the car stopped.

Cookie had a good spot. His room took up the southwest corner facing the rear court where there was a reasonable amount of quiet and enough of a breeze that wasn't contaminated by the dust and exhaust gases on the street side.

I knocked twice, heard the bedsprings creak inside, then Cookie yelled, 'Yeah?'

'Mike, Cookie. Get out of the sack.'

'Okay, just a minute.'

The key rattled in the lock and Cookie stood there in the top half of his pajamas rubbing the sleep out of his eyes. 'This is a hell of an hour to get up,' I said.

'I was up late.'

I looked at the second pillow on his bed that still had the fresh imprint of a head, then at the closed door that led off the room. 'Yeah, I'll bet. Can she hear anything in there?'

He came awake in a hurry. 'Nah. Whatcha got, Mike?'

'What would you like to have?'

'Plenty. Did you see the papers?' I said no. 'I'm not so dumb, Mike. The D.A.'s giving out a song and dance about that triple kill in Islip. Me, I know what happened. The rags gotta clam up because no names are mentioned, but you let me spill it and I'll clean up.'

I sat down and pulled out a butt. 'I'll swap,' I said.

'Now wait a sec, Mike . . . '

'There aren't any rough boys this time. Do something for me and you'll get the story. Right from the beginning.'

'You got a deal.'

So I told him straight without leaving anything out and he was on the phone before I was finished talking. Dollar bills were drooling out of his eyes and the thing was big enough to get a direct line to Harry Bailen himself. I told him not to play the cops down and when he passed it down with the hint that more was yet to come if it was played right, the big shot agreed and his voice crackled excitedly until he hung up.

Cookie came back rubbing his hands and grinning at me. 'Just ask me, Mike. I'll see that you get it.'

I dragged in on the smoke. 'Go back a ways, Cookie. Remember when Charlie Fallon died?'

'Sure. He kicked off in a movie house on Broadway, didn't he? Had a heart attack.'

'That's right.'

'He practically lived in them movies. Couldn't tell if he was in the classiest playhouse or the lousiest theater if you wanted to go looking for him.'

I nodded that I knew about it and went on, 'At the time he was either married or living with a woman. Which was it?'

'Umm . . . ' he tugged at one ear and perched on the edge of the bed. 'Nope, he wasn't married. Guess he was shacking with somebody.'

'Who?'

'Hell, how'd I know? That was years ago. The guy was woman-happy.'

'This one must have been special if he was living with her.'

His eyes grew shrewd. 'You want her?'

'Yep.'

'When?'

'As soon as you can.'

'I dunno, Mike. Maybe she ain't around no more.'

'She'll be around. That kind never leaves the city.'

Cookie made a face like a weasel and started to grin a little bit. 'I'll give it a spin. Supposing I gotta lay out cash?'

'Go ahead. I'll back it up. Spend what you have to.' I stood up and scrawled a number on the back of a match-book cover. 'I'll be waiting for you to call. You can reach me here anytime and if anybody starts buzzing you about that story your boss is going to print, tell them you picked it up as a rumor and as far as I'm concerned, you haven't seen me in a month of Sundays.'

'I got it, Mike. You'll hear from me.'

He was reaching for his shorts when I closed the door and I knew that if she was still there he'd find her. All I had to do was wait.

I went back to Marsha's apartment, went in and made myself a drink. She was still asleep. I knew how she felt.

It wasn't so bad this time because somebody else was doing the work. At least something was in motion. I picked up the phone, tried to get Pat and missed him by a few minutes. I didn't bother looking for him. The liquor was warm in my stomach and light in my head; the radio was humming softly and I lay there stretched out watching the smoke curl up to the ceiling.

At a quarter to eight I opened the door to the bedroom and switched on the light. She had thrown back the covers and lay there with her head pillowed on her arm, a dream in copper-colored nylon who smiled in her sleep and wrinkled her nose at an imaginary somebody.

She didn't wake up until I kissed her, and when she saw me I knew who it was she had been dreaming of. 'Don't ever talk about me, girl, you just slept the clock around too.'

'Oh . . . I couldn't have, Mike!'

'You did. It's almost eight P.M.'

293

'I was supposed to have gone to the theater this afternoon. What will they think?'

'I guess we're two of a kind, kid.'

'You think so?' Her hands met behind my head and she pulled my face down to hers, searching for my mouth with lips that were soft and full and just a little bit demanding. I could feel my fingers biting into her shoulders and she groaned softly asking and wanting me to hold her closer.

Then I held her away and looked at her closely, wondering if she would be afraid like Ellen too. She wrinkled her nose at me this time as if she knew what I had been thinking and I knew that she wouldn't be afraid of anything. Not anything at all.

I said, 'Get up,' and she squirmed until her feet were on the floor. I backed out of the room and made us something to eat while she showered, and after we ate there was an hour of sitting comfortably watching the sun go back down again, completing its daily cycle.

At five minutes to ten it started to rain again.

I sat in the dark watching it slant against the lights of the city. Something in my chest hammered out that this, too, was the end of a cycle. It had started in the rain and was going to end in the rain. It was a deadly cycle that could start from nothing, and nothing could stop it until it completed its full revolution.

The Big Kill. That's what Decker had wanted to make.

He made it. Then he became part of it himself.

The rain tapped on the window affectionately, a kitten scratching playfully to be let in. A jagged streak of lightning cut across the west, a sign that soon that playful kitten would become a howling, screaming demon.

At seven minutes after ten Cookie called.

There was a tenseness in my body, an overabundance of energy that had been stored away waiting for this moment before coming forward. I felt it flow through me, making the skin tighten around my jaws before it seeped into my shoulders, bunching the muscles in hard knots.

I picked up the phone and said hello.

'This is Cookie, Mike.' He must have had his face pressed into the mouthpiece. His voice had a hoarse uncertain quality.

'Go ahead.'

'I found her. Her name is Georgia Lucas and right now she's going under the name of Dolly Smith.'

'Yeah. What else?'

'Mike . . . somebody else is after her too. All day I've been crossing tracks with somebody. I don't like it. She's hot, Mike.'

The excitement came back, all of it, a hot flush of pleasure because the chase was still on and I was part of it. I asked him, 'Who, Cookie? Who is it?'

'I dunno, but somebody's there. I've seen signs like these before. I'm telling you she's hot and if you want her you better do something quick.'

'Where is she?'

'Not twenty-five feet away from where I'm standing. She's got on a red and white dress and hair to match. Right now she's doing a crummy job of singing a torch song.'

'Where, dammit!'

'It's a place in the Village, a little night club. Harvey's.'

'I know where it is.'

'Okay. The floor show goes off in about ten minutes and won't come on for an hour again. In between times she's doubling as a cigarette girl. I don't like some of the characters around this place, Mike. If I can I'll get to her in the dressing room. And look, you can't get in the back room where she is if you're stag, so I better call up Tolly and have her meet us.'

'Forget Tolly. I'll bring my own company. You stick close to her.' I slapped the phone back, holding it in place for a minute. I was thinking of what her face would be like. She was the woman in the compound with me, the other one watching the play. She was the woman Lou Grindle found worth cursing in the same breath with Fallon and Link and me. She was the woman somebody was after and the woman who could supply the answers.

From the darkness Marsha said, 'Mike . . . '

My hands were sweating. It ran down my back and plastered my shirt to my skin. I said, 'Get your coat on, Marsha. We have to go out.'

She did me the favor of not asking any questions. She snapped on the lights and took her coat and mine out of the closet. I helped her into it, hardly knowing what I was doing, then opened the door and walked out behind her.

We got on Broadway and drove south while the windshield wipers ticked off the seconds.

The rain had grown. The kitten was gone and an ugly black panther was lashing its tail in our faces.

The bars were filling up, and across town on the East Side an overpainted redhead in last year's clothes would be rubbing herself up against somebody else.

A guy would be nursing a beer down at the end of the bar while a pair of drunks argued over what to play on the juke box.

The bartender would club somebody who got out of line. The floor would get damper and stink of stale beer and sawdust.

Maybe the door would open and another guy would be standing there with a bundle in his arms. A little wet bundle with a wet, tousled head.

Maybe more people would die.

'You're quiet, Mike.'

'I know. I was remembering another night like this.'

'Where are we going?'

I didn't hear the question. I said, 'All the way it's been Fallon. Whenever anything happened it was his name that came up. He was there when Decker was killed. He was there when Toady died. He was there when Grindle died. He was there at the beginning and he's right here at the end. There was a woman in it. She disappeared after Fallon died and she's the one we're going to see. She's going to tell us why she disappeared and why Toady Link got so important and when she tells that I'll know why Decker made his own plans to die and kissed his kid good-by. I'll know why Teen sat there and watched me being cut up and know what was so important in Toady's apartment. I'll know all that and I'll be able to live with myself again. I went out hunting a killer and I missed him. I never missed one before. Somebody else had a bigger grudge and cut him down before I had a chance, but at least I have the satisfaction of knowing he's dead. Now I want to know why it happened. I want to make sure I did miss. I've been thinking and thinking . . . and every once in a while when I think real hard I can see a hole no bigger than a pinhead and I begin to wonder if it was really Today I was after at all.'

Her hand tightened over mine on the wheel. 'We'll find out soon,' she told me.

★ ★ ★

A rain-drenched canopy sagging on its frame braced itself against the storm. Lettered on the side was HARVEY'S. The wind had torn a hole in the top and the doorman in the maroon uniform huddled in the entrance to stay dry. I parked around the corner and locked the car, then dragged my raincoat over the two of us for the run back to the joint.

The doorman said it was a bad night and I agreed with him.

The girl in the cloakroom said the same thing and I agreed with her too.

The headwaiter who was the head bouncer with a carnation didn't say anything. I saw Cookie over at a corner table with another bleach job and let muscles make a path through the crowd for us until we reached him.

Somewhere, Cookie had lost his grin. We went through the introductions and ordered a drink. He looked at me, then at Marsha and I said, 'You can talk. She's part of it.'

The blonde who looked like a two-bit twist caught my attention. 'Don't mind my getup. I can get around better when I act like a floozie. I've been on this thing with Cookie ever since he started.'

'Arlene's one of Harry's stenos. We use her once in a while. She's the one who dug up the dame.'

'Where is she, Cookie?'

His head made a motion toward the back of the bandstand. 'Probably changing. The act goes on again in a few minutes.' He was scowling.

The blonde had a single sheet of paper rolled up in her hand. She spread it out and started checking off items with her fingernail.

'Georgia . . . or Dolly . . . is forty-eight and looks like it. She was Fallon's girl friend and then his mistress. At one time she was a looker and a good singer, but the years changed all that. After Fallon died she went from one job to another and wound up being a prostitute. We got a line on her through a guy who knows the houses pretty well. She took to the street for a while and spent some time in the workhouse. Right after the war she was picked up on a shoplifting charge and given six months. Not two weeks after she got out she broke into an apartment and was caught at it. She got a couple years that time. She got back in the houses after that to get eating money, broke loose and got this job. She's been here a month.'

'You got all that without seeing her?'

The blonde nodded.

'I thought you were going to speak to her, Cookie.'

'I was,' he said. 'I changed my mind.'

He was staring across the room to where Ed Teen was sitting talking to four men. Only two of them were lawyers. The other two were big and hard-looking. One chewed on a match-stick and leered at the dames.

My drink slopped over on the table.

Cookie said, 'I thought you told me there wouldn't be any rough stuff.'

'I changed my mind too.' I had to let go of the glass before I spilled the rest of it. 'They see me come in?'

'No.'

'They know you or why you're here?'

Cookie's ears went back, startled. 'Do I look like a dope?' His tongue licked his lips

301

nervously. 'You think . . . that's who I been crossing all day.'

I was grinning again. Goddamn it, I felt good! 'I think so, Cookie,' I said.

And while I was saying it the lights turned dim and a blue spot hit the bandstand where a guy in a white tux started to play. A girl with coal-black hair stepped out from behind the curtains and paused dramatically, waiting for a round of applause before going into her number.

I couldn't wait any longer. It was coming to a head too fast. I said, 'I'm going back there. Cookie, you get over to the phone and call the police. Ask for Captain Chambers and tell him to get down here as fast as he can move. Tell him why. I don't know what's going to happen, but stick around and you'll get your story.'

I could see Cookie's face going white. 'Look, Mike, I don't want no part of this. I . . .'

'You won't get any part of it unless you do as you're told. Get moving.'

I started to get up and Marsha said, 'I'm going with you, Mike.'

All the hate and excitement died away and there was a little piece of time that was all ours. I shook my head. 'You can't, kid. This is my party. You're not part of the trouble any more.' I leaned over and kissed her. There were tears in her eyes.

'Please, Mike . . . wait for the police. I don't want you . . . to be hurt again.'

'Nobody's going to hurt me now. Go home and wait for me.'

There was something final in her voice. 'You won't . . . come back to me. Mike.'

'I promise you,' I said. 'I'll be back.'

A sob tore into her throat and stayed there, crushed against her lips by the back of her hand. Part of it got loose and I didn't want to stay to see the pain in her face.

I nudged the .45 in the holster to kick it free of the leather and tried to see across the room. It was much too dark to see anything. I started back and heard Marsha sob again as Cookie led her toward the front. The blonde had disappeared somewhere too.

12

A curtain covered the arch. It led into a narrow, low-ceilinged alcove with another curtain at the far end. The edges of it overlapped and the bottom turned up along the floor, successfully cutting out the backstage light that could spoil an effective entrance.

I stepped through and pulled it back to place behind me. The guy tilted back in the chair, put his paper down and peered at me over his glasses. 'Guests ain't allowed back here, buddy.'

I let him see the corner of a sawbuck. 'Could be that I'm not a guest.'

'Could be.' He took the sawbuck and made it vanish. 'You look like a fire inspector to me.'

'That'll do if anybody asks. Where's Dolly's room?'

'Dolly? That bag? What you want with her?' He took his glasses off and waved them down the hall. 'She ain't got no room. Under the stairs is a supply closet and she usually changes in there.' The glasses went back on and he squinted through them at me. 'She's

304

no good, Mac. Only fills in on an empty spot.'

'Don't worry about it.'

'I won't.' He tilted the chair back again and picked up the paper. His eyes stayed on me curiously, then he shrugged and started reading.

There was a single light hanging from the ceiling halfway down and a red exit bulb over a door at the end. A pair of dressing rooms with doors side by side opened off my right and I could hear the women behind them getting ready for their act. In one of them a man was complaining about the pay and a woman told him to shut up. She said something else and he cracked her one.

The other side was a blank beaverboard wall painted green that ran down to the iron staircase before meeting a cement-block wall. It must have partitioned off the kitchen from the racket that was going on in back of it.

I found the closet where the guy said it would be. It had a riveted steel door with an oversize latch and SUPPLIES stenciled across the top. I stepped back in the shadows under the staircase and waited.

From far off came the singer's voice rising to the pitch of the piano. Down the hall the guy was still tilted back reading. I knocked on the door.

A muffled voice asked who it was. I knocked again.

This time the door opened a crack. I had my foot in the opening before she could close it. She looked like she was trying hard to scream. I said, 'I'm a friend, Georgia.'

Stark terror showed in her eyes at the mention of her name. She backed away until the fear reached her legs, then collapsed on a box. I went all the way in and shut the door.

Now the figure from the mist had a face. It wasn't a nice face. Up close it showed every year and experience in the tiny lines that criss-crossed her skin. At one time it had been pretty. Misery and fear had wiped all that out without leaving more than a semblance of a former beauty. She was small and fighting to hold her figure. None of the artifices were any good. The red hair, the overly mascaraed eyes, the tightly corseted waist were too plainly visible. I wondered why the management even bothered with her. Maybe she sang dirty songs. That always made a hit with the customers who were more interested in lyrics than music.

The kind of terror that held her was too intense to last very long. She managed to say, 'Who . . . are you?'

'I told you I was a friend.' There was another box near the door and I pulled it

306

over. I wanted this to be fast. I sat down facing the door, a little behind it. 'Ed Teen's outside.'

If I thought that would do something to her I was wrong. Long-suffering resignation made a new mask on her face. 'You're afraid of him, aren't you?'

'Not any more,' she replied simply. The mascara on her lashes, suddenly wet, made dark patches under her eyes. Her smile was a wry, twisted thing that had no humor in it. 'It had to come sometime,' she said. 'It took years to catch up with me and running never put it behind me.'

'Would you like to stop running?'

'Oh, God!' Her face went down into her hands.

I leaned on my knees and made her look at me. 'Georgia . . . you know what's happened, don't you?'

'I read about it.'

'Now listen carefully. The police will be here shortly. They're your friends too if you'd only realize it. You won't be hurt, understand! Nobody is going to hurt you.' She nodded dumbly, the dark circles under her eyes growing bigger. I said, 'I want to know about Charlie Fallon. Everything. Tell me about Fallon and Grindle and Teen and Link and anybody else that matters. Can you do that?'

I lit a cigarette and held it out to her. She took it, holding her eyes on the tip while she passed her finger through the thin column of smoke. 'Charlie . . . he and I lived together. He was running the rackets at the time. He and Lou and Ed worked together, but Charlie was the top man.

'It . . . it started when Charlie got sick. His heart was bad. Lou and Ed didn't like the idea of doing all the work so they . . . they looked for a way to get rid of him. Charlie was much too smart for them. He found out about it. At the time, the District Attorney was trying his best to break up the organization and Charlie saw a way to . . . to keep the two of them in line. He was afraid they'd kill him . . . so he took everything he had that would incriminate Ed and Lou, things that would put them right in the chair, and brought them to Toady Link to be photographed. Toady put them on microfilms.

'Charlie told me about it that night. We sat out in the kitchen and laughed about it. He thought . . . he had his partners where they could never bother him again. He said he was going to put the microfilms in a letter addressed to the District Attorney and send it to a personal friend of his to mail if anything ever happened to him.

'He did it, too. He did it that same night. I remember him sitting there doing all his correspondence. It was the last letter he ever wrote. He intended to wait awhile, then tell Lou and Ed about it, but something else happened he didn't foresee. Toady Link saw a way to work himself into the organization. He went to Ed and told him what Charlie had done.

'That's . . . where I came into it. Lou came for me. He threatened me. I was afraid. Honest, it wasn't my fault . . . I couldn't help myself. Lou . . . would have killed me if I didn't do what he said! They wanted to kill Charlie so they wouldn't be suspected at all. They knew he had frequent attacks and had to take nitroglycerin tablets and they made me steal the tablets from his pockets. God, I couldn't help myself! They made me do it! Charlie had an attack the next day and died in the theater. God, I didn't mean it, I had to do it to stay alive!'

'The bastards!' The word cut into her sobbing. 'The lousy miserable bastards. Toady pulled a double-cross as long as your arm. He must have made two prints of those films. He kept one himself and let the boys know about it, otherwise they would have knocked him off long ago. That was his protection. That's what Teen thought I took out of his apartment!'

Georgia shook her head, not knowing what I was talking about, but it made sense to me. It made a damn lot of sense now.

I said, 'After Fallon died . . . what happened? What did the District Attorney do?'

'Nothing. Nothing happened.'

The evil of it was like the needle-point of a dagger digging into my brain. The incredible evil of it was right there in front of my face and needed nothing more than a phone call to make it a fact.

All along I had tripped over that one stumbling block that threw me on my face. I had missed it because it had been so goddamn small, but now it stuck out like a huge white rock with a spotlight on it.

I grabbed Georgia by the arm and lifted her off the box. 'Come on, we're getting out of here. Anything you want to take with you?'

She reached out automatically for her hat and purse, then I shoved her out the door. The hallway was empty. There was no guy in the chair down under the light. A pair of tom-toms made the air pulsate with a harsh jungle rhythm that seemed to enjoy echoing through the corridor as if it were in its natural element.

I didn't like it a bit.

The red exit light pointed the way out. If

Ed Teen was waiting to see Georgia he was going to have a long wait. Maybe he thought he was the only one looking for her and he didn't have to hurry. I pulled the door open and stepped out ahead of her, feeling for the step.

The voice behind the gun said, 'This the one, Ed?'

And Ed said, 'That's the one. Take him.'

I was keyed up for it. There was no surprise to it except for them. A gun is a gun and when one is rammed in your ribs you aren't supposed to scream your guts out while you slam into a woman in the darkness and hit the pavement as the flame blasts out above your head.

The .45 was a living thing in my hand cutting its own lightning and thunder in the rain. I rolled, scrambled to my feet and ran in a crouch only to roll again. They were shouting at each other, running for the light that framed the end of the alley. The bright flashes of gunfire at close range made everything blacker than before. I saw the legs go past my face and grabbed at them, slashing at a head with the barrel of my gun. Back in the shadows Georgia's voice was a wail of terror. There was the sound of other feet hugging the wall and for an instant a shape was there in the frame. I had time to get in one shot that sparked off the brick wall then a body slammed into mine that was all feet and something heavy that pounded at my head.

The cursing turned into a hoarse wheeze when my fingers raked across a throat and held on. But a foot found my stomach and my fingers slid off. They had me down on my back; an arm was under my chin wrenching my head to the side and the guy was telling the other one to give it to me.

Before he could a siren moaned and wheels screamed on the pavement. There was only that one way out. They ran for it and I saw them stop completely when the beams of three torches drenched them. Georgia was still a shrill voice buried under the shadows and Pat was calling to me. His light picked me out of the rubble and he jerked me to my feet.

I said, 'She's back there. Go find her.'

'Who?'

'Fallon's old girl friend.'

He said something I couldn't catch and went back for her, letting me lean up against the wall until my breath came back. I heard him in there behind the garbage can, then he came back with her in his arms. She hung there limply, completely relaxed.

I didn't want to ask it. 'Is she . . . dead?'

'She's all right. Passed out, I think.'

'That's good, Pat. You don't want anything to happen to her. Right now she's the most precious thing you have. The D.A. is going to love her.'

'Mike, what the hell is this about?'

'She'll tell you, Pat. Treat her nice and she'll tell you all about it. When you hear her story you're going to have Ed Teen just a step away from the chair. He was an accomplice before the fact of Fallon's murder and she's the girl who's going to prove it.'

I followed him back to the street, my feet dragging. The two boys were trying to explain things to a cop who didn't want to listen. Pat passed Georgia into a car and told the driver to get her down to headquarters. He looked at the big boys and they started to sweat. The rain was beating in their faces, but you could still tell they were sweating.

I said, 'They're Teen's men, Pat. Ed was here to supervise things himself. He was real smart about it too. I had a man trying to run down the woman while Ed was doing the same thing. He guessed who was doing it. He came to make sure I didn't get away with it. He's gone now, but you won't have any trouble picking him up. An hour ought to do it.'

The crowd had gathered. They fought for a

look, standing on their toes to peer over shoulders and ask each other what had happened. Cookie was on the edge and I waved him over. He had my coat in his hand and I put it on. 'Here's the guy I was telling you about, Pat. I'd appreciate it if you'd let him in on the story before it gets out to the papers. Think you can?'

'Who's going to tell the story . . . you?'

'No . . . I'm finished, kid. It's all over now. Let Georgia tell it. She had to live with it long enough; she ought to be glad to get it off her chest. I'm going home. When you get done come on up and we'll talk about it.'

Pat made a study of my face. 'All this . . . it had something to do with Decker?'

'It had a lot to do with Decker. We just couldn't see it at first.'

'And it's finished now?'

'It's finished.'

I turned around and walked through the crowd back to my car. The rain didn't matter now. It could spend its fury on me if it wanted to. The city was a little bit cleaner than it was before, but there was still some dirt under the carpet.

Back uptown I found a drugstore that was open all night and went into the phone booth. I dialed the operator and got a number out on the Island. It rang for a few minutes and the voice that answered was that of a tired man too rudely awakened. 'Mr. Roberts?'

'Speaking.'

'This is Mike Hammer. I was going to call you earlier but something came up. If you don't mind, there's something I'd like to ask you. It's pretty important.'

His voice was alert now. 'I don't mind a bit. What is it?'

'During your term in office you conducted a campaign to get rid of Fallon and his gang. Is that right?'

'Yes, quite right. I wasn't very successful.'

'Tell me, did you ever have any communication from Fallon about that?'

'Communication?'

'A letter.'

He thought a moment, then: 'No . . . no, I didn't.' Then he thought again. 'Now that you mention it . . . yes, there was a peculiar incident at one time. An envelope was in my waste basket. It was addressed to me and had Fallon's home address on it. I recognized the address, of course, but since he lived in an apartment hotel that was fairly prominent I didn't give it another thought. Besides, Fallon was dead at that time.'

'I see. Well, thanks for your trouble, Mr. Roberts. Sorry I had to bother you.' It was a lie. I wasn't a bit sorry at all.

'Perfectly all right,' he said, and hung up.

And I had the answer.

I mean I had all of it and not just part of it like I had a minute before and my brain screamed a warning for me to hurry before it was too late even though it knew that it was already too late.

I cursed the widow-makers and the orphan-makers and every goddamn one of the scum that found it so necessary to kill because their god was a paper one printed in green. But I didn't curse the night and the rain any more. It kept the cars off the street and gave me the city for my own where red lights and whistles didn't mean a thing.

It gave me a crazy feeling in my head that pushed me faster and faster until the car was a mad dervish screaming around corners in a race with time. I left it double-parked outside my apartment and ran for the door. I took the stairs two at a time, came out on my floor with the keys in my hand reaching out for the lock.

I didn't stop to feel the gimmick on the lock. I turned the key, shoved the door open and pushed in with my gun in my fist and she was there like I knew she'd be there and it wasn't too late after all. The nurse was face down on the floor with her scalp cut open, but she was breathing and the kid was crying

316

and pulling at her dress.

'Marsha,' I said, 'you're the rottenest thing that ever lived and you're not going to live long.'

There was never any hate like hers before. It blazed out of those beautiful eyes trying to reach my throat and if ever a maniac had lived she was it. She dropped the knife that was cutting so neatly into the sofa cushion and got up from her crouch like the lovely deadly animal she was.

I looked at the partial wreckage of the room and the guts of the chairs that were spread over the floor. 'I should have known, kid. God knows it slapped me in the face often enough. No man would cut up a cushion as neat as that. You're doing almost as nice a job here as you did in Toady's place. You're not going to find what you're looking for, Marsha. They were never hidden. You couldn't believe that everybody's not like yourself, could you? You had to think that anybody who saw those films would try to make them pay off like you did.'

She started to tremble. Not from fear. It was an involuntary spasm of hate suffusing her entire body at once. I laughed at her. Now I could laugh.

Her mouth wasn't soft and rich now. It was slitted until it bared her teeth to the gums.

'You don't like me to laugh, do you? Hell, you must have laughed at me plenty of times. Woman, when you were alone you must have laughed your damned head off. You know, it *was* funny the way this thing went. I based everything I had on a false premise yet I wound up with the right answers in the long run. You had me talked into it as nicely as you please.

'*All this time I thought Decker had made a mistake in apartments.* Like hell! Decker knew what he was doing. They had your place cased too well to make any mistake.

'But just to see if I'm right, let's go back to the beginning. I haven't got a damn thing to stand on but speculation, yet I bet I can call every turn right on the button. What I have got will hold you until we can dig up the real stuff though. We may have to go back a way, but we'll get it and you'll burn for it.

'You were even nice enough to give me a lot of hints. There you were out in Hollywood in a spot most girls would give their right arms to be in and there was only one drawback. You weren't big time. You weren't going to get to be big time, either. You were one of that big middle class of actors who were okay, but not for the feature films. Then a man came along who gave you a hard time and you got sour on the world.

'Right then you were ripe for the kicker. You were shaking hands with the devil and didn't know it. Back in New York a guy named Charlie Fallon was writing a batch of letters. One was a fan letter to you. The other was to the District Attorney with enough evidence on microfilms to put a couple of racketeers where they belonged. Old Charlie was feeling good that night. He felt so good that he got his envelopes mixed and those films came to you.

'That was just before your secretary died, wasn't it? Yeah, I can tell that much by your face. She was all for turning them in to the authorities and you put the kibosh on that. You saw a way to get yourself a lot of easy dough. That man came in handy too. When you knocked off that secretary you made it look like a suicide and it wasn't hard to explain away at all.

'Now let me speculate on what happened right here in New York. The D.A. got a letter, all right. It was from Fallon, but it contained a fan letter to you. Teen and Grindle put out a lot of cash to have a pipeline in where it counted and they had a slick cop watching the mail for that letter. When they got it they must have turned green because it didn't take much thought to figure out what had happened. All they could do was to sit back

319

and see what you would do.

'You did it. You came around with your hand out and they greased it to whatever tune you called. For ten years that went on. Even the time checks. It's a lot of years, too. Hell, you know what blackmail is like. It grows and grows like a damned fungus. Ed and Lou had two of you on their necks. When Toady Link made those films for Fallon he made a copy for himself. But at least he added something to the outfit. Then one day one of you put too much pressure on the boys. One of you had to go. Toady probably pulled the squeeze play. Since he knew all about it anyway they told him that if he could lift those copies you had he'd make out better himself.

'That's where Decker came in. Good safe men are hard to get for those jobs. Toady located Decker somehow and had Mel Hooker steer him right into a trap where he had to play ball with Toady or else. They figured it out nice as you please and never stopped to figure out what can go on inside a guy's mind.

'Decker had been through the mill and he wasn't setting his kid up to have any part of it. In his own way he was a martyr. He knew what he was going to do and knew he'd die for it. When he lifted that stuff from your place I think he planned to take it straight to

320

the police. He didn't move fast enough though. So he did the next best thing. He stuck those films where they'd probably be found and went out and died.

'You know the rest of it from there, Marsha. I don't have to tell you any more, do I? I shot my mouth off to you and spilled it about Toady, so you went up there to see him yourself. You did a nice job of bumping him. Nice and clean. Maybe in those ten years you figured it all out for yourself, and if you didn't think Toady had those films you were going to get his copy. Yeah, me and my big mouth. You hung on like a leech and kept giving me the old sex treatment just to know where you stood. And I fell for it. You sure learned how to act these last ten years, all right. I thought it was pretty real.

'What gets me is the way you thought that I had them all this time. You couldn't get that out of your head. You thought I had them and Teen thought I had them. They were worth a million bucks on the open market and I didn't look like a guy who'd throw it away. You even went to the trouble of getting a copy made of my keys while I was asleep, didn't you? Tonight you used them. Tonight you had to take a look to be sure because you knew that when I talked to Fallon's old girl I was going to know the truth!

321

'Yeah, everybody was looking for those pictures. That's what should have tipped me off. Toady searched Decker's apartment and I thought Toady or his boys searched mine. That was where I kept tripping up. That was the one fault in the whole picture. *When Toady drove that car he never had time to see who I was at all, so how could he know where I lived? You, Marsha, were the only other person at the time who knew I had gone over Decker's body right after he was shot because I told you that myself.*

'That was a nice set-to up here that night. Want me to guess who it was? It was that jerk from the theater . . . the kid with the broken arm who's so much in love with you that he'd do anything you ask. He got me with that damn cast.

'Where is he tonight? He'd like to be in on this, wouldn't he?'

All that pent-up hate on her face turned into a cunning sneer and she said, 'He's here, Mike.'

I started to move the same time she started to talk and I wasn't fast enough. I had a glimpse of something white streaking toward my head just before it smashed the consciousness from my body.

Long before my eyes could see again I knew what would be there when I opened

322

them. I heard the kid crying, a series of terror-stricken gasps because the world was too much for him. I pushed up from the floor, forced my eyes open and saw him huddled there in the corner, his thin body shivering. Whatever I did with my face made him stop, and with the quick switch of emotions a child is capable of, he laughed. He climbed to his feet and held on to the arm of the chair babbling nonsense at the wall.

I raised my head and caught her looking at me, a spiteful smile creasing her face. She was a big beautiful evil goddess with a gun in her hand ready to take a victim and there wasn't a thing I could do about it. My .45 was over there on the table and I didn't have the strength to go for it.

Jerry was in a chair holding his broken arm to his chest, rocking back and forth from the pain in it. One side of the cast was split halfway.

Then I saw the junk on the floor. The suit I had thrown away and the kid's overalls that had been stuffed in the bottom of the can. And Marsha smiled. She opened her palm and there were the films, four thin strips of them. 'They were in the pocket of the overalls.' She seemed amazed at the simplicity of it.

'They won't do you any good, Marsha.

Teen's finished and so are they. Your little racket's over.' I had to stop for breath. Something sticky ran down my neck.

'They'll serve their purpose,' she said. 'Somebody else might guess like you did, but they'll never know now. Those Toady had I destroyed. These will go too and only you will be left, Mike. I really hate having to kill you, but it's necessary, you know.'

There was none of the actress in her voice now. There was only death. She had finished acting. The play was over and she could put away the smiles and tears until the next time.

I swung my head around until my eyes were fixed on Jerry. He stopped rocking. I said, 'Then I guess you'll have to marry Jerry, won't you? He'll have you trapped like you had Ed and Lou trapped. He'll have something you'll pay dearly for, won't he?'

I think she laughed again. It was a cold laugh. 'No, Mike. Poor Jerry will have to go too. You see, he's my alibi.' Her hand went out and picked up my gun. 'Everyone knows how crazy he is about me. And he's so jealous he's liable to do anything . . . especially if he came up here and caught us together . . . like tonight. There would have been gunplay. Unfortunately, you killed each other. The nurse was in the way and she died too. Doesn't that make a good story, Mike?'

Jerry came out of his chair slowly. He had time to whisper incredulously, 'Marsha!' The .45 slammed in her hand and blasted the night to bits. She watched the guy jerking on the floor and threw the gun back on the table. The rod she held on me was a long-barreled revolver and it didn't tremble in her hand at all. She held it at her hip slanting it down enough to catch me in the chest.

She was going to get that shot off fast for the benefit of the people who were listening. She was killing again because murder breeds murder and when she had killed she was going to put the guns in dead hands and go into her act. She'd be all faints and tears and everyone would console her and tell her how brave she was and damn it all to hell, her story would stand up! There wouldn't be a hole in it because everything was working in her favor just like when she killed her secretary! It would be a splash in the papers and she could afford that.

The hate was all there in my face now and she must have known what I was thinking. She gave me a full extra second to see her smile for the last time, but I didn't waste it on the face of evil.

I saw the kid grab the edge of the table and reach up for the thing he had wanted for so long, and in that extra second of time she gave me his fingers closed around the butt safety and trigger at the same instant and the tongue of flame that blasted from the muzzle seemed to lick out across the room with a horrible vengeance that ripped all the evil from her face, turning it into a ghastly wet red mask that was really no face at all.

We do hope that you have enjoyed reading this large print book.

Did you know that all of our titles are available for purchase?

We publish a wide range of high quality large print books including:
Romances, Mysteries, Classics
General Fiction
Non Fiction and Westerns

Special interest titles available in large print are:
The Little Oxford Dictionary
Music Book
Song Book
Hymn Book
Service Book

Also available from us courtesy of Oxford University Press:
Young Readers' Dictionary
(large print edition)
Young Readers' Thesaurus
(large print edition)

For further information or a free brochure, please contact us at:
Ulverscroft Large Print Books Ltd.,
The Green, Bradgate Road, Anstey,
Leicester, LE7 7FU, England.
Tel: (00 44) 0116 236 4325
Fax: (00 44) 0116 234 0205

Other titles published by
The House of Ulverscroft:

ONE LONELY NIGHT

Mickey Spillane

Mike Hammer's on the prowl for international thugs, on the lookout for military secrets, and on the make with a treacherous society doll too tempting for her own good.